I0638359

UNAWARE

A Suspense Novel

By

SUSAN P. BAKER

Copyright

ISBN: 978-0-996-2021-5-2

Disclaimer

This book is entirely a work of fiction. Any resemblance to any person whether alive or dead is purely coincidental and unintentional on the part of the author.

For my oldest grandson, Andrew.

ACKNOWLEDGMENTS

The author would like to express her appreciation and thanks for the assistance provided by Bill and Judy Crider (deceased), John Hunger, Margaret Anderson, and the members of the First and Second Galveston Novel and Short Story Writers Group, and Saralyn J. Richard.

Chapter One

MARTIN

*L*ieutenant Martin Richardson pushed his cold, half-eaten shrimp po-boy aside and kicked back in his leather chair, propping his bad leg up on his desk. He glanced at his cell phone for the umpteenth time. Still nothing from his little sister. His stomach burned with anger. If the asshole had harmed her before she could get to that woman lawyer's office, he was a dead man.

Joe Morales, Martin's ex-partner, arrived at the top of the stairs with a stocky man in tow. Joe seated the man next to a desk and glanced toward Martin's office. Two other officers brushed past him, escorting two women toward the lineup room. A skinny kid of about fifteen, handcuffed to an old wooden desk chair, struggled to pull his hand free and uttered epithets at everyone who scooted by him. A sobbing woman perched in a chair on the other side of Joe's desk. Earlier, she'd told Martin she wouldn't talk to anyone but a female officer, so Martin had sent for Sergeant Loyola, who was taking her sweet time in getting there.

1

Joe stuck his head in the door. "Lieutenant, this guy's house is across the street from the store on 39th. I think he saw the boys that killed the owner. You want to be in on the questioning? He's pretty scared."

"Thanks, Joe." Martin rubbed his calf where a shotgun blast had damaged it when he'd been a rookie many years earlier. He appreciated Joe's asking, though it wasn't required for the Lieutenant to be at the interview. "Get him a cup of coffee. I've got a couple of calls to make, and then I'll be in there." He reached for the phone. He'd like to grab a bite to eat with Joe later and catch up on things. In the last two years, Martin had lost two partners: Joe, when Martin had made lieutenant, and Liz, when she'd dumped him and moved to California with her best friend.

His insides were hollow with dissatisfaction. He was finally making decent money. He was over his wife's splitting on him. They should have never gotten married in the first place. The years he'd spent getting a college degree instead of working his way through the ranks had paid off. And now he didn't like it. He missed the streets. He had no personal life. He was thirty-two. Childless. And didn't even have prospects.

He did know a lot of women. The ones at Frank's Gym often flirted with him. The trouble was—Martin's sisters had said—he was too picky. He should have remarried within a year of Elizabeth's taking a hike. Martin finished his calls and pulled his leg down. He spun around in his chair. Maybe the summer heat was making him restless. He wanted a relationship. Remembering what his divorce therapist had said before he'd quit seeing him—that it would happen when it was right—he told himself to be patient. He sure was tired of waiting, though.

He didn't think he was particularly picky. He wanted an educated woman. Divorced was okay, but no kids. He wanted his own. He wanted a woman who had the guts to stand up for herself without being aggressive. He wanted intelligent conversation. If she also wanted to walk on the beach and go to the theater, not just the movies, that would be okay, too, as long as she didn't complain when he watched football.

Pulling himself up to his full six feet, Martin walked into the patrol room, feeling like an intruder. He hadn't been talking to the murder witness five minutes when his baby sister, Ginny, topped the stairs. He jerked his thumb toward his office and followed her with his eyes as she went in and closed the door. She'd been crying. Hell, every time he saw her lately she'd been crying. What was it this time?

"All right, Mr. Jackson," Martin said, clapping the witness on the shoulder, "I guarantee you that if you can ID those two boys, we'll keep them in detention. Okay?" He shook the man's hand. "Talk to Detective Morales here. He can explain to you how the system works."

Martin walked back into his office and closed the door behind him. Ginny sat in one of the chairs opposite his desk. She stared at her lap and thumbed through a stack of papers. Her long, straight blond hair had tangles on the left side, which he recognized was from twirling her hair around her forefinger like she had when she was little. Patting her on the head as if she were a puppy, he rounded his desk and perched on the edge, facing her.

"Why didn't you call? I was worried."

She looked up with red-rimmed eyes. "I'm sorry. I forgot to charge my phone again."

He hated the whiny tone in her voice and swallowed back a harsh comment. "So what'd she say? Will she take your case?"

Ginny nodded. Mascara smears down her cheeks made her look like a clown in full makeup. "She's going to file a protective order."

"So what's wrong? Isn't that what we wanted?"

"Yes. I'm just afraid of what he'll do when he gets served the papers. He'll kill me. I know him." She wiped her nose with her fingers.

He handed her his handkerchief. "He isn't going to do that, Sis. I won't let him. What do you have there?" He stared at the papers in her lap.

Ginny wiped her nose and eyes. Black smudges transferred to the handkerchief. "A copy of the contract and interview sheet Mrs. Armstrong had me fill out. She says we're common law married because we lived together and told people we were married. We did talk about being married." Tears coursed down her face again. "We have to get a divorce."

"I thought these days if you were common law you could just split up and be divorced after awhile."

"But I'm going to have a baby, and if I don't get a divorce, it'll be illegitimate. I don't want my baby to be a bastard." She burst into tears.

Outrage struck him like a wallop to the stomach. "A baby. Shit." He jumped off the desk. "Didn't you use protection?"

She raised her head, tears streaming. "I know it was stupid. He said it wouldn't hurt just one time to do it without a condom."

"And you're just gullible enough to do anything that monster says, right? What have I told you from the very beginning?" He poked his finger at her face. "You shouldn't have gotten involved with someone so much older than you. There was a reason he wasn't already with somebody else."

Ginny pushed his hand away. "All right, Martin. I said I knew it was stupid. What do you want?" She blew her nose again and glared at him.

"For you to get an abortion."

Her eyes grew large and round. "No. Never. I can't believe you would even suggest such a thing."

"Aw, c'mon, Sis. If you have that baby, you won't get rid of that creep for the rest of our lives. Do you want that?" His heel banged against his desk, making a deep metallic noise. "Do you want him beating you, stalking you, making you miserable forever? You'd better think about it. You can always have another kid when you settle down with someone decent."

"No. I won't murder my baby." She cupped her stomach as if she were holding an infant. "You can ask me anything, but not that. I won't kill my baby."

How could he make her understand? Having lost their parents when Ginny was still a minor, he and their older sister, Mary, had raised her. He'd spent those years instilling in her all his values, teaching a naïve little girl how to reason things out. Her irrational behavior, her willfulness, her pigheadedness frustrated him. "Jesus H. Christ. Have you gone off the deep end? How much pregnant are you anyway? A week? A month? It's not a baby, yet. It's a ... a ... thing ... a mass of cells."

"I don't care what you say." Ginny crossed her arms. "I will never murder my baby."

"Stop saying that. What's got into you, anyway?"

She stared at the floor.

He looked out the window at the patrol room. Everything out there appeared normal. It ought to be a madhouse, to complement what was going on in his office and in his gut. It was hard enough to think about that creep laying a hand on his baby sister, much less having sex with her, but to even think that he would be father to Martin's niece or nephew. God. The poor kid would never have a chance. Sellers would make all of their lives miserable. There had to be a solution. He focused his attention on Ginny again. "Okay. Here's what you can do. Give it up for adoption."

Ginny shook her head, her hair flying. "How could I do that? Give up my own child to strangers? How could you ask me to do that?"

"You're being hardheaded. You can't just keep the baby. Can't you see you have to sever all connections to the man?"

"You don't understand. Alan's mother abandoned him when he was a little baby. How could I do that to his son?"

"Easy. The kid would be better off with two parents who loved him and wanted him and didn't beat on each other."

"I never hit Alan."

"I know that. It was just a 'for instance.' You know what I mean."

She covered her face with her hands. "I don't know what to do."

"What did the lawyer say?"

"She made me a list of options." Ginny pulled a sheet of paper from the stack and handed it to him.

1. Abortion.

2. Adoption with father's consent.

3. Adoption without father's consent. Perjury.

4. Don't tell the father. Keep the baby.

5. Don't tell the father. Give the baby to a relative to raise.

6. Divorce and name him as the father. Ask for child support.

7. Divorce and don't mention the baby. Name the father on the birth certificate. Don't tell the father.

8. No divorce. File a paternity suit a year after separation and after the baby is born. Ask for child support but no possession time for the father due to his violent history.

9. No divorce. After the baby is born, ask the father to sign a waiver of interest in the child and keep the child.

10. Divorce. List the baby as a child of the marriage. File a termination of parental rights suit and ask the father to sign an affidavit of relinquishment. Terminate his rights.

"There're enough options here," he said, handing the paper back.

"I know. She said she'd let me know if she thought of anything else."

"What else could there be?"

Ginny shrugged. "But she's going to file a divorce with the protective order. She said there's a sixty-day waiting period in Texas, and we might as well start it running. If we decide not to go through with it, we can dismiss it later."

"Is she putting the baby in?"

"Not right now. She wants me to think everything over. She said we could add the baby later if we wanted to."

"What does she think you should do?"

Ginny hugged herself. "She wouldn't say. She said it's a personal decision between my doctor and me."

Martin pulled Ginny into his arms. "And so it is, Sis."

Chapter Two

DENA

"Just what do you think you're doing?" Dena pulled the well-chewed stem of her thick glasses from between her teeth, feeling like a criminal as she faced her cousin, the senior partner in the firm. She had hoped to get away from the office before he found out.

Just as she started to reply, he said, "You've been retained on a wife-beating case?"

Dena stroked the indentations her glasses left on the bridge of her nose. Meredith and her big mouth. "Yes, Luke, I have, and the politically correct term is 'family violence.'" She held her palm up and out to stop his rant. "Before you say anything else, let me explain."

"I thought we agreed we wouldn't practice domestic relations in this firm."

She rested her clasped hands on top of the Texas Family Code. She'd been reviewing the updates on the chapter on protective orders to see whether the legislature had made any significant changes. She stared at him, unable to respond as quickly as she wanted.

He towered over the front of her desk, his jowly face flushed. "It was my father's agreement with your father, your father's agreement with me, and I thought it was my agreement with you. It's a long-standing tradition in this firm that we do not practice family law."

Dena glanced inside her roller bag. From where he stood, Lucas couldn't see the contents. She threw a pen on top of the Petition for Divorce, the Application for Protective Order, and the Ex Parte Protective Order, and zipped up the front pocket. First thing the next morning, she would file the suit at the courthouse. "You don't understand, Lucas. This young woman's husband is so violent that someone had to take the case immediately. She didn't have time to go to anyone else."

"What part of 'We do not practice family law' don't you understand?"

Dena pressed her fingers to her lips to stop harsh words from spewing forth. She'd wanted to tell her cousin for a long time that family law was all she'd ever wanted to practice. Her compulsion didn't make any sense. She couldn't explain it. It was just the way she felt. All other areas of law seemed boring by comparison, except maybe criminal defense.

Okay, so she had gone to him on false pretenses. She had tacitly agreed not to take family law cases. She'd been sure she could get him to change his mind. Now it had been a year, and he hadn't. She wanted to understand his rationale, look behind this unyielding position that it just 'had always been that way.'

"What was I supposed to do, throw her out? I was the third attorney Ginny had gone to. No one else would take her case. She was desperate. It was late in the day ..."

"Did it occur to you there was a reason they wouldn't take her case?"

"You don't have to be sarcastic."

"It seems I have to be a lot more than that with you, Dena Barlow Armstrong. Did you or did you not make an agreement with me when I said I'd take you into the family firm?"

"Did you have garlic for lunch, Lucas?"

He gritted his teeth. "Did you or didn't you?"

Dena put her glasses on and stared down at her desk. What would it take to change his mind? What was he afraid of? Did he think something terrible would happen if one of the two lawyers in the firm took family law cases? Or was he just afraid their firm would become known as a 'domestic relations' firm? Would that sully the Barlow name? She just didn't get it.

"Did," she answered, not looking up.

"And did you or did you not sign up a family law case today?"

"Today? Yes, Ginny Sellers gave me a check for five thousand dollars from her brother. A five thousand dollar retainer, Lucas." Dena sure wasn't going to mention the other cases she'd taken that apparently their legal secretary hadn't told him about.

Lucas' expression didn't change. "Did you or didn't you?"

"Did." She had to restrain herself from rolling her eyes when answering him.

"So did you or did you not commit a breach of our agreement?"

Dena closed her laptop and slid it into the roller bag inside pocket. She zipped the bag and yanked up the handle in preparation for her departure before looking at him again. Why did he have to cross-examine her like she was a defendant on the witness stand? And why did she sit there and let him do it? She despised herself when she showed no more gumption than a larva.

Determination glinted in his eyes. He wouldn't stop until he convinced himself she had knuckled under to him one more time. The silence of her office sucked in other noises like a vacuum cleaner. The phone rang. The central air-conditioning unit clicked on. And Meredith-the-Traitor tapped the keys on her computer. If Dena had hired her, she'd have fired her for squealing to Lucas. Why Meredith had chosen to tell on Dena this time, Dena didn't know. Maybe family violence scared her.

"Did."

"And did we, or did we not, after you first came aboard, after that first disastrous case you took, discuss what would happen if you breached our agreement again?"

He always went back to that first incident. Okay, so she had been too trusting. She gritted her teeth. "We did." Ready to head for the door, Dena grabbed the handle of her rollerboard and waited for Lucas to stop blocking her exit. She wanted to avoid a major confrontation. She wasn't really frightened that their business relationship might end. She just hadn't put all her plans in motion yet. Though she had always loved Lucas like a big brother, she was sick of him bullying her. She would be leaving, but on her own terms. In the meantime, arguing with him was her least favorite activity, and one she made every effort to avoid.

"Just what do you think you're doing?"

Dena bit back the smart retort that was on the tip of her tongue. "I'm leaving. Going home." She studied Luke's face, anticipating the reprimand. That was exactly what it was, a reprimand. She was sick to death of this.

"I don't mean going home, and you know it." He peered at her through half-glasses perched atop his wide, up-turned nose. "You can't leave now. We have to talk about this. The minute I turn my back ..."

"It wasn't the minute your back was turned, Lucas. You and I are partners. Partners. It's not fair for you to dictate what kind of law I can practice." Dena's stomach churned. "I really have to go home now. The kids are waiting for me. We can discuss this another time."

To her surprise, he crab-stepped toward his own office. "We're going to have to discuss this further. If not today, then soon ... very soon."

"We will." But not yet. She just needed a little more time. She glanced past him into his office, thinking of saying something about the pigsty he worked in. That was something they sorely needed to discuss. She kept thinking he would straighten it up, but he never did. His office was cavernous, at least twice the size of hers. The stacks of files and papers sprouted upward like ancient stalagmites. Dena shook her head and made her exit. Soon none of that would matter anymore. "Goodnight, y'all."

As she pulled the door shut, he called after her, "I'm not sure I want a partner who does domestic relations. Think about it."

She laughed. If only he knew how much she had thought about it.

Chapter Three

ALAN SELLERS

lan Sellers lay on his bed, exhausted. A sense of calm enveloped him as it always did when he awakened after he had lost his temper, an all's-well-in-the-world feeling, until he focused on his surroundings, the trashed bedroom. He clenched his teeth. They ached, as they always did, the result of his constant anger.

Ginny had left him. He had been home for lunch a while before he realized it. She hadn't made the bed before she left the apartment. He had required her to always make the bed. The breakfast dishes weren't washed either, the bacon grease smell already stinking up the kitchen.

At first, he thought she had simply gone to work in a hurry, that she was either pretty pissed off or else was playing games. Maybe she thought she would come home at the end of the day and something would have changed.

He had driven over to the longshoremen's hall to see about work. Told her he would run some errands. Told her to call him later. Told her he would be home at lunchtime. After coming home and seeing the stinky breakfast dishes and the bed, he thought she was rebelling because of his discipline of her the night before. A little bit later, when he'd been taking a piss, he saw her make-up kit was gone from the bathroom shelf along with her toothbrush and hairbrush. His face grew hot. He zipped up his pants and ran to the closet. Most of her clothes were gone. Bitch. His eyes darted around the bedroom. Her dresser drawers stood gaping like big hollow mouths. Pretty much everything that was hers was gone from the top of the dresser.

He found no note. Most of the others had at least left a note. Not all of them, not what's-her-name ... Patsy. But that had been years earlier, and the details blurred in his memory. They all could have been more understanding if they'd tried. Trouble was, they didn't bother trying. All women were the same. They all left in the end.

He'd had hopes for Ginny Richardson. She was younger than the other girls. He'd thought if he got one before her ideas were solidly formed, before she had strong beliefs as to what she was supposed to do, he could train her to be the kind of girl he wanted. He had tried that before with limited success, taught one girl what made him angry, what set him off, what she was supposed to do, and how not to push his buttons and make him mad. He'd thought if Ginny understood, if she did what she was told, things would work out.

Women had different ideas from when he was growing up. They wanted more independence. More say-so in how things went. He wasn't sure, but that's what he thought. He had been rolling that around in his mind like a tiny rubber ball, going over it and over it.

He could be loving. He had shown all of them he could make them feel like queen of the world. It was not just the sex, though he knew he could make them feel stuff they'd never felt with anyone else, but also when they'd go out with him. When they walked somewhere, he always made sure to be on the street side and let them take his arm. When they went to dinner, he'd open the doors, pull out their chairs, order for them, be attentive, and always pay. At clubs, he would order their drinks and never leave them alone. He'd only go to the men's room when they'd go to the ladies', and then he'd hurry so they wouldn't be alone when they came out. He'd dance with them whenever they got that I-want-to-dance look on their faces, not waiting for a hint.

Once they moved in with him, he paid the bills and gave them an allowance. He would take them shopping and give advice on what they should wear, including shoes and jewelry. He was generous, giving back what he could from their salaries to be sure they didn't feel like they didn't get enough spending money.

But, in spite of everything, there was one thing he had learned: women always leave.

His father had warned him. One of his oldest memories was a statement by his father. *Never trust a woman. Women never stick around.* Sellers had grown up an only child. A motherless child. *Your mother left you. Your mother didn't love you. Your mother abandoned you. She had to be punished. After she got her punishment, your mother died.*

Sellers dragged himself off the bed and went back into the kitchen where he plucked a longneck out of the fridge. After twisting off the cap, he went to the window overlooking the street. Hospital shift workers were walking to their cars. The long pull he took from the bottle felt good going down his gullet.

When he was little, Sellers had believed everything his father told him. At the daycare, though, he saw other kid's mothers come pick them up. He thought those kids must not have fathers.

Maybe the kids whose mothers picked them up lived someplace without the fathers. When he had asked his father about that, his father told him not to contradict and belted him across the room. After that, Sellers had kept such thoughts to himself.

In middle school, Sellers once got up the courage to have a girlfriend. It hadn't lasted long. She had broken up with him when he told her she couldn't talk to other boys. He had only meant for her to be his alone. She hadn't understood why he wanted things that way.

He didn't try girls for a while after that. He watched them. He studied them. He saw how other boys acted with them. He tried to figure out the things girls liked, and the things girls didn't like. He didn't have anyone to talk to about it, so he just watched and listened to other guys.

He heard girls talk to each other when they didn't know he listened. He'd be at his locker or in the cafeteria at the next table or at a school dance. He thought he had it all figured out, only he never told his father.

The other thing he'd been afraid to tell his father, when his father had been alive, was that he'd looked for his mother. A long time ago, he went down to Houston City Hall and asked them how you found out about a dead person. They gave him an address in Austin where he could write for a death certificate. He had written, but no one with his mother's name had a death certificate, at least not in Texas.

He'd always wondered whether his father had lied to him. His father had always taken the belt to him when he was little if he asked about his mother. He couldn't ask him how she died. Inside, deep inside himself, Sellers wondered whether his father had hit his mother. Maybe he had even killed his mother. Or maybe his father wasn't really his father. Maybe he had stolen

Alan when he was little and just made up the story of his mother. But he knew his mother's name. At least, he supposed the name he'd heard when he was little had been his mother's.

After he grew up and got his own place, he contacted the Bureau of Vital Statistics in all the states surrounding Texas. None of them had anyone who died who had the same name as his mother.

Now, just a few days ago, he got a copy of his birth certificate. He wanted to be sure his mother's name was right, to be sure his father hadn't changed anything on the copy he had of his birth certificate. The name had been correct except there was a middle name that wasn't on his copy. It had to be the name his mother was born with, her maiden name.

This new idea was one reason he was sorry Ginny had run out on him because she acted like she was happy he was looking for his mother. Anyhow, he'd gone online and requested a death certificate for his mother in her birth name. And, instead of waiting this time, he had also contacted those other states. He felt like he was getting close to what had really happened to her.

And now, Ginny's leaving was a setback. He'd had high hopes for them. He'd thought he could put what he'd done to his father out of his mind, like what happened to his last girlfriend— what's her name—and start new with Ginny, and maybe when he found out what happened to his mother, he could settle down and start his own family.

He played the what-if game with himself. What if his mother was not really dead? What if he could find his mother? What if she was nice, and everything was his father's fault? What if she wanted to be with him? What if she loved him?

Or, what if she was dead? What if everything his father had said was true? What if she had been a horrible person and abandoned him and hated him and his father? How would he feel?

What if he found her alive, and she was sickening, a crack whore or somebody like that?

And, what if he had a sister or brother somewhere? If he did and he found them, would they tell him about his mother? Would they like him?

Ginny had helped him search, and now she had left him. Well, he'd get over it. He'd always gotten over it. One more woman leaving him wasn't going to kill him, which couldn't necessarily be said for them.

Chapter Four

DENA

When Dena pushed open the fire door and stepped outside, a gust of hot, humid air enveloped her. The sizzling sidewalk penetrated the soles of her shoes as she walked two blocks down Postoffice Street to the parking garage. Summers in Galveston were best spent at the beach or in a pool, but she wasn't in a position to go to either.

She drove down Seawall Boulevard, glancing occasionally at the breaker line where the sun sparkled on the water. The scene was typical for Galveston Island. Darkness wouldn't descend for another couple of hours. Desperate surfers tried to catch the last good waves of the day. Children built sandcastles and splashed in the water. Adults waded out and played in the breakers.

From Twenty-first Street to the West End, rollerskaters, skateboarders, and bicyclists dominated the seawall. West of Sixty-first Street, runners and walkers took over. The thirty-plus mile island almost burst with people. As nice as it was to see visitors enjoying themselves, her favorite times of the year were late fall and early spring. While there were still tourists trying to catch a few rays of sunshine, there were occasional spots of isolation where an islander could enjoy herself and remember the reasons for living on the Gulf coast.

She turned off the boulevard and pulled into the subdivision where she lived with her family. Two of the neighbors mowed their lawns. Another's automatic sprinkler system had come on and some laughing little children, fully clothed, ran in circles through it, soaked to the skin.

She parked in the garage, but before she could get out of her car, Paul, her six-year-old son, started jumping up and down outside the driver's side window. He wore denim shorts, tennis shoes, and a Houston Rockets tee shirt with a large orange stain down the center. "Mommy. Mommy." When she got out, he flung himself at her.

Dena swept Paul into her arms. She gave him a big hug and kissed him in the wrinkles of his neck. Her nose told her it was Kool-Aid on his shirt. She'd have to get it off him in a hurry and into a pail to soak. "How's my great big Paul?" She nuzzled his ear, kissing and biting it as he giggled.

"I had a really, really good day, Mommy. Juliet says you're home early. Why are you home early?"

Dena set him down on the floor. She retrieved her purse and roller bag and walked with him into the house. "Mommy was tired of working today. Is it okay with you if Mommy comes home before dark sometimes?"

"I like you to come home early, Mommy." Paul grinned at her. "Can we go out to eat?"

She tousled his hair and stroked the soft line of his little cheek. Except for his eyes, which were the same hazel as hers, Paul was the spitting image of his father. "Let me deliberate on that for a few moments." She smiled at her son, a swell of pride and joy in her chest. She knew it was silly, but often when she looked at her kids she realized what a miracle children were and felt pleased she'd been gifted with them.

"What's that mean?" Paul's large eyes gazed at her.

"It means I'll have to ask Daddy."

"Daddy not home yet," the little boy said.

"Daddy *is* not home yet," she corrected him.

"Noooo." He shook his head.

"Where's your sister?"

"In the bathtub. Want me to tell her and Juliet you're home? Want me to get 'em?"

"Let me change my clothes and then I'll find them," she said, leading him by the hand. "What did you do today?"

"Juliet helped me read stories after camp." He pulled away and ran down the hall.

She felt a pang. She should have been there reading the story, not the *au pair*, but she and Zack had always *agreed* she would work outside the home. The almighty dollar. Zack loved it more than he did her, and she knew it.

To be fair, after her father had died, Zack had given her a choice. She could stay home with the kids if she would put her inheritance in both their names and deposit a lot of it to their joint account so they could increase their level of living. Some choice. If something ever happened to their relationship, there'd be a presumption that the money was community property. She'd be left with only half of it—if the court gave her that much. Thanks, but no thanks. She'd finally agreed to name him trustee in the event something happened to her. The children would be the beneficiaries.

Now, over four years later, she was glad she hadn't given her inheritance to their community estate. She didn't know what it was—whether he was having an affair or just wanted to move on—but something was up with Zack. She didn't really care because she was ready to move on, herself. She only hoped he hadn't figured that out yet. Their relationship had deteriorated to the point where she was making plans to get out of it, just like the law practice with Lucas. She had a plan, but she wasn't ready to go forward just yet. Soon, but not just yet.

Before going to find Melissa and the *au pair*, Dena stopped in the bedroom and slipped off her shoes. The soft, cool carpet under her bare feet felt heavenly after the hot pavement. The bed looked so inviting. If she could lie down for just a few minutes ... But Super Mom, as Zack sometimes called her and not always in a pleasant tone of voice, didn't get to rest when she arrived home. Super Mom had to be there to take over where the *au pair* left off. Over the years she'd tried to talk Zack into helping, but the responsibility always fell back on her. And while she had been attending law school, it had been no different. And, of course, she had still been expected to contribute the same amount of money to the household budget as she had before she quit teaching. Lucky for her, three years of that contribution hadn't made any real dent in what her father had left her.

"Hello, Mrs. Armstrong."

She turned at hearing the accented voice. The *au pair* held five-year-old Melissa wrapped in a fluffy, white bath towel. "Hello, Juliet." Dena took Melissa from her. "Hi, Sweetie." Dena breathed in the aroma of baby shampoo. Melissa's auburn locks, the same color as Dena's, had been toweled into tightly wound curls.

"Hi, Mommy. I took a bath." Melissa hugged her mother around the neck.

"You're home early," Juliet said.

"Yes, for a change. I had a bit of an argument with my cousin. You know how he can be sometimes. Has Zack called?" Zack didn't like her sharing their personal life with Juliet, but Dena didn't care. Juliet was more like a younger sister than an employee.

"No one has called today," Juliet said. "Do you want me to prepare dinner tonight?"

"I don't think so, Juliet. I think we'll take the children out to eat since Zack has only one more night in town. Thanks for offering though." She didn't add that she'd be relieved for him to be gone for a few days. Juliet already knew that. "By the way, how are summer classes going?"

"Fine, Mrs. Armstrong. It is harder for me to sit in the classroom in the summer, though. I would prefer to be at the beach since it stays light so late." She shrugged one shoulder. "You would like me to dress Melissa before I leave?"

"Please," Dena said. She snuggled Melissa for a moment. "Mommy will be in to get you in just a minute." She sent her back to Juliet.

"Okay, Mommy," Melissa said. "See you in just a minute."

Juliet seemed wistful, but the girl had always been one to share her problems when she was ready so Dena would wait until that time came, if it did. She closed her bedroom door so she could change clothes.

Shedding her jacket and skirt, she hung them up on wooden hangers. They could go for pizza or hamburgers if Zack wasn't in one of his moods and insisting on a big dinner. He was more moody than not, lately. She hated it because it made it harder for her to be pleasant around him. Often she just wanted to yell at him to get out, that she was tired of putting up with him and whatever his issues were. Any intimacy between them had disappeared a long time ago. What had happened to the affectionate and funny and comforting man she'd married?

After slipping on a pair of jeans, a yellow cotton sweater, and a pair of sandals, she heard whispers and giggles coming through the door. She jerked it open.

"Boo." Paul jumped at her, laughing, the roses in his cheeks blooming. Melissa, her red-brown curls bouncing around her face, clapped her hands and shrieked.

"Oh, I didn't hear you out there," Dena said. "You startled me, Paul."

"Did I really, Mommy?" Paul giggled. "Really, really?"

"Oh yes." She bent down and touched the end of her son's nose. "You scared me. You were so quiet I didn't know you were there." She wrapped an arm around each child, hugging them.

"Have you decided yet?" Paul pulled back and peered into her face. "Can we go out to eat?"

"I told you we'd have to ask Daddy. When he gets home, we'll ask him if we can go for pizza, okay? He should be here any minute."

"Oh, boy," Paul yelled, jumping up and down. "I'm gonna go watch for him out the window."

"No, you go wash your hands and face and put on a clean shirt. Give that Kool-Aid one to Juliet to wash. I'll go watch out the window." She picked up Melissa. Paul ran down the hall to the children's bathroom. "You're getting heavy, my girl. Pretty soon Mommy won't be able to pick you up any more."

"Pretty soon I'll be all grown up," Melissa said.

A car pulled into the driveway, and its engine cut off. She carried Melissa into the den where they peeked through the mini-blinds. They watched as Zack's lean frame unfolded from the white Lexus SUV he'd insisted he had to have. His light brown hair glistened in the evening sun. He glanced around the neighborhood and waved to some neighbors. He gave the impression of being in a good mood, though Dena could tell by the way he held his head and the bend of his shoulders that all was not as it appeared.

She sighed and released Melissa to run greet her father. This would be their last night together for more than a week. She couldn't wait for him to be gone, for the tension in the house to leave with him. Dropping the mini-blinds, she walked to the kitchen door leading to the garage. When he came inside, the garage door groaned in the background as it closed.

"Hello."

"Daddy," Melissa called out.

"Why is the garage door open?" He ran his fingers through one of Melissa's ringlets and patted her cheek.

Dena flexed her jaw and reigned in her anger. "I guess I didn't close it when I got home. Paul met me in the garage."

Zack's dark eyes glared down at her. "I've told you a hundred times, Dena. One of these days someone is going to waltz inside and rape you or Juliet and kill all of you, and it will be because you were too damn trusting to close the garage door. What do I have to do to convince you?"

"Don't talk like that in front of the children."

Melissa looked from one to the other of them.

"I apologize. I figured you'd be home pretty soon anyway." Seemed like the men in her life were always fussing at her. She couldn't wait to put some distance between herself and them, to be her own boss in every sense of the word. "I'll try harder to remember."

"You've got to start taking things more seriously. How many times do I have to tell you that everyone out there in the world is not like you and I?"

"Me," she said. "You and me."

Zack shot her a dark look. "I don't know what I'm going to do with you." He brushed past her, dropping his briefcase on the table. At the wet bar in the far corner of the den, he started mixing himself a drink. Melissa had followed him and stood next to him staring up. "Where's Paul now, anyway?"

The air filled with the smell of bourbon. "Getting cleaned up." She crossed the room and picked up Melissa. "The kids want to go out to eat."

He held a bourbon and water in his hand. "So you're not going to cook again?" He sipped his drink.

Dena bit her lip. He seemed to be deliberately goading her. He knew she hated the smell of bourbon. It reminded her of vomiting up bourbon and Coke at college. Backing away, she dropped into her rocking chair, Melissa on her lap. Juliet hadn't left yet, and Melissa wasn't so young that she didn't at least pick up on harsh tones of voice even if she wasn't old enough to understand what was going on. An argument wasn't what she wanted, anyhow. What she wanted was to have something to eat, play with the kids, put them to bed, and work on the files she'd

27

brought home, before going to bed herself. "I can cook if you want. Paul just asked me before I ever got out of the car. I think he wants to go for pizza at Mario's."

Zack set his glass down on the counter and bent down, putting his face very close to hers, spewing bourbon breath. "I don't give a damn what Paul wants to do, but if it will keep this family happy the last night before I leave, I'm in agreement."

Melissa reached out to him. "Pick me up, Daddy."

"Daddy. Daddy." Paul came around the corner and jumped into Zack's arms before Zack had a chance to take Melissa from Dena. "Can we go eat pizza?" Paul grabbed Zack's cheeks one in each fist, pulling Zack's face toward his.

Melissa said, "Yea, pizza."

Zack's laugh was strained, but the kids took no notice. "Are you paying for it?"

"I don't got no money, Daddy," Paul said, still holding onto his father's cheeks and staring into his eyes, nose-to-nose.

"I don't *have any* money," Dena said.

Zack shot Dena another grim look.

"Daddy's got money," Melissa said, clapping her hands. "Daddy. Mama. Let's go get pizza."

Dena chewed on her lower lip. In spite of the way she felt about Zack, the kids loved their father, and he clearly loved them as well. It would be hard on the kids to take them away from their father, but their growing up around the increasing hostility between their parents wouldn't be any better. "Guess majority rules."

Zack looked from one of the children to the other. "Anything to make my children happy, huh, kids?" He glanced at Juliet who stood in the background. "You can come too, if you want."

Paul hugged his father's neck. "Thank you, Daddy."

"No thank you, Mr. Armstrong," Juliet said, clutching her purse to her chest. "I have a class tonight. Have a pleasant evening together."

Dena walked Juliet to the front door. When she returned, she caught a glimpse of the children in her husband's arms. For just the barest moment she felt like an outsider peering through a window, a taste of what it would be like when she and Zack divorced. More than likely, there would be split custody. The children's time would be divided between the parents. Grimacing, Dena resolved to make a fair deal for both of them when the time came. The children shouldn't be deprived of either parent, and the parents should put the best interests of the children first.

Chapter Five

ALAN SELLERS

Searching for a parking space, Sellers drove around the lots close to the Justice Center several times before breaking down and leaving his car across the street. He wore tan slacks and a flowered shirt, not tucked in, and his running shoes. The summer heat and humidity caused him to break a sweat before he ever got to the door. He clutched the papers he'd been served by some red-headed girl two weeks earlier. He hadn't heard from Ginny, and the redhead surprised him outside his apartment. He hadn't expected court papers, especially ones that said what those did.

Now, when he pushed through the glass doors, he found people waiting to go through metal detectors. He raked his damp, thinning hair with his fingers when he stopped at the end of the line. July in Texas always made him feel like a sausage link frying on a grill.

His watch indicated he only had about two minutes before he'd be late. He didn't even know what courtroom the case was in. He felt for the handle of the fillet knife in his back pocket under his shirttail. He'd have to stash it somewhere, and he didn't have time to go back to his car. He hurried back outside where he ditched the knife in the ground under a clump of pink-flowered bushes. He hoped no one would notice the handle sticking out of the dirt.

Moments later, he elbowed his way in front of other people, mumbling about being late for court. He emptied his pockets into a plastic container on the counter and stepped through the archway. "Which way to domestic relations court?"

"Lemme see your papers." A deputy looked at the documents and then said, "Up the elevator to six then down the hall to the right."

"Thanks, Buddy." Sellers stuck his hand between the elevator's closing doors, forcing them to open back up. He dumped his keys and change into his pockets as he rode.

There were two courtrooms on six. He opened the door to one. A bunch of men in jail clothes sat in the front. He recognized their jumpsuits from when he was in the county jail.

Jogging to the other end of the hall, he flung open the door just as Ginny stepped down from the witness stand. She walked toward a table where another, somewhat older woman stood. He stepped into the courtroom.

Ginny's straight blond hair hung to her waist, shining in the fluorescent lights. She looked like a teenybopper. He walked to the front of the courtroom, past the bench seats where Mary, Ginny's bitch of a sister, sat. When Ginny turned toward him, and her eyes flared wide, Sellers felt like he'd already won the first round. He started to wave but remembered what she had filed on him and the things the papers said. Bad enough she had filed for divorce when they weren't even married, but that protective order thing made him sound like a wife-beater. The other woman faced the bench, and Ginny tugged on the woman's sleeve.

"He was finally served this time, Your Honor, but he hasn't shown up." She turned in response to Ginny, her face registering his arrival with a flicker of a frown. She wasn't much bigger than Ginny, but he could tell she was a lot older, about the same age as him. She wore large black-framed glasses, which made her eyes look really big. "Never mind, Your Honor, he's here now."

Sellers looked past the woman lawyer at the thin-faced, gray-haired judge. The judge scowled behind his own glasses, his lips pressed together, tight as a vise.

A black man the size of a bear stepped toward Sellers. He had a badge on his jacket pocket. Sellers' stomach turned over. He should have hired a lawyer.

"Very well, Mrs. Armstrong," the judge said. "Call your next witness."

"Alan Sellers," the attorney said. Ginny gave him a lot of space and walked to one of the tables.

"Mr. Sellers, step up here to the witness stand," the judge said. "Raise your right hand. Do you solemnly swear or affirm that the testimony you are about to give will be the truth, the whole truth, and nothing but the truth, so help you God?"

Sellers almost laughed aloud at how much the judge looked like the grim reaper in that black robe. His gray hair faded into a face as pale as bleached bones. His eyes were dark and sunken in their sockets. "Yes, Sir, Your Honor." He heard a tremble in his voice and hoped no one noticed. No way did he want them to think he was scared of what they might do to him.

The judge's eyes followed him as he sat down. The big bear-like man stood next to the witness box and said in a low, rumbling voice, "Roll your chair up to that microphone so you can speak right into it."

Sellers obeyed and glanced at the deputy for approval.

The officer's forehead furrowed, and he grunted at Sellers. He stepped back and sat in a chair near the door to the hallway. His jacket fell open, exposing a side arm in a shoulder holster.

Sellers shivered.

The judge turned his attention to the lawyer. "Proceed, Mrs. Armstrong."

Under the cover of the witness box, Sellers rubbed his sweaty palms on his pants. Everything was dim and dreamlike. The clock on the wall ticked as the second hand circled around. The time between seconds seemed like minutes. When his eyes met those of the lawyer's, he had the distinct feeling he knew her or had seen her before. He glanced away, then back.

"Isn't it true you first beat your wife about two weeks after you moved in together?" The lawyer had sat down at one of the long tables. Ginny rolled her chair up next to her.

Alan hadn't dreamed much since he was a kid. He knew everyone dreamed, but he rarely remembered he even had a dream, much less what it had been about. Sitting there in the witness box, he recalled dreaming of his mother. He'd been a little boy and had wet the bed. He tiptoed as quietly as he could to the hall closet for dry sheets, but his father came out of his room and backhanded Alan into the wall. The occurrence had been a frequent one. Eventually, he quit dreaming of her. Later, he quit wetting the bed. Sometime, he didn't really remember when, he had quit dreaming altogether. His father hadn't quit backhanding him, though.

Shaking off the rush of memories, he focused on being in court. His eyes met those of the lawyer again. Behind those thick glasses, the color of her eyes was difficult to make out. They looked light brown or green, maybe even hazel, like his. Her face came into focus. A scowl drew her eyebrows together.

What were they going to do to him? His discipline of Ginny hadn't been that bad. Not like when his father had hit him. He tried to catch Ginny's eye, but she had slid her chair behind the lawyer where he couldn't see her. Would they give him jail time?

"Mr. Sellers?" He heard the judge's deep voice again. "Mr. Sellers. You don't have to testify. But if you don't wish to testify, you must step down. You have the right not to incriminate yourself, Sir."

Sellers came to his senses, staring into the lawyer's eyes. He cleared his throat. Ginny peeked around the lawyer's shoulder. "What was the question?"

Chapter Six

DENA

"Isn't it true you first beat your wife about two weeks after you moved in together?" Dena repeated and stared at Alan Sellers, waiting for an answer. Something was familiar about him, something disconcerting she couldn't quite put her finger on. Although sure she'd never met him before, she couldn't shake the feeling that she knew him. She'd figure it out eventually. It would probably be one of those things she'd wake up in the middle of the night remembering.

"Mr. Sellers," the judge said again. "Mr. Sellers, if you don't wish to testify you must step down. You don't have to incriminate yourself, Sir."

"I'll answer," Sellers said. His eyes pierced Dena to the core.

"Isn't it true?" Dena had written her cross-examination questions on a legal pad since she hadn't performed a cross-examination in a family violence case. Although she wanted to be a great litigator someday, she knew she had a long way to go. This early in her career, she hoped she looked self-confident, even if she didn't always feel that way. Alan Sellers' eyes darted around the courtroom as if searching for an escape route. Finally, he said, "No, Ma'am."

Dena inhaled and continued, "Isn't it true, Mr. Sellers, that on the night you and Ginny moved into your own apartment from her sister's, you got drunk, accosted your wife in the kitchen where she was cooking your dinner, yanked her head back by the hair, tried to pour beer down her throat, and when she wouldn't swallow, you dumped it all over her and threw her to the floor?"

"No, Ma'am. That's not true." The muscles flexed in his jaw.

"And after you threw her to the floor, you tore off her shorts and tried to rape her." Dena's heart pounded. Her hands shook, so she put them in her lap. After a moment, she smoothed the hem of her brown skirt and pulled it down over her knees. She glanced from Sellers to Ginny. As slight as Sellers was for a man, Ginny was even smaller, not more than five feet tall. She looked hardly old enough to date, much less marry a man in his early thirties.

"No, Mrs. Armstrong, that didn't happen, and if Ginny told you that, she's a liar. I never touched her that she didn't want me to." His face softened. He turned in his chair toward the judge. "Judge Johnson, I never did that. Make her stop saying I did those things."

"Young man," the judge said, "you said you wished to testify. Mrs. Armstrong has the right to question you in the manner in which she has been proceeding." He nodded at Dena. "Go ahead, Counsel."

"Thank you, Your Honor," Dena said, hiding a smile. "Now, Mr. Sellers, to give credit where credit is due, you didn't rape your wife the night y'all moved into your apartment, did you?"

"No, Ma'am," he said, sitting a bit straighter in his chair and folding his hands on the counter in front of him.

Dena adjusted her glasses and looked down at the legal pad resting on the table beside her. She made a check on the paper. "You didn't rape your wife the next night either, did you?"

"No, Ma'am. I didn't." He visibly relaxed.

"Or the next?"

"No, Ma'am." A confident smile grew on his face.

Dena's voice grew louder as she spoke. "In fact, isn't it true you didn't succeed in raping your wife until approximately four weeks ago? And wasn't that after you had beaten her so severely—"

"No."

"—so brutally, that she could scarcely see out of either eye? And isn't it true you forced her to have sex with you at the point of a fillet knife with which you have threatened her on several occasions?"

"No, Ma'am. I never did."

"May I approach the witness, Your Honor?" Dena rose, holding two glossy eight-by-ten, black and white photos.

The judge nodded. "Certainly."

"How do you explain your wife's appearance in these pictures, Mr. Sellers?" Dena spun the pictures down on the counter in front of him like she was dealing from a deck of cards. "If you never hit your wife, how could she possibly have turned up at the hospital looking like this?" She pointed with her fountain pen at Ginny's face in the photographs.

Sellers' tan face paled when he glanced at the prints. His eyes swept past Dena and stopped on Ginny. "Oh, Honey," he said in a sorrowful voice, "who did this to you?"

Heat flared in Dena's cheeks. Surprised at her own anger, she said, "Come on, Mr. Sellers. Are you going to sit there and tell Judge Johnson that you never touched your wife?" Her face was so close to his that she could smell his body odor. He stank like rotten meat. "Do you understand the nature of the oath you took before you got on the witness stand?" She snatched the pictures from in front of him and took them to the bench where she handed them up to the judge. Ginny had already testified to them before Sellers' arrival. Taking several long strides back to the table, she threw her pen down.

"I'd never hurt Ginny," Sellers said, almost in a whisper. "I love her." He leaned forward and stared at the girl. "I love you, Ginny. Why are you doing this to me?"

Dena shook her head and gazed down at her notes. She had to give the guy credit. He had some nerve. At the very least, he could act like he was sorry, instead of pretending he hadn't done it. She couldn't understand why he even submitted himself to the embarrassment of testifying. He'd have been better off if he'd defaulted. She turned and patted Ginny on the arm. "Only a few minutes longer," she whispered.

Ginny's little-girl face was as white as her husband's had turned. Her hands trembled. Her sky blue eyes watered. Ginny's sister watched the proceedings from a bench in the back of the courtroom. Mary, who was an older, chunkier version of her sister, gave a thin smile when Dena glanced her way.

Turning back to face the man in the witness chair, Dena sighed like she was long suffering. "Mr. Sellers, do you know why we are here today?"

"To get divorced?"

She could tell the judge wasn't buying his stupid act. He heard cases like the Sellers' all day, every day. Still, Dena found herself growing angry that Sellers would assume anyone would believe him. She hated it when the other party didn't get an attorney. She had to work twice as hard. "No, Mr. Sellers, we are not here to get the divorce. We're here today for the judge to decide whether or not to grant a permanent protective order and to make some temporary orders in your divorce case. Do you have any idea of what I'm talking about?"

"No, Ma'am," he said.

Dena studied the fringe on the Texas flag that hung down from a pole next to the bench. "You remember the papers with which you were served prior to coming to court? The ones that instructed you, among other things, to show up here today for this hearing, if you wanted to defend this suit? The ones that ordered you to stay away from Ginny and not threaten her and that type of thing?"

"I couldn't find her. I didn't know where she was for the longest. How could I threaten her?"

"I'm not saying you did, *after* the protective order was served on you. I'm just asking whether you remember those papers, and what they said?" His dumb act was so disgusting.

"Yes, Ma'am," he said, all innocence.

"Do you have any objections to the judge entering an order very much the same as the first one? An order prohibiting you from all the same things?"

"Yes, I object." He turned to the judge again. "Judge Johnson, I'm not going to hurt Ginny. I never hurt Ginny."

"Then you won't object to the order being entered, Mr. Sellers." The judge glanced at Dena. "Anything else, Counsel?"

"Just a few more things, Your Honor," she said.

"Continue."

"Mr. Sellers, Ginny is asking for temporary alimony while this cause is pending," Dena said.

"I ain't gonna pay her nothin'."

"You will if I order it, Mr. Sellers," the judge said, his forehead furrowed.

"How much money do you bring home each month, Mr. Sellers?" Dena poised to write down his answer.

"I'm unemployed at the present." He crossed his arms.

"You're getting a disability check each week, true?" Dena wanted to approach the witness stand and whack him across the head.

"Yeah," he said, shifting in his chair, his face turned away from the judge.

"And your check is about five hundred a week, is it not, Mr. Sellers?"

"I'm not giving her any money. She withdrew all my money out of the bank when she left, and I want it back." Dena felt like shouting, but she held back. "Is your check five hundred a week?"

"Yes." His eyes widened.

Dena chewed on the end of her pen. Could he tell how nervous she felt? "And don't you have a personal injury lawsuit pending?"

"Yes."

"The money Ginny drew out of the bank was the last of a prior lawsuit you had settled, correct?"

Sellers stared down at his hands. The muscles in his jaws worked overtime. "Yes," he said finally.

"And didn't the two of you charge thousands of dollars' worth of meals, jewelry, and property on her credit cards, much more than that withdrawal from your account would cover?" Dena scooted her chair more in front of Ginny so he couldn't see her.

"Yeah," Sellers answered. He twisted around, his eyes searching the courtroom.

"And you charged a lot of liquor on those cards, too, didn't you?"

Sellers looked toward the jury box and didn't answer.

Dena looked where he was looking to see if he saw anything in particular. Another deputy stood next to the end of the box. He was cleaning his fingernails with a pocketknife. She was anxious to get through with the examination. There was something about Sellers. She wanted to get far away from him as soon as possible. She repeated her question. "Didn't you, Mr. Sellers? Didn't you charge alcohol on her credit cards?"

"Yes, Ma'am."

"Don't you think you should share the responsibility of repayment?"

He shrugged.

"Answer out loud," the judge said.

"I guess so," Sellers said, staring at the backs of his hands.

"Ginny is also asking that you turn over certain personal property that belonged to her prior to the marriage. Do you have any objection to turning over what was hers before marriage?"

"I can't," Sellers said and stared Dena straight in the eye.

"What do you mean by that?" She met his gaze, but her heart beat loudly in her ears.

"I don't have it any more."

"Why not?"

"Simple, Mrs. Armstrong," he said, "the day I discovered that Ginny was gone, I was so upset I ran off and left the door unlocked and someone came in and stole most of it."

There was a sharp intake of breath behind Dena. She reached back and patted Ginny's knee. "Did you file a police report?"

"I've been meaning to, but I've just been so upset I haven't gotten around to it. I will, though, don't you worry, Mrs. Armstrong." The courtroom had grown so quiet that Dena could hear the bench creak in the back when someone shifted his weight on it. The back door behind her opened and closed. Ginny blew her nose. "Do you expect me to believe that everything Ginny brought with her into the marriage no longer exists? Her china, her crystal, her books?"

"You can believe anything you want."

"Answer the question," the judge said, his voice flat.

Dena recognized the anger in the judge's voice. She would have to hurry before the judge lost patience with the whole proceeding.

"Are you saying that everything Ginny brought into the marriage no longer exists?"

"No." He turned and looked the judge in the eye and shook his head. "Judge, I'll give her what's left, but I can't give her what ain't there."

Dena removed her glasses and rubbed the bridge of her nose. She'd just have to deal with property later. Ginny could count herself lucky she got out in one piece.

Standing, she addressed the court. "That's all, Your Honor. But I'd like to argue if you think it's necessary."

"It's not. All right," he said, addressing the courtroom. "The protective order is granted for two years. Mr. Sellers, if you go anywhere near your wife, if you call her, harass her, communicate with her in any fashion, send her flowers, cards, letters, try to contact her through mutual friends, harm her or threaten her in any way, or go within two-hundred yards of a place you know her to be, I will not only put you in the jail, but I will put you under the jail for six months for each violation. I am ordering you to mail two hundred dollars per week to her lawyer's office beginning this Friday—"

Sellers, hovering over the microphone like he could swallow it, said, "Your Honor, don't I get a chance to tell my side of it? You said I'd get a chance to have my say." His voice, in a high-pitched squeal, bounced off the back wall.

"Son, I don't think you need to perjure yourself further, do you? Right now, I'm giving you a break, but if you press me to proceed, I may be inclined to request the district attorney's office to file charges on you for your perjured testimony, as well as for assault on your wife."

Pointing his forefinger at Sellers, the judge continued with what sounded like a standard lecture, his tone pretty harsh. Dena watched Sellers. He was about to burst.

Dena packed her roller bag and waited for the judge to leave the bench. When he did, Dena, Ginny, and Mary hurried from the courtroom. When they got on the elevator, Dena turned and saw Sellers. His staring eyes went right through her. When the doors began to close, he snapped his finger at them as if he were firing a gun.

Chapter Seven

DENA

"Thank God it's Friday," Meredith said, stubbing out a cigarette in an ashtray inside her desk drawer when she saw Dena. "The phone's been ringing off the hook. The computer is giving me trouble. The printer ran out of toner, and I spilled the refill on top of my shoes."

Dena coughed, the smoke burning her throat and eyes. "Good morning, Meredith. You've been at it again." She left her roller bag in front of one of the chairs opposite Meredith's desk and stepped out of her pumps. Anger threatened to turn her face red. Lucas refused to make Meredith go outside to smoke, saying he was afraid she'd quit, and that she was too good a legal secretary to lose her.

Dena flipped on the air filter that sat on the coffee table. "Could you just do this one thing for me if you insist on breaking the law?" A gray film covered the vent so she turned it back off, unplugged it, went into the storage room, replaced the inside filter, and wiped the vents clean. When she returned she said, "If you're going to smoke, the least you can do is keep the filter in good working order."

"Sorry, Mrs. Armstrong," Meredith said, with a touch of sourness in her voice.

"It's not good for the computer or the printer," Dena said. "And what kind of impression do you think it gives the clients?"

"You don't have to get so bent out of shape over it. I'm going to quit. I swear."

"Sure, when hell freezes over." Dena knew Meredith wouldn't quit smoking or quit her job. They gave her very good benefits she wouldn't necessarily receive at another law firm. And anyway, another law office would probably fire her the first time she lit up.

"It's so dadgum hot outside. I can't stand to smoke out there."

Dena sat down and rubbed a sore spot on one of her feet. Meredith had been working for Luke when she had arrived on the scene. What Dena wanted didn't carry much weight. Luke had hired Meredith right out of junior college and trained her himself. He wasn't about to get rid of her just because she smoked, not to mention the fact that he liked a pipe occasionally himself. And he sure wasn't going to enforce their rule that she only smoke outside. The situation was just another reason Dena wanted to open her own office.

"Feet hurt?" Meredith looked down at Dena's feet.

"I guess I'm going to have to make the transition to lower heels soon. Sometimes I hate being short."

"Here." Meredith waved a pink message slip at her. "You got a call this a.m. from a Martin Richardson. Says he's Ginny Sellers' brother. Wants you to call him back before you go to lunch."

Just as Dena reached for the message, the door opened, and a man stuck his head inside. "I'm looking for Dena Armstrong."

Dena brushed her hair out of her face, pushed her skirt down over her knees, and stood. "You found her. What can I do for you?" The man had to be a good six feet tall with sandy brown hair and light brown eyes. His nose looked like it had seen the wrong side of a fist more than once. His summer suit was wrinkled and his tie hung loose. Dena found him appealing and, from the look on Meredith's face, so did she.

He let the door close behind him and held out his hand. "I'm Ginny Richardson's brother, Martin."

"Oh ... Ginny *Sellers* ... nice to meet you." Her fingers tingled when they shook hands. "It's Lieutenant, isn't it?"

"Yes, Ma'am." He looked down at her, his expression at first serious, but then a smile tugged at his lips. "Could we go into your office for a few minutes?"

"Certainly." She dreaded putting her shoes back on. The carpet was soft under her feet. She had known the heels were too high but had worn them anyway since she'd bought them to match her brown suit. They made her legs look great. She picked them up and took the handle of the roller bag, leading the way into her office.

Dena's father would have died before he let the courthouse crowd see him without his coat and tie. He had expected the same formality of all lawyers and often remarked on how casual their attire had become. But her father wasn't there, and she pushed his voice out of her head. She stepped behind her desk and sat down.

"So what can I do for you?" She indicated he should take a chair. She didn't know why, but now she wished she'd bothered decorating her office. Other than her framed law license and diploma and a couple of pictures of the kids, the walls were bare. The bookcases held few law books, since now just about everything was available online.

Zack had accused her of being too tight with her inheritance money, and maybe she was. What was it about Martin Richardson that made her feel self-conscious? For some reason now she had a desire to purchase a painting or two and some plants to make the place feel more hospitable. The bowl of irises appeared rather stark on the table in the corner.

Having closed the door behind him, he sat opposite her. Staring into her eyes, he said, "Ginny said she was going to court this morning, and since I was in the vicinity, I thought I'd drop by to see how it went." He leaned forward in the chair, as if he were anxious.

"The judge gave us what we asked for and lectured Sellers. The clerk gave him a copy of the protective order." She started twirling a pen.

"Was she all right when you left her?"

"She's okay. We walked down together, and I watched until she and your other sister drove away." She'd let Ginny tell him about Sellers' pointing his finger at them like he was holding a gun.

"I haven't heard from her. I guess I worry 'cause she's the baby of the family." He shrugged as if to say he couldn't help it.

"She's not great about answering her cell phone, but I don't understand Mary not answering hers."

"It was close to lunch time. They probably went to get something to eat. I wouldn't worry." Her own stomach rumbled a bit. She hadn't eaten.

"What about Sellers? Did you see him anywhere after the hearing? He's a nut, you know."

"He didn't get on the elevator with us. I think the judge put the fear of God into him. I doubt he'll try anything else."

"The judge ... was he pretty tough?"

"Like I said, he lectured him and warned him of the consequences. So is there a problem?" Was he second-guessing her?

"That's just the kind of thing that will cause Sellers to be even more angry."

"He is a little weird, but the judge let him know in no uncertain terms he'd put him and I quote 'under the jail' the first time he tried anything."

"Just the same, let me give you my phone numbers at the station and my cell so you can call me if that creep shows his face." He reached into his jacket pocket.

"Sure, if it'll make you feel better, Lieutenant, but I don't think there's anything to worry about. Most of these guys are only brave when they're alone with their partners. You know that."

Martin wrote his numbers on the back of a card and handed it across the desk to her, his long fingers brushing hers. She glanced at him to see if the contact was deliberate but saw no sign of it in his eyes. God, what was wrong with her? She wasn't even divorced yet.

As she set it next to her computer, he said, "I want you to keep those numbers with you as long as you're representing Ginny. I won't rest easy until this whole thing is over. I don't trust the guy. If anything at all suspicious happens, I want you to call me a-sap."

He sounded like an army sergeant giving orders, but she tried not to let it bother her. "I'll be glad to. I'll plug the numbers into my computer and phone. It's nice to know Ginny has a brother who cares so much about her."

"Thanks, but I want you to call if you see anything suspicious around your office or house. I think you need to be aware of your surroundings at all times until this case is closed."

A shiver tickled the back of her neck. "I'm sure you're mistaken, Lieutenant. There'd be no motivation for the man to harm me. It's your sister you should be worried about."

He cleared his throat. "I know, Ma'am, but there's something about the guy that's just not normal. I can't put my finger on it, but I've felt that way since I first met him. I think he's a sociopath. No telling what he'll do. Besides, I ran a background check, and he's got a history of assaults."

Dena stared at him for a moment. Was he a beer short of a six pack? Or was Sellers really a danger? "Did you look to see who the assaults were on? Perhaps he was only defending himself."

"Not yet, but I intend to." He towered over Dena's desk, staring down at her.

"Lieutenant, I'm not trying to offend you, but you do seem to be overreacting."

"Maybe you're right, Ma'am, but it still doesn't hurt to be careful. I don't want anything to happen to her…or you either."

"Neither do I. If you're trying to frighten me, you're not doing a bad job. I promise I'll exercise the utmost caution." Dena walked him to the door. He had a slight limp, which made her wonder if something had happened to him in the line of duty.

"Thanks, Mrs. Armstrong. That's all I want." They walked through the reception area together. "I'm sure you'll do right by my sister. I've heard, for a new lawyer, you're pretty good. That's why I sent her to you."

"Well, thanks. I hope I live up to your expectations. Your sister's a nice young lady and lucky to have a brother who cares about her the way you do." She reached out to shake his hand, a bit closer than the first time. He smelled of sweat mixed with something musky, a far cry from the horrible odor emanating from Sellers when he was on the witness stand.

He held her hand a moment longer than normal, but she didn't pull away. She was gratified he didn't use a bone-crushing grip on her like a lot of men did. His hand wasn't very soft, but his grip was reassuring and warm. "Nice meeting you, Ma'am."

"You too, Lieutenant. Take care now." Something rang a bell inside her. What was wrong with her? She walked back into her office. The outside door opened and closed. She shut her door, wanting a few minutes to herself before Meredith burst in full of questions.

She pulled up Ginny's information in her contacts and put Martin's numbers in the notes section. She started to throw his card into the trash, but thought better of it, and put it into her billfold. Moments later Meredith cracked her door.

"What'd he want, *Ma'am?*" Meredith was poised at Dena's open door with her hand balled up as if to knock.

"He's just worried about his sister. I told him she got away okay." Dena loosened the string tie around her neck and reached for a bottle of water from the small refrigerator behind her desk. "He says Alan Sellers is crazy."

"Hey, Mrs. A, do you think Sellers would really rip her guts out with his fillet knife like he said?" Meredith hunched her shoulders, her mouth twisted around like she was in pain.

"I don't know," Dena said, laying her glasses aside and raking her hands through her thick hair. She shook out two ibuprofen from a bottle that lived on a corner of her desk and swallowed them with water. "She thinks he would. Remember how scared she was?"

"Yeah. She jumped every time the door opened."

"Poor kid," Dena said as she closed her eyes, hoping Meredith would see that she needed a few moments to herself.

"I felt sorry for her," Meredith said.

"Me, too." She leaned back in her chair and clasped her hands in her lap, but didn't hear Meredith budge. Meredith knew Dena, on occasion, would take a catnap.

"Hey, Mrs. Armstrong, what'd you think of that brother of hers? Whoa, isn't he a hunk?"

Dena opened her eyes. "I tried not to notice, but there was something about him."

"Well, he got me all hot and bothered. Did you see his limp?"

"I'll bet there's a story there."

"Me, too, Mrs. Armstrong, *Ma'am*." Meredith cackled as she closed the door on her way out.

Chapter Eight

MARTIN

*L*ater that afternoon, Martin Richardson stopped working on an offense report in mid-sentence when Ginny showed up, skirting between desks to get to him. He was helping out in the main squad room because Charlie Gardenia had gone home sick with food poisoning. As if that wasn't bad enough, "Tex" Plummer had been in a wreck on the seawall, which turned out to be a nine-car rear-ender pile-up, blocking traffic for half a mile to the east, which wasn't so hard to do in Galveston in the summertime. He turned to the petty thief sitting beside the desk and said in a gruff voice, "Stay right here. I'll finish with you in a minute."

The little man said, "I ain't going nowheres, Lieutenant. I done told you that. You just tell me what you want me to do. You want me to sit here and wait for you? I'll sit here all day if that's what you want me to do. You don't have to tell me twiced."

"All right," Martin said, stepping into the aisle. He reached for his baby sister, giving her a bear hug. "It went okay, huh?" He glowered at the prisoner and led Ginny into his private office.

"Everything was perfect, except now Alan's saying someone broke in and smashed my stuff." Ginny tossed her head, her hair flying.

"You're just lucky to get away from him." He perched on the corner of his desk. "If you'd have listened to me in the first place…"

"Don't start." She stamped her foot. "If one more person tells me I should never have moved in with him in the first place…" She sat on the edge of a chair and crossed her arms.

"All right," he said. "Where's Mary?"

"Waiting for me down in the car. I just wanted to run up and tell you, so you wouldn't worry."

"I already talked to your lawyer."

"You didn't. She's going to think I'm a big baby. First Mary comes with me to court, and then you call her."

"I didn't hear from you, and I wanted to know what happened." Martin didn't correct her. He didn't want to hear what she would say if he told her he'd actually gone to Mrs. Armstrong's office. "She seems pretty nice."

Her eyes lit up. "She's the best. You should have seen her rip him up on the witness stand. There was nothing he could say that would have done him any good. She was great."

"I'll have to watch her in court sometime. Mitchell Trailor's wife had her for her lawyer, and she ripped him a new one, too. That's why I sent you to her."

"You didn't tell me that." She giggled and tossed her long hair over her shoulder. "Remind me not to mention her to Mitchell the next time I see him."

He stood, hoping she'd understand it was time to leave. He had a lot of work to do. "Well, now you know. Hey, it's great to see you laughing again, Gin."

She studied the tops of her shoes. "I wasn't laughing in court. He still scares me to death. I could hardly look at him."

He put a finger under her chin and lifted her face. "Don't worry, Sis. Mary and I will take care of you." His eyes bored into hers. "He's never going to hurt you again."

Ginny clasped her brother's hand to her cheek. "Thank you," she said in a soft voice. "Thank you for everything." She squeezed his hand and jumped up, her old bouncy self. "You're the best. Well, I've got to go. Mary's double-parked outside, and I don't want her to get a ticket." She grinned and headed for the door.

He touched her arm. "By the way, where have y'all been? Court's been over for quite a while."

"Lunch and then we poked around the shops on The Strand."

"Women." He wanted to fuss at her for not calling but thought it better to save it for another time. "See you later, kid."

She walked back through the crowded office, dodging some other police officers and the desks. She was so young. If only he'd been able to talk her out of seeing that bum. The only thing he could do now was make sure she was safe until it was all over. He'd never let her make the same mistake again.

Glancing at the little guy he'd been talking to in the squad room, Martin remembered the report he'd been filling out when his sister had arrived. He went back to the computer. "Okay, let's finish this and get you booked in."

Chapter Nine

ALAN SELLERS

Sellers browsed in the front windows of an antique store on Postoffice Street that stood catty-corner from Dena Armstrong's office building. He wanted to see if Ginny would come out. After having found the address of the lawyer on the bottom of his papers, he had decided the best place to find Ginny after the hearing, and away from Mary, would be at her lawyer's place. He wanted to talk to her. He wanted to try to reason with her. He wanted to find out why she had said they were married.

He'd stood outside every shop and café on each side of the street down from the lawyer's office. He'd sweated all day. He could smell himself. The pavement had heated up the bottoms of his shoes. He ate a bowl of gumbo at a place next to what used to be a sandwich shop.

At least it had been cool in there. When he figured he had worn out his welcome, he went into an art gallery with big picture windows so he could see out. After a while, the man inside had crowded him so much Sellers left and went into the shop next to it. After waiting for hours, Ginny hadn't come out.

She might not have gone back to her lawyer's, but he didn't want to think about that possibility, because if true, what would he do? He couldn't call her at Mary's. Mary wouldn't let her talk to him. Mary had never liked him. He didn't like her either. Or Martin. He had never liked any cops, especially big ones, and Martin ranked with the tallest, if not the biggest.

If he couldn't talk to Ginny, he at least wanted to follow her. That lawyer and the judge had made him so mad that after court he not only hoped to find out what Ginny was doing and who she was doing it with, but he might even scare her a little.

Where did she plan to live after she left Mary's? He had gone to Mary's one night late and seen Ginny's car there and figured she lived there for the present, but it wouldn't be forever. He figured she still lived with Mary since she came to court with her, but he wanted to see for himself. What if she had already found another place to live?

Thoughts swirled around in Sellers' mind like little whirlpools. He wanted to punish Ginny for what happened in court. He couldn't believe the judge and the lawyer thought they could tell him what to do, thought they could talk to him like they had and get away with it. Did they think he wouldn't get them back for that?

A part of him wished his father hadn't died. They wouldn't have dared treat him so badly if his father had come to court with him. His father would've called some of his union buddies and someone would've called the judge and none of that protective order stuff would've ever gotten off the ground.

Too bad his father wasn't alive.

His father would've worked a deal with that lawyer. His father wouldn't have let anyone push him around. But his father was deader than dirt, and he really didn't like thinking about what caused him to be that way.

Sellers pretended to be looking at some junky furniture in the antique store window but stared across the street, though he didn't have much hope Ginny would still show up.

Judges were supposed to be fair. At least, judges were supposed to act like things were fair. He wondered how that judge could've dared let that lawyer talk to him like he wasn't worth scraping off the bottom of her shoe. The judge and the lawyer didn't act like they cared what he had to say. What about his side? He'd worked out a whole story to tell, and they didn't let him, and that really pissed him off. Slamming his fist into his palm, he tasted bile, as his insides spun around with anger. Could that judge have gotten some money from Martin to fix Ginny's case? It'd be just his luck to get a judge like that.

Sellers had been planning on telling the judge that Ginny stole his money out of the bank. Ginny had no right to it or the DVD player or the TV she took, and the judge ought to make her give it all back. To top it off, now the judge ordered him to pay alimony. When did they get alimony in Texas? The judge must have decided they were married, like the papers said.

Just what did Ginny say on the witness stand? She couldn't have been there more than a few minutes. He wasn't that late. Now he moved across the street to the next antique store. This one had its whole storefront across from the lawyer's office. He'd be able to see real good.

The more he thought about it, the more pissed he got. He wouldn't have to pay alimony if something happened to Ginny. Pleased at the thought, he began to play with that idea. He picked up a mallard bookend from an old desk and pretended to look at it as he watched the door across the street. Once a person did something serious, it didn't take too much to do it again.

"May I help you, Sir?"

Sellers looked into eyes the color of bluebonnets and then focused on the person talking to him. She had a halo of dark hair and large, even teeth, but could have been as old as his mother. "Nah, just looking," he answered, setting the bookend back on the spindly desk.

"No problem," she said. "Please let me know if I can show you anything." She moved away, toward the back of the store.

The shop people probably thought he was going to steal something. He shoved his hands in his back pockets and moved slowly between the furniture and display racks in front of the windows that went all the way across. After a few minutes of listening to the sappy music they were playing and breathing in some sweet candle smell, his anger faded, replaced by a grim determination to get revenge. If he did it right, he could get away with almost anything, including putting that lawyer in her place, six feet under.

Mama. Sellers' vision blurred, and he saw himself as a little guy, just out of diapers, standing on tiptoes and staring out a window in search of his mother, a mother who never answered his cries.

What made him remember that?

Clearing his throat and focusing on the building across the way, he pretended to brush his hair off his forehead as he wiped at his eyes and glanced around to be sure no one watched. It might take him all afternoon, but if Ginny never came out, he would just have to find out where that lawyer lived. He smiled a smile that did not spread to his eyes.

After six that evening, he sat in his car on Twenty-second Street, still watching the building. The lawyer finally rewarded him by pushing through the door in the company of a fat white man in a white suit. Scooting down in the seat, Sellers watched over the edge of the car door as they rounded the corner, crossed the street, and walked out of his sight. He started his father's Cadillac and eased down to the corner of Twenty-second and Market, turned right, and found an open spot across the street from a parking garage. He spotted her in a little black Ford sedan when she came out. She headed south in the direction of the seawall.

He stayed back so she wouldn't see him, but she wasted no time pulling ahead by three car-lengths and speeding toward the beachfront. He stomped on his gas pedal and tried to catch her as she turned west on the seawall. The summer tourist traffic slowed them down on the boulevard as drivers ogled everything from bikini-clad females on roller-blades to surfers catching waves. To be on the safe side, Sellers kept an eye on her and remained a fair distance behind. Even if Ginny-the-Bitch had told Mrs. Armstrong what his car looked like, he had covered himself. She wouldn't know him in his daddy's white Cadillac. He had taken it out of storage after his own car's air conditioner had quit, and he'd put it in for repairs. At least that was one thing Ginny wouldn't get out of him. His father had left the Caddy to him, and if it hadn't reminded him so much of that night his father had died, Sellers would've been driving it a long time ago. He didn't think Ginny even knew about it.

He trailed the lawyer all the way down the seawall, past the hotels, past Sixty-first Street where the fast food joints were, past the Wal-Mart Supercenter. After that, he had to work to keep up with her as she cut in and out of traffic. The traffic used to thin out after Sixty-first, but in the past decade or so even more condos and hotels and restaurants had been built.

He banged on his steering wheel. Damn. Why didn't she slow down? Lawyers. They could probably get their tickets fixed while people like him had to pay his or hire one of them to fight it. He accelerated so he wouldn't lose her.

She turned right and drove down the slope of the seawall toward the north. The cars in front of him were driving in slow motion. When the driver in front of him hit his brakes, Sellers came to a halt. His neck grew hot. He slammed his fist on the steering wheel again, blasting the horn. The other cars pulled around both cars. The people in front of him had stopped right where she had turned. One of them held up a map.

He blasted them with his horn again and gripped the steering wheel, his knuckles turning white. He pounded the dashboard and stuck his head out. "Son-of-a-bitch," he yelled. The people pulled up past the turn so he could get by. Gunning his engine, he swerved around the corner, down the slope, and stopped at the stop sign. The Ford had disappeared.

Chapter Ten

DENA

Dena and Zack sat perpendicular to each other at a table in an Italian restaurant. A red and white-checked cloth covered the table. A single red candle burned down next to a breadbasket, the aroma of garlic filling each breath she took. There had been a time when she chose to sit across from Zack so she could gaze into his eyes, but that time was long past. Now she positioned herself so she could watch the children punching in songs at the jukebox. Paul could read just enough to think he knew what each song was about.

Dena kept the hand closest to Zack in her lap and the other hand resting next to her wine glass. Conversation had been sporadic as it usually was lately unless he was chastising her about something, which seemed like everyday. He cleared his throat.

Dena glanced from the jukebox to him and waited. He was probably going to tell her he was going out of town again. She was long past caring. In fact, now she relished the time with him gone. She sipped from her glass of red wine.

"You know how I'm fixing to go out of town? Well, I'm going to El Salvador for a week after I get home from this trip."

"Let me see if I have this straight," she said, hiding the relief that danced in her stomach. "You've only been home a week, and you're leaving again tomorrow. So when you get home next week, you'll be home a week and then go again?"

"Yep. That's not a problem for you, is it?"

She shrugged and twirled the nearly empty wine glass between her fingers. "Nope." It used to be a problem. Once upon a time, she'd get a pain in her chest when she heard he'd be leaving. She'd been so in love that she wanted him to be home as much as possible. "The kids will miss you." She felt his eyes on her but didn't look at him.

"If it wasn't for the money, I wouldn't have to be gone so much."

Dena ignored the comment about the money and pulled off a piece of bread, biting a big hunk out of it. She felt all mixed up inside. One minute she was sad. The next, angry. Then, suspicious, distrustful. She drew a deep breath, not wanting another argument, trying to keep her feelings inside. It didn't work. "Are you sure you aren't going off visiting another woman?"

His face blanched. "What the hell's that supposed to mean?" The muscle in his jaw flexed.

She hadn't intended to say that. Somehow it just slipped out. She had thought it, sure, in the deep recesses of her mind, but never intended to say it to his face. She could have bitten her tongue the moment it slipped out. Laughing, she tried to pretend it was a joke.

"That's not funny." He took a long swallow from his wine glass and, grabbing the bottle, refilled his glass more than halfway. "If you'd give up some of that money of yours, I wouldn't have to work so hard."

The old money issue was raising its ugly head like a deadly snake. She wasn't going to let that comment go. "You mean you wouldn't have to work so hard if you didn't buy cars like that Lexus."

His face had grown blotchy. "I deserve it. I do work hard. You think all the travel I do for my job is easy?"

"My job isn't easy either, Zack. Most people's jobs aren't easy. That's why they call it work."

"Yeah, well our lives would definitely be a lot better if you'd share some of your inheritance with your family."

Dena rolled her eyes. "Not that again. By going to law school and making more money than I did as a teacher, I am sharing it."

Throwing down his napkin, Zack pushed back from the table. "Yes, that again. It's time you thought about how you could help the whole family if you'd just get off it, especially help yourself. Did it ever occur to you that you could do something with that money besides pay for law school? You could do something with your office. You could fix up the house. You could spend a little on the kids. Hell, just look at yourself in the mirror sometime. You could stand to spend some money fixing yourself up, too." He rose and stalked in the direction of the kids.

A heat wave swept her body. Damn him. Since when had he thought there was something wrong with the way she looked? She hadn't heard that one before. Glancing down at her hands, she examined her fingernails in the candlelight. Her nails were different lengths, unpolished, and even a bit ragged. All the paperwork she processed every day and all the water she put her hands in every night didn't help. She could opt for a manicure occasionally. Maybe she could get her hair done more often and do something different with it. She could ask John, her hairdresser, for his opinion. Wait a minute. Why did she care what Zack thought, anyway? He was fixing to be history … just as soon as she could put her plan in motion.

Chapter Eleven

ALAN SELLERS

"You'll never get away from me," he whispered into the phone. "I know where you are, and I'm coming to get you."

"Alan, please leave me alone." Ginny moaned. "All I want are my few things you have left and for you to leave me alone."

"No. I'll never let you go. You belong to me." He liked hearing her plead. It made him feel in charge. Kicking back in his recliner, he took a long swallow of beer.

"Please, let me go," Ginny begged. "I don't want to belong to you any more."

"I don't care what you want." He laughed under his breath. He wanted to make sure she couldn't sleep at night. She'd never know when he might show up at the door or a window.

"Alan, quit calling me. I've got a protective order against you. You're not supposed to call me." Ginny's voice cracked as she cried out the words.

"Ginny, hang up the telephone. Just hang up on him," Ginny's sister, Mary, hollered from another room.

His cell went dead. He tapped the little telephone symbol on his cell again, a redial.

"We're going to get a recorder," Mary said into the phone after it had rung once. "Alan, she doesn't want to talk to you. Leave her alone."

He didn't say anything. He knew better than to let Mary hear his voice. That would make it two against one. He could just see that old judge putting him 'under the jail' as he had put it, based solely on what Ginny and Mary said.

"Alan, I know you're there. You can't scare me like you do Ginny. Stop calling," Mary yelled.

The line went dead one more time. Sellers tapped the symbol again. He could see Ginny in his mind's eye, her eyes all red from crying, her face wet, and her hair streaming down around her shoulders.

Someone picked up the phone and Sellers heard: "Don't answer it, Gin. Just let it ring." Mary's voice. Then he heard: "I can't let it ring. It's driving me crazy." Sellers grinned and waited for her to speak to him. She said, "Alan, stop calling. I'm not changing my mind."

"You'll never get away from me," he said in a quiet monotone.

"Didn't you hear what my lawyer and the judge told you? You're under a protective order, which you're violating by calling me."

"I don't care what they said. I'm going to kill you, Ginny. I'm going to kill you and your lawyer and your sister and anyone who gets in my way. You'll see. You'll never get away from me."

"Your number shows up on my phone, Alan," Ginny said. "I've got evidence you've been calling me, so you'd better quit it." The line went dead again.

Sellers's chest grew tight. He didn't really think anyone could tell it was him from the number of the throwaway phone he'd bought. He'd have to buy a couple more, just to be on the safe side.

Chapter Twelve

DENA

"Lucas." Dena stood in the doorway of his office. When he looked up, she said, "We need to talk when you have some time."

Lucas threw down his pen. "Now is as good a time as any. What is it?"

Closing the door behind her, Dena went to one of the two leather chairs that faced his desk, picked up the stack of files from the seat, and sat down with them in her lap. "I need some money." His office smelled of stale pipe smoke. She felt a little headache coming on, over her right eye. That always seemed to happen when she ventured inside Lucas's office. She didn't know whether it was physiological or psychological and didn't care. All she knew was that it hurt and as soon as she got out of there, she'd have to pop some painkillers.

"Don't we all," he said and chuckled at his own joke, his broad front teeth glistening.

"I'm not joking, Lucas. I want to cash in some of my inheritance."

Lucas sat up straighter. "I thought we agreed that after you got through paying for law school, you wouldn't spend any of that. I thought you wanted to save it for your old age or for the kids." He sipped coffee from a Styrofoam cup. "Yuck, cold," he said and threw it into the wastebasket.

Dena drew a deep breath. She'd known there would be an argument, and she was ready for him. "I know what I said. I changed my mind. How soon can you cash some of my stocks?"

"The market is doing well right now. You'd be a fool to cash anything in." He gripped the edge of his desk and pushed himself back.

"Some bonds then," she said, determined he would do as she wished.

He eased out of his executive chair, the leather groaning from the strain, sidestepping the stacks of books on the floor, and stood over her. "They're locked in. What's gotten into you?"

Why did men always like to stand over her? Weren't they bigger than her already? "Just because you're executor of my father's estate doesn't mean you can tell me what to do with my money." She kept her tone even and met his eyes with a determined look.

In the past, she'd been unable to have a confrontation about personal matters without getting defensive or teary-eyed. She was determined to overcome her timidity. She did fine when dealing with other people's business, but when it came to her own, she had trouble holding it together. "I've let you manage things all these years, but if you won't do as I ask I'll go to Probate Court and demand an accounting."

"For heaven's sake, tell me what you have in mind." His labored breathing made her wonder how long it would be until he had some kind of attack. He weighed well over two hundred and fifty pounds, and he wasn't very tall. She had no desire to mother him, and she had quit mentioning his health some time back.

"Calm down, Lucas." She waved him back to his chair. "Sit down, and let's talk about this civilly. You want a drink of water or something?"

"No, I'm all right. Listen, you know your father wanted me to safeguard that money for you. You know how he felt about Zack getting his hands on it."

She pressed her lips together. "Let's not go into that again. My father was very patronizing toward me, but you don't have to be."

"No, really. Is it for him? Is he pressuring you to spend it? Tell me what's going on." He coughed, a hard hacking sound in the back of his throat, and spit something into his handkerchief.

Dena suppressed a gag reflex. She stared out the window behind his desk. How could she tell Lucas she needed money to start her own law practice? She could tell him she was planning on leaving Zack, but she didn't want to. She wanted to play her hand close to her chest...wanted to get everything in place before anyone found out. There would be no talking her out of either one. No stopping her from becoming the free and independent woman she'd longed to be since before she went to law school.

Taking a deep breath, she squared off with her cousin. "It's not for him, okay? He doesn't even know I'm talking to you. It's a surprise."

"For what? Just tell me that."

She shook her head. "No. It's not that I don't trust you, but I want to keep my business to myself."

"For heaven's sake," he said. "How much money are we talking about?"

Dena pulled a piece of paper from her jacket pocket and glanced at it. "A hundred and fifteen thousand, three hundred and fifty dollars."

"Now you've really got me curious. When do you need this money?"

"Give or take a couple of months, but I wanted to give you plenty of notice, you know, to make the best possible arrangements."

"And you won't tell me what it's for?"

She just stared at him. No way was she going to tell him about the small office building she wanted to put a contract on or that the sum of money she was asking for included the price of a full set of office furniture for her new office.

As for Zack, she'd figured out the cost of a dinette set, bedroom suite, and living room suite of furniture for an apartment for him plus bunk beds and chests of drawers for the kids for the second bedroom of his apartment. Once the divorce got to the end stage, she'd withdraw more money to buy him out of his share of the house.

Lucas shook his head. "You know if you do this every couple of years you won't have anything left by the time you reach retirement age."

"I'm making very good money right now, Lucas. In the next few years, I should start making a lot more, you said so yourself. I'll invest some of it." She wasn't about to give up. She knew he had to do what she wanted. It was her money, and there was nothing he could do about it.

He hooked his thumbs in his vest pockets and sighed, his sunken eyes resting on her face. After a few moments, he said, "Sounds like you're determined to go through with it."

She relaxed a bit when his tone changed. "I've been thinking about this for a long time."

He rocked back in his chair. "Look, I have a better idea. You know that old warehouse a couple of blocks over where we store our files? Why don't we sell it instead of cashing in anything?"

Taken aback, Dena said, "That old building? I haven't been over there in ages. You'd sell a piece of real estate?" She'd never considered that. She'd thought he'd never part with any of the precious real estate that had been left to them by their fathers. Each of them owned a fifty-percent-undivided interest. Lucas had always managed it for a modest fee, much less than they would have had to pay a real estate management company. He enjoyed dealing with tenants and leases and that sort of thing. To her, it was all very boring and tedious.

"We've got that antique mall on the bottom floor anyway, and those two guys who run the mall have been saying for a long time they might want to buy if the price was right."

Dena jumped up, energized. "Property has always been like a sacred cow to you. Not that I'm saying no. Go ahead, sell." Putting his files down in the chair, she headed for the door before he changed his mind.

"Real estate in Galveston is doing very well right now. We could make good money on it." Lucas cleared his throat. "But, there are a few minor details we have to discuss..."

Oh, oh, here it comes. She turned back and faced him. "Like…"

"Don't look so skeptical. Nothing bad. It's just that we've been using it for storage all these many years. In order to sell it, or even to place it on the market—"

"Anything," she said interrupting. "I'll do whatever it takes."

"You'll need to get rid of all your father's old files and make other arrangements for your own. Oh, and your grandmother's furniture and—"

"Okay, Lucas. I'll do it."

"It's not going to be so easy. There's a lot of stuff there. You'll need some help."

She tempered her smile, relieved they could reach some sort of compromise without any harsh words. "I can be very resourceful when I want, you'll see. How long do I have to get it done?"

"How about September first?" He was smiling, too, like there was something she didn't know, but she didn't care. "Don't go over there alone, you'll need plenty of help. And don't come back and tell me you've changed your mind—"

"Don't worry, I won't." She pulled his door open. "See you, Luke. And hey, thanks." She blew him a kiss and fled back into her office. Collapsing into her chair, she laughed into her hands. It had been easier than she'd thought. Now all she had to do was line up some help without Zack knowing what was going on. She reached for the phone to call her friend, Ellen, and breathed a big sigh of relief.

Chapter Thirteen

MARTIN

$\mathcal{M}$artin deliberately waited until the end of the week and a payday before approaching his captain, thinking at least that way he had a shot at Boyd's being in a good mood. On top of that, he waited until after lunch when he knew the captain would have been to the bank and eaten at DeLaRosa's. Perhaps the cap wouldn't have the energy to get mad or, if he did, not to yell too loud. As soon as he saw Boyd drop into his chair, Martin launched himself. Knocking cn the doorjamb, he said, "Captain, may I see you for a few minutes?" The guys often kidded Martin about how formal he sounded sometimes. He didn't mean to. It just came out that way about half the time, especially when he was nervous or wasn't thinking about it.

"Sit down, Richardson." Boyd belched. "That hot sauce. It gets to me, you know?" Boyd was a balding, half-black, half-Latino man that Martin guessed was somewhere in his sixties. He kept his exact age a secret, as if he was afraid it would be used against him. He was a couple inches shorter than Martin but built like a refrigerator. In fact, he was fond of telling stories of how he used to play tackle on his high school football team. Nobody ever got past Ildefonso Boyd. He belched again.

"Yeah, not to mention the refried beans." Martin studied the front of the desk before him, waiting for the right opening.

The captain laughed. "Right. So what can I do for you? Everything going okay? I heard about your sister. She okay?"

Martin jerked his head up. "What did you hear?" He wondered if the cap could know about her having a baby. Martin still meant to talk her out of it.

"About that Sellers creep, you know. She shoulda filed charges. We could've straightened him out." He pulled a penknife from his pocket and opened it up and started picking at his teeth. "You know his old man was a big shot in the longshoreman's union in Houston in his day."

"He made a point of telling us that when she first started going out with him."

"Hell, that didn't hold any water with us. We jailed his butt lots of times when he used to come down here trying to throw his weight around. 'Specially when he'd go out on the beach, like around the beginning of each summer, and get drunk and ogle the girls, you know?"

"Yes, Sir."

"And once he beat up a woman at East Beach right in front of a crowd. Tore her bathing suit off her and everything."

Martin flinched at the thought that Sellers had been raised by a man like that. "What a bastard."

"Yep. Anyway…" Boyd kicked back in his chair.

"Captain," Martin said, hating to interrupt the captain's reverie but afraid he'd lose his chance if he didn't speak up. "There's something I wanted to talk to you about."

Boyd sat upright, a wistful smile on his face. "Those were the days, though, Richardson, last century. A lot of stuff went down. You should've been there."

"I believe you, Sir."

The captain closed his knife and slipped it into his pants pocket. "So what is it?"

"Captain, you know how I've been lieutenant about two years?"

"What, you want my job? Get in line."

Martin shook his head. "No, Sir. It's not that." He stared solemnly at Boyd. He wondered if he'd get mad and start hollering in Spanish. Martin hated it when Boyd did that. If he was going to get yelled at, he wanted to know what was being said. "I don't want *my* job. What I mean is, I was wondering if I could quit?"

"Quit the force? You're handing in your resignation?" The captain slammed his palm down on the top of his desk. "After what—"

"No. No, just being lieutenant. I'd like to go back to being sergeant. I'd like to go back on the street. Sir."

"You're kidding me. I don't believe it. You want to give it up and go back on the street?"

"Yes, Sir, if that's all right with you and the chief." Martin consciously breathed in deeply. He had felt like he couldn't get his breath all during the conversation until that point.

"Have you talked to the chief?" Boyd cocked his head.

"No, Sir. I thought protocol called for me to speak to you first." Martin was surprised at Boyd's non-reaction. Maybe it was going to be a delayed one.

"Of course." His eyebrows drew together. "You know something like this has never happened before. At least, not in my memory. You want to tell me why, Richardson? Here I was thinking of you as captain after I'm gone, and you don't even want to be lieutenant. Just tell me why." He stroked his closely cropped mustache as he waited for Martin to answer.

Martin cleared his throat. "A lot of things, Cap. I miss the streets. I don't like to have to reprimand the other guys. And the politics, I hate the politics."

"Chief isn't going to be happy about this. She brags on you all the time. You're one of the few cops with a college degree, a four-year college degree."

Grimacing, Martin said, "I know. I've thought about this for a long time. Would you talk to her about it for me?"

"When do you want to do it?"

"Yesterday would be all right with me."

"It won't be that easy, I hate to tell you. What's she going to do to replace you? It'll take time to fill your spot. You know all that stuff. I wouldn't get my hopes up that it'll be real soon if I was you, Richardson."

"But you'll start the ball rolling, won't you, Captain?"

"Anxious to get out there in the hot summer sun, are you?"

Martin snorted with laughter. "Yeah, I'm looking forward to sweating again." He stood. "Thank you, Sir."

Captain Boyd shook his head. "I think you're nuts, but it's your life. I'll let you know as soon as I know something myself."

The captain stood and reached out his hand to Martin. Surprised, Martin took it. He didn't think he'd shaken the captain's hand since he'd made lieutenant. It was an odd feeling, ominous somehow.

Chapter Fourteen

DENA

After tucking Melissa into bed, Dena sat on the edge for a few moments and gazed at her daughter's face as the child's features relaxed into sleepiness. She sang a lullaby in hushed tones and caressed the baby-soft cheek. A sudden outpouring of love, like a powerful electrical surge, sprang from Dena's being. She scooped her daughter into her arms, cradling the five-year-old against her chest. Stroking her hair, Dena whispered, "I love you, Baby Girl."

The child squealed and squirmed, so Dena released her, laying her back down. Melissa's mouth made a large O as she yawned. "Nite, nite, Mommy."

"Nite, nite, Baby," Dena said as she stood. "I've got to go tuck Paul in now." She leaned down and kissed her.

Melissa scooted under the covers as Dena checked the window to make sure it was locked. She put out the light and pulled the door almost all the way closed.

Across the hall, Paul was sitting on the bed and playing with his airplanes. "You're supposed to be in the bed, Paul, not on the bed," she said, trying to be stern. He was so cute she had a hard time being strict with him.

"Mommy, read me a story," he said, getting under the covers with his airplane.

"Okay, which one do you want to hear tonight?" She walked to his overcrowded bookcase.

"*Little Engine That Could.*"

Dena had already pulled the book from the shelf, guessing it would be his choice. Nine times out of ten, it was. She sat next to him. "You sure you want to hear this old story again?"

"Yes, Mommy, it's my best one." Paul's knitted eyebrows and tightly pressed lips gave her a glimpse of the serious adult he would become.

She stretched out on his bed next to him, her arm around his shoulders. He smelled like Ivory soap. When the story ended, he rubbed his eyes and cuddled up to her. She hugged and kissed him. She had to resist an urge to lie there on the edge of his bed and hold him for a while. He and Melissa were the only children she would ever have. Zack had made sure of that. He'd extracted an agreement from her early on that they would stop after two, even if they had been of the same sex, saying it was too expensive to have many. Zack had wanted her to get a tubal ligation, but she had refused. She told him if anyone was going to be sterilized, he would have to do it. And he did.

Paul pulled his covers up to his neck and turned over, facing the wall. Dena kissed the back of his head and whispered goodnight. Glancing at his window, she stepped over and checked behind the fire engine curtains to make sure it was locked, too. She turned out his light and closed his door all but a little so he could have some light from the hall the way he liked it.

She checked the locks on the front door, unlocking them and relocking them. She walked around the house to the back doors, checking them, and peered into the garage to make sure the door was down even though she knew she'd left it that way. She put out most of the lights, leaving the outside ones burning.

After she took a hot shower, she pulled on a long, white granny gown and slipped into bed. She realized she was adhering to a ritual she'd adopted, but it made her feel better. She punched the power button on the TV remote just to get some noise into the room and picked up her Kindle. When she'd been young, when she'd been childless, she'd often read more than a book a week. Now, she was grateful for the two or three pages she could get through before she put out the light.

Reaching out to her bedside table, she tugged on the top drawer to make sure it was still locked. It was. She patted the top of the table as though to reward it for behaving well and turned her attention to her novel, the volume of the TV drowning out the noises of the night.

Chapter Fifteen

ALAN SELLERS

He moved around his apartment like a football player on the sidelines of a close game, never able to sit in one place for more than a few moments. He had put his plan into action, but it wasn't as simple as he'd thought it would be. He'd called Ginny. He'd cried for her. He'd begged her. He'd promised her. But she didn't react like she should have. She'd hesitated. He could hear her sister, Mary, in the background. She needed to shut her fat mouth.

He began shadow boxing. "Pow." A left to Mary's eye. "Bang." A right to Ginny's mouth. Dancing around on the balls of his feet, he could see himself circling the lawyer, ready to move in for the kill. Then in his mind's eye, he saw Martin in the background. What he wouldn't like to do to her brother.

Dropping onto the sofa for a moment and then bouncing up on his feet again, Sellers continued to move around the room. He'd told Ginny to call him back in an hour, but it had been an hour and a half. He wanted to know why. Had Mary stopped her? He'd asked her to give him her decision. She'd better call, or she'd be sorry. She'd be sorry anyway. He slammed one fist into the other. The phone rang, startling him. He drew a deep breath before picking it up, straining to sound casual, reining in his anxiety about what she would say. "Hello," he said, his voice too loud in his own ears.

"Alan?" Ginny's soft, little-girl voice sounded breathless. He could picture her in some boxers and a muscle tee shirt, her long, blond hair flowing around her small breasts.

"Hi, Babe. Glad you called." He tried to sound friendly and confident. She would crawl back to him. He just knew it. Women were like dumb little lambs. They needed a man to keep them in line, like a shepherd.

"Alan, I thought it over, and I called my lawyer. Did you really mean it when you said you'd get help for your drinking problem?"

She sounded scared. He felt good knowing he had power over her. He'd reassure her. Convince her of his good intentions. Sweet-talk her, just like before they moved in together. "Sure, doll, anything you want. Just come back to me 'cause I'm lonely for you." He almost laughed aloud. "You're the best thing that ever happened to me." He had her where he wanted her.

"I miss you, too. I want to come back …"

"Oh, I'm so glad." He tried to sound sincere. "I knew once you thought things over, you'd see it my way." He laid down on the sofa and stared at the ceiling.

"Wait a minute. I've been wondering, who are you going to go see?"

He frowned at his cell phone. "I don't know, Honey, you come back, and we'll decide together. I'll go to whoever you want. Your lawyer got any suggestions?"

"I don't know. I haven't asked her," she said.

Sellers realized his work was cut out for him. He had a plan, but maybe it wouldn't be as easy as he thought. "Well, come on home, and we'll make an appointment together to ask her."

"I'm not coming back until you get help. After you've been to counseling or AA or whatever, we can talk about it, okay?"

"No, not okay. I want you back now, Ginny. I love you and miss you. I'm lonely for you." He could feel the burn rising inside him.

"No. You have to understand. I can't come back now. My lawyer said for me not to go back until you get some help. Martin told me there's a batterers' program you can go to and AA meetings all over town."

He'd like to tell Martin to go to hell. "Honey, I wouldn't be this way if it wasn't for you. Don't you understand that? You come back, and we'll go together. We'll help each other." He felt like he stood on the edge of a cliff and could fall either way.

"No. You have to do it yourself. You have to prove to me that you really mean what you say, and then I'll come back."

A vein pounded in his forehead. He hadn't been this angry since the day she'd left. "Ginny, Darlin', you don't understand. I need you to help me. You don't know what you mean to me. If you really loved me, you'd come home now and help me get through this. I can't do it alone."

"Yes, you can. You can do it——"

"Baby, come home. It'll be so much easier for me if you're here cheering me on. You do love me, don't you? Don't you want to help me?" His pulse raced like one of those dogs that used to race at that track on the mainland. If he could only hold on.

"Of course I love you. That's why I'm doing this. It's the best thing I can do. For us."

He couldn't hold on. A dam-like feeling burst inside of him. "You're so stupid. I don't want you anyway. Nobody wants you. All you know how to do is spread your legs," he bellowed into the phone. He felt like he'd just careened over a cliff and couldn't find anything to grab onto to stop himself. Finally, he said, "You and your prissy lawyer. I'll get you for this. You'll be sorry. I'm gonna cut your face off, and when I'm through with you, I'm gonna do her, too. You better be looking over your shoulder, because the first time you don't, you're dead—"

"Don't …" She sobbed into the phone, and that pleased him.

"I ain't listening to you no more. You just remember what I said." Breathing hard, he clicked off his phone and threw it across the room. After several moments, the flame began to fade. He picked up his fillet knife from the coffee table and danced his fingers along the razor-sharp edge he'd spent hours honing. His sullen expression evolved into a sneer.

Without his even knowing it, the knife had become an extension of himself. No longer simply a tool, more like another limb. He had it so sharp now that he could separate skin from flesh easier than peel from a grape.

He would catch Ginny when she least expected it. It might take some time. But what else did he have? He made a promise to himself and to his father, whose voice he heard inside his head. "Yes. I'm going to have the time of my life."

Sliding his knife's cutting-edge over the callus on his thumb, he drew a thin line of blood as he continued thinking of what he would do to her. It wasn't often he didn't get what he wanted, though since his father had died it had become more frequent than he liked.

At the realization that Martin had gotten involved on top of Ginny staying at Mary's house, and a woman lawyer wielding more power over Ginny than he did, Sellers got mad again. No one was gonna get between him and Ginny and his plans. No one. Not her brother or her sister. And for sure not that lawyer.

Chapter Sixteen

MARTIN

$\mathcal{A}$ week after Martin had been in Dena Armstrong's office, he was waiting to testify in a criminal case when she came rushing from the direction of the elevators. He'd been reviewing his notes from the murder investigation and talking to his ex-partner, Joe Morales. She all but knocked them down in her determination to get where she was going. Martin waylaid her. "Whoa."

Armed with the handle of her roller bag in one hand and an inch-thick file in the other, her focus lay elsewhere. She stopped and stared at him a moment as if trying to figure out who had spoken to her.

"Lieutenant Richardson," she said, her face lighting up. "Hi." Glancing at Joe, then in the direction of the courtroom, and back to Martin, she said, "Ah, waiting to testify?"

"Yes, Ma'am." She looked good. Her reddish-brown hair had been flying as she hurried toward them. Her large-framed glasses made her face look like a little mouse's. She was almost as tiny as his sisters. She wore little in the way of make-up, but her cheeks and lips were rosy. Her suit stopped just a bit above her knee. Her legs weren't bad.

Facing backwards, she walked away from them. "Well, nice to see you. I'm running late." She shrugged as she scrambled to enter the other courtroom and called, "Bye now," in a loud whisper.

"Not bad," Morales said when Martin turned back to him.

"My sister's lawyer."

"I see." Morales raised his eyebrows.

"No, really…she's married, but she seems like a nice lady." Martin knew Joe watched his face for a reaction. Joe didn't say anything more and Martin didn't either. Glancing at the door through which she'd passed, he wondered when she'd be coming out. He wouldn't mind talking some things over with her.

The door of the first courtroom opened a minute later. "Hey, Richardson, you're up." The first assistant district attorney, a man only a bit older than Martin, held the door. Martin clapped his hand on Morales' shoulder and headed inside toward the witness stand.

At four o'clock, Martin's testimony concluded, and the judge released him from the subpoena so he could leave the courthouse. He exited the courtroom and nodded at Morales. The rules forbade them from discussing what had been said. Joe was testifying next.

Martin walked down the hall. When he cracked open the other courtroom door, Dena Armstrong huddled at the counsel table with an older male. A woman, who Martin assumed was the wife since they were in family court, sat on the witness stand. Another woman, tall, thin, dressed in a white, double-breasted pantsuit, wrote on the Panaboard with red marker. Martin tiptoed into the courtroom.

The judge acknowledged him with a glance and a raise of her eyebrows. He inclined his head and smiled the briefest of smiles. They knew each other slightly. He'd had to testify before her a couple of times on juvenile cases. Besides that, the judge had come to the Pig Pen, the police officers' union hall, and asked for their endorsement when she ran for election.

The other attorney glanced at him and continued her Q & A. Mrs. Armstrong gave no indication she'd even heard anyone in the back of the courtroom. She scribbled on a yellow legal pad. He listened to the testimony. When it became Mrs. Armstrong's turn to question the wife, Martin enjoyed watching her cross-examination, though she seemed too nice. She politely led the woman through a list of property the woman agreed her husband could have, too politely, in Martin's opinion. He began to wonder whether she had been the right choice for Ginny. What if she wasn't assertive enough? What if she wimped out on Ginny? Ginny didn't seem to think that of her, but what if Ginny just didn't know any better? He listened closely to see whether he needed to reconsider his choice of attorneys for his sister.

"Isn't there anything else you'd be willing to let Harold have?" Her voice rose. "How about the shirt off his back?"

"Objection, argumentative," the other attorney said as she jumped up from her chair.

Martin's interest picked up.

"Mrs. Armstrong, you know better than to be sarcastic with witnesses. I won't tolerate argumentative questioning. Sustained."

Dena stood. "Sorry, Your Honor, withdrawn. All right, Mrs. Tyler, let's go over a few other things, then."

The woman sat a bit straighter in the witness chair.

"You want the house."

"I owned it before the marriage. It's my separate property."

"Yes, Ma'am, but didn't you and Harold install a twenty-five thousand gallon swimming pool since marriage? And isn't it paid for?"

"Well, yes, we did. He didn't want to, but I've always been a swimmer. He complained every time we had to make a payment. He didn't—"

"Objection, nonresponsive," Mrs. Armstrong said, standing.

"Sustained," the judge said. "Mrs. Tyler, just answer the questions as put to you and don't elaborate. Your attorney gets another chance in a moment."

Mrs. Armstrong sat back down. "Okay. You want to be fair to your husband, don't you, Mrs. Tyler?" Just as the woman started to answer, Dena said, "Strike that." She rifled through some papers on her table. "Okay, you added a pool. You remodeled the kitchen. You added a guestroom and bathroom. And you remodeled the master bedroom and the bathroom. Your home is now worth three hundred and fifty thousand dollars. Isn't that what you put on your inventory form, Mrs. Tyler?"

The woman glanced at her attorney. "Yes, I guess."

"And it was valued at the time you bought it at one hundred five thousand dollars?"

"Yes, but that was many, many years ago."

"I understand that, Ma'am, but don't you think in light of the improvements, fully paid for, to your separate property home that Mr. Tyler should be entitled to a seventy-five thousand dollar rental property house that only has twenty-thousand dollars equity?"

"Not after what he did, Mrs. Armstrong."

Mrs. Armstrong stood again. "Pass the witness, Judge. I'd like to argue if you think it's necessary."

"Mrs. Warren, any more questions?"

"No, Your Honor, we rest."

Relieved to hear her actually score some points, Martin listened to the judge's rendition and waited while Mrs. Armstrong packed her roller bag. She approached the back of the courtroom, followed by her client.

Her eyes sparkled, the edges crinkling up into tiny smile wrinkles when she saw him. He thought his being there pleased her. He knew it was probably all in his mind, but he felt good about it anyway. As she walked closer to him, she turned and shook hands with her client.

"'Bye, Mr. Tyler. I'll call you when I get the decree from Ms. Warren." Her client stepped past them, and Mrs. Armstrong turned her attention to Martin. "How long were you back there?"

"Long enough to hear that the judge shafted Mr. Tyler," Martin replied.

Mrs. Armstrong laughed and, in a confidential tone, said, "Not really. She only gave the wife sixty percent. The evidence showed the husband had been screwing around on her, spending money on girlfriends, and he makes twice as much money as she does. He's lucky the judge didn't give the wife what she asked for, but the house was hers before marriage, and they have no children."

Martin chuckled. "Oh. I guess I should have come in earlier."

Mrs. Armstrong inched toward the exit. "Is there something I can help you with?"

Martin hurried around her and opened the door. "I just thought we could visit a minute. I have some questions. Want to get some coffee downstairs?"

"Yuck, out of those machines? God, no. But I'm going back to my office if you want to stop in at the coffee house down the way from it. And please call me Dena."

"All right, Dena." He liked the way her name sounded rolling off his tongue. Hey. What was wrong with him? She was a married woman. Still... "Let me take that stack of files from you."

"Okay." Her eyes crinkled again. He couldn't decide whether they were green or hazel or blue or a bit of each. He looked through her lenses, which were every bit as thick as her eyelashes. "'Bye, Marie," she called to the other attorney, who was still in deep conversation with the wife.

"'Bye. I'll try to get that decree to you by the end of next week, and I'll expect the Quadro from you around the same time."

"Quadro? What's that?" Martin glanced from one attorney to the other.

"Qualified Domestic Relations Order," Dena said. "To divide retirement. She got a chunk of that."

They rode the elevator down and walked past the metal detectors and out the front doors. The minute they hit the sidewalk that led around to the parking lots, the August heat enveloped them like a cloud. "Hang on a minute," he said. Slipping off his blazer, he draped it over one arm and loosened his tie.

"I hate the summers here," Dena said when they started walking again.

"Fall and spring are the best, though." He realized he was walking ahead of her and slowed down. She'd never be able to keep up with his normal pace.

"I like it when that first cold front blows in. Not that it makes it cold." She smiled up at him.

"But the air smells different. And the temperature does drop a few degrees." He stared down at the top of her head. The hot summer breeze blew her hair away from her face, and he could just make out her perfume. Vanilla and orange. She didn't seem so small when they talked. He liked her. She was really easy to talk to.

He handed her the files when they reached her car. She put them in the front seat and her roller bag on the floor in the back. They agreed to meet at Mod Coffee Shop on Postoffice Street.

When he arrived, she was standing at the counter, placing her order. He got in line behind her. She ordered a chai tea and a slice of carrot cake. She looked over her shoulder. "I know I shouldn't, but what the heck?" She smiled like she knew she was being a wicked little girl.

She's a married woman. A married woman. He stepped away from her, giving himself some space and ordered a black coffee.

They walked into the room next to the serving bar area. The chairs and tables were funky and battered, but it was easy to get comfortable. Dena pulled off her jacket and laid it over the back of a chair. Martin pulled his tie off and slung on the seat next to him. Several students were bent over computers, a couple mumbling to each other. Outside on Postoffice Street, people strolled by, most of them in shorts and short-sleeved or sleeveless shirts and sandals.

Dena kicked off her shoes. "God, that feels better."

Martin remembered when he'd arrived unexpectedly at her office the week before. She'd been in her stocking feet then, too. She certainly didn't stand on formality, and he didn't mind. "I like this place," he said, glancing around. "I don't get to come here often … have to suffer with the coffee at the station."

"Do you go to the Artwalks?"

"Used to when I worked on the street. I had this beat years ago, but things have really changed since then. You?"

"Used to, before the kids were born. Well, I went a couple of months ago when my husband was out of town. Took my son. He's too little to understand most of the paintings, but he had a good time." She forked a piece of carrot cake into her mouth and made eye contact.

She had kids. Well, what did he expect? "I probably wouldn't understand the paintings either."

She swallowed and said in a low voice, "Most of the time I don't either. Once I commented to a friend about whether the so-called art was art, and the artist was standing within hearing distance. My bad. So I keep my mouth shut … that is, if I ever get to attend Artwalks at all."

"So you have a kid." It was more a statement than a question. The way her eyes lit up when she mentioned her son, he could tell she loved the boy.

"Two. Paul is six. Melissa's five. What about you?"

"Nah. My wife left me before we had any." He shrugged and took a swallow from his coffee.

"Count yourself lucky. You could be stuck with child support and a wife that gives you nothing but trouble."

"Yeah, I know." He forced himself to relax. Neither of them spoke for several moments. Martin remembered the implication Morales had made in the courthouse hallway. What would it be like to be married to someone like Dena Armstrong, a mother of two and a lawyer? She had good looks and a good sense of humor. Nice hair and she dressed well. If he couldn't have her, maybe he could find someone like her. He forced himself to focus on the reason they were there. "You know, Mrs. Armstrong … Dena, Ginny has decided to keep the baby."

"So that's what this is about?"

Smart, too, Martin thought. "I've been trying to talk to her about it. So has Mary. We were wondering—"

"No way." She shook her head.

"It's just that we thought if you were to suggest the abortion, she might listen."

She kept shaking her head. "I don't get involved in people's personal decisions. Nope. The most I'd ever do would be to give her Planned Parenthood's phone number at her own request."

"But—"

"No, Lieutenant Richardson."

"Martin."

"Okay. No, Martin. It's not even open to discussion."

Stubborn, too. He picked up his coffee again and sipped. Well, that could be a good trait when it came to a person maintaining her convictions. He looked into her eyes and caught her watching him. Why was she doing that? What was wrong with him? It was like he had some schoolboy crush on his teacher. He had to quit fantasizing. Married women, especially with two kids, well...the words *off-limits* described them best. There *must* be someone else like her out there. "All right. I just thought...well, you know. You're not angry, are you?"

She shook her head. "I understand. I really do. But next time I'm going to make you buy my tea and cake."

"It would be an honor, Ma'am," he said, ducking his head.

"Thank you, Sir. Now is there anything else I can do for you?"

Martin wanted very much to give her an honest answer but restrained himself. "You could spend a few minutes explaining those ten options you gave my sister."

"Now that I'll be glad to do, Lieutenant ... Martin," she said. She ate the last bit of cake and slapped the saucer and fork down on the table.

Martin looked down into his coffee cup. Damn, she was just too good to be true.

Chapter Seventeen

DENA

Wednesday afternoon, Dena had agreed to catch the telephone while Meredith worked on some discovery materials they had to get into the mail before the end of the day. Dena sat at her own desk with the speakerphone turned on so she could get some work done, too. Theirs being a so-called one-girl office, they all had to make compromises, however answering the telephone happened to be one area where Luke would not cooperate unless the call was on his cell phone. He would rather the phone lines not be answered than to lower himself to picking up for a secretary.

Luke's attitude was a constant source of irritation to Dena, who thought everyone ought to pitch in and do anything that needed doing. The fact that Lucas felt there was a line between attorney and secretary, that he would not deign to cross, annoyed Dena to no end. So, as usual, Dena already found herself in a foul mood when she picked up line one. "Barlow and Barlow. Dena Barlow Armstrong speaking."

"This is Alan Sellers."   Dena recoiled from the set like she'd seen a snake come out of it. Making an effort to calm her jittery hands and keep the surprise and disgust out of her voice, she said, "What can I do for you, Sir?"

"I called her today, Mrs. Armstrong. I called her, but I didn't mean to, really I didn't. It just happened. I had a few drinks, so I called her, but I didn't mean what I said. Please don't put me in jail, Mrs. Armstrong."

Dena squinched up her face. A perfect end to a perfect day. She wished he had his own attorney. If he had his own attorney, she couldn't talk to him. Ethically, it would be a violation. When *pro se* litigants called, though, since they were acting as their own attorneys, she had to speak to them. She hated *pro se* litigants with a passion she rarely felt for anything else in the world. "What did you say to her, Mr. Sellers?" Dena kept her tone as sweet as she could.

"I can't remember everything I said, Mrs. Armstrong. I had a few drinks and got carried away. But I didn't mean it. I'm sorry. I won't do it again."

He sounded like an adolescent boy, half soprano-half tenor. Odd for someone not much older than her—early thirties, if memory served.

"What did you say, though, Mr. Sellers? Tell me what you said to her."

"I said some crazy things, Mrs. Armstrong. But I didn't mean them. Honest. I didn't mean to call. Won't you believe me? I won't do it again. I'm sorry. I won't call her again. I promise. You know I wouldn't really hurt her."

When she was first married, Dena thought she would never get tired of hearing herself called Mrs. Armstrong. Now it was a different story. She tried to keep the irritation out of her voice. "Did you threaten her, Mr. Sellers?"

"I don't know. If I did, I didn't mean it. I just wanted to talk to her. Please don't put me in jail, Mrs. Armstrong. I don't want to go to jail. I won't do it again. I promise I won't."

A tiny stabbing sensation began in her left temple. She rubbed it. "Mr. Sellers, calm down please."

"I'm calm. I'm calm. I just wanted you to know. I didn't mean it. I'm sorry. I just want a friendly divorce. I won't do it again."

"Oh, so now you want a friendly divorce? Did you upset her?" She stabbed the pen she held into the deskpad and drew a stick figure with horns.

"No, I don't think so. I don't know. I know I'm not supposed to call her, but I couldn't help it. Will you tell her I'm sorry? Are you going to put me in jail, Mrs. Armstrong?"

The pain in Dena's temple pierced farther into her head, moving into her left eye, causing a tremor. She took a deep breath. "If you promise it won't happen again, I won't take you back to court, but you must stop calling her."

"Okay. I promise. I just got carried away. I just had a few drinks, that's all. They just got to me, that's all. I don't want to go to jail."

"Okay, Mr. Sellers." Dena rubbed her eyes. She could feel mascara come off on her fingers. "I'm going to call Ginny and tell her you won't do it again. If you do, I *will* file on you. You're under a protective order and can go to jail just for the act of calling her, not to mention contempt of court for violation of a protective order. Do you understand?"

"Yes, Ma'am. I won't do it again. By the way, I haven't gotten my copy of the papers yet from court. Are you going to send me the papers?"

"I already have, Mr. Sellers. You sure you didn't get them? You are a week past due on the temporary alimony."

"No, I swear. Did you mail them to my apartment?"

"First of last week." She knew he was lying, but she couldn't do anything about it.

"I'll check the mail again today. Do they include what she wants to settle this case, Mrs. Armstrong?"

"I haven't received that information from Ginny yet. I'll let you know when I do." Would he ever shut up?

"Okay, Mrs. Armstrong. And thanks. Thanks a lot. You have my promise that I won't do it again. I don't know what got into me. I knew I wasn't supposed to call her. I knew it, but I couldn't help it. You tell her I'm sorry, okay? You know, I wouldn't hurt a fly."

Dena no more than hit the button disconnecting them than the other line began ringing. She reached for it when what she really wanted to do was reach for her bottle of ibuprofen. "Barlow and Barlow."

"Mrs. Armstrong? It's Ginny Richardson, er, Sellers."

"Oh, hey, I just got off the phone with your—with Alan. He apologized for calling you and promised he wouldn't do it again if I promised not to put him in jail this time." God, she had the worst headache. Where was the bottle of ibuprofen that was supposed to be on her desk?

"I'm sorry," Ginny said in a little girl voice. "Are you going to have him arrested?"

"You want me to?"

"I don't know. He was pretty scary."

"What did he say?"

"Oh, man, like everything was all my fault. Like I was a...you know ... yucky words I don't use. He cussed me. He called me all the ugly things he could think of." Her tone of voice sounded dismissive.

"You don't sound very upset."

"Yeah, I was, but, you know, I guess I'm starting to get used to it. The funny thing is that when I didn't let it creep me out, he sounded aggravated."

"That's a great way to handle him, Ginny. I think he must get his kicks from the way you let it upset you in the past. Maybe he'll quit now."

"Yeah. That's what Mary said."

"I told him if he'd promise not to do it again, I wouldn't file on him. I hope that's okay with you. Actually, I'm not sure the judge would jail him for contempt over a couple of phone calls. And the D.A. has more things to worry about than filing misdemeanor charges over a phone call. But if I press it, I'm sure I could get them to."

"Let's wait. I don't want to go to court if it's not going to do any good. We can hold this over his head, can't we? Did he say anything else?"

"The check's in the mail." Dena grabbed her purse out of her lower desk drawer and dug around in it for her other bottle of painkillers.

"Oh, sure. I'll bet he never pays me that alimony."

"*That* the judge will put him in jail for."

"Oh. Good."

"He also wanted to know if I had the list of things you wanted."

"I'm working on it, Mrs. Armstrong. I'll send it as soon as possible. Now that I'm out of the apartment, it's hard to remember everything that was there."

"I know," Dena said. "But the sooner we get the list to him, the sooner we can get this thing over with. You know there's a sixty-day waiting period on a divorce. This is already the sixth week."

"I forgot. I guess 'cause it took so long to get him served for the first hearing. Shoot, I could be divorced in three weeks or less?"

"If we get everything done. By the way, have you decided what to do about the baby?" She finally found the bottle and dropped her purse back into the drawer.

"Oh, I don't know. If I didn't tell him, and he found out later that he had a kid, I'm scared what he might do."

"Uh-huh," Dena muttered. Martin and Mary were really working on the girl, she could tell.

"I'll let you know about that soon, too. I'm going to a counselor tomorrow to talk it over."

"Okay. But get me that list. Right now it sounds like he might give you everything you want."

"I'll let you go. There's just one more thing I want to tell you. I wasn't going to, but Mary and Martin said you should know."

"What's that, Hon?"

"The last few times Alan called threatening me? Well, uh, he said he's going to kill you, too."

That evening, after dinner and after they had put the children to bed, Dena and Zack sat in front of the television, though Dena's mind was elsewhere. She chewed her lower lip as she thought about what Ginny had said. Though a bit frightening, it didn't compare to the time the previous winter when Zack had been out of town and a man had followed her home.

At least now, if someone did come after her or her kids in her own home, she had protection. She had her thirty-eight. She had even gotten one of the assistant D.A.s to take her to the firing range for practice. He had shown her how to hold the grip of the gun with one hand supporting the other. Her aim was straight and steady. She'd hit the target every time. Not that she believed Sellers would really attempt to harm her. Silly thought.

Zack stared at her. "Something the matter?"

She didn't want to sound like a clingy female. All her feelings of equal rights for women, all her arguments that women were just as good as men, those things made it difficult for her to admit, even to herself, that she might need protection.

"Dena," he said when she didn't respond. "Something on your mind?" He cocked his head. "What is it?"

Not that she thought he'd really care, but since he was persisting, she'd tell him. "I was just thinking about Ginny and Alan Sellers' case."

"Is there something special about it?"

"I had to file a protective order on the guy, because he beat his wife so badly. Today he called the office."

"Really?" He turned his full attention on her. "Why did he call you?"

"He violated the protective order. I guess he wanted to tell me what he did before Ginny, that's his wife, did. He sounded sort of irrational, repeating himself over and over."

"Luke told me you keep taking those cases even though you're not supposed to. I agree with him. You need to stop doing family law if it's going to upset you."

Why did Zack suddenly care? If she died, he'd be trustee of her money. Her insides twisted. What a morbid thought. "It's not that bad."

"You're acting like it is, sitting there and staring into space."

They're eyes met. "I was just thinking about what else Ginny Sellers said. But I probably shouldn't tell you, if you're going to side with Luke."

"I won't say anything to Luke if you don't want me to."

"Well...Alan Sellers apparently told his wife he wants to kill me."

Zack drew a sharp breath. "You kidding me?"

"I was kind of frightened at first, but now I'm just mad. I'm not going to be intimidated by something like that."

"What a stupid jerk. What did he tell her that for?" He'd been scanning the newspaper. He folded it and set it aside. He sounded like he actually cared.

"Because he's a stupid jerk."

"You don't think he really means it, do you? He was probably just blowing off steam."

Dena couldn't decipher the look on Zack's face. "Yes, but some really creepy thoughts went through my mind and with what my client's brother said," Dena shivered, "I just couldn't help getting a bit nervous about it for a few minutes." Dena stared at her lap. She was kneading her hands into her thighs. She stopped, resting them palms down. She didn't want Zack to know it made her worry just a little.

"What did the girl's brother say?"

She should have kept it to herself. There was nothing Zack could do about it. He was gone most of the time. "Martin said Alan Sellers is crazy. He told me to call him if I see any sign of Sellers anywhere."

"Wouldn't it make more sense for him to take out his anger on his wife?"

"Yeah. I'm sure he doesn't mean it. Sometimes I just get the creeps, though."

"You're usually a good judge of character. What do you think? Is he a mental case?"

"I didn't think so when we were at the courthouse. He just had a mean look about him."

"Why change your mind just because someone involved with him thinks so? That's not like you."

She shook her head. "I know this sounds silly, but there's just something about him I can't put my finger on."

"You and your feelings. If you want, I'll go by and check on the guy myself. Where does he live?"

Why the sudden concern? Was he worried about the kids? "In an apartment on the East End someplace. You don't need to do that."

"Yeah, I do. We may have our problems, but I'm not going to let anything happen to you, even if I have to take care of the guy myself. What's his address?"

She wanted to laugh. The thought of Zack going over to Sellers' apartment was ludicrous.

"Just give me his address and see what I do."

"All right, sure, Zack. If you really want it, Meredith can get it for you out of the file."

"Okay." He stood and stretched. "Well, if you feel creepy when I'm gone, you can call Bob. I'm sure he'll come right over."

"I have my gun, too." As soon as she said it, Dena knew it was a mistake.

With one long step, Zack was in front of her, leaning down over her with a hand on each arm of her chair. His grim face was so close she couldn't see him clearly.

"You promised to keep your pistol locked up."

An electrifying jolt swept through her, and Dena reared back. She hadn't seen him this angry in a long time. "I do keep it locked. I'm just saying—"

"Are you leaving the night table drawer unlocked at night when I'm not here?" His breath still smelled of dinner, but the second time around. "Do the kids know you have a gun in there?"

She pushed him away. "God no, Zack. I'm just saying—"

"Because if I find my children have access to a gun, I don't know what I'll do. At the least, I'll get rid of it."

"All right. I get the message. Go to bed."

He stood and backed away, his nostrils flaring, his eyes penetrating. "Just remember what I said."

"I'm sorry. I don't even look at it anymore, I swear."

His breath slowed. "I apologize for getting so riled up. It's late. I'm tired. And I do worry about you and the kids when I'm gone."

She reached a hand out to him.

He touched her shoulder before he left the room. "Goodnight."

"Goodnight. I'll be in later," she said, over her shoulder, but he was already gone. What a conversation. At first, he acted like he might still have feelings for her. Could he? She didn't think so, but she'd been wrong before. And to get so angry about her gun. What was that about? She'd promised to keep it under lock and key, and she had. The kids didn't know about the gun and even if they did, they didn't know where she hid the key.

Maybe he was just going through some midlife change, which would explain how cold he'd been to her lately. Maybe something else was going on. If there was, she didn't have a clue what it could be. They barely talked to each other anymore. She picked up the remote and started flipping through the channels, looking for something entertaining to get her mind off the discussion they'd just had.

Chapter Eighteen

ALAN SELLERS

*T*wo days after Sellers had telephoned Ginny's lawyer, a white guy sat in a white Lexus SUV across the street from his apartment. The same car had driven by the afternoon before. He went into the bedroom to see if he could get a better look, but the oleander bushes cast impossible shadows across the car's windshield.

Sellers' curiosity grew as the hours passed. Who was the man looking for, him? Or could he be looking for Ben, who lived in one of the upstairs apartments? He couldn't quite believe it could be that bitchy black nurse downstairs who worked at the University of Texas Medical Branch. Even funnier to think the man could be trying to get something on her retarded son.

Living near the medical center, Sellers often saw a bunch of different cars parked in every available free spot in the neighborhood. Usually, the same people got there early every day and monopolized the spaces. Being used to seeing the same cars over and over, Sellers knew the Lexus was not one of those cars. Though a different vehicle occasionally wouldn't be that weird, two days in a row, especially with a man sitting in it all day, that was unusual.

Sellers ate his bowl of corn flakes and took his shower. The man was still there. He pulled on his jeans and a black muscle shirt. The man was still there. Finally, he slid his leather belt through the loopholes of his jeans and put on his steel-toed cowboy boots. When he looked out the window again, his hazel eyes met the man's dark ones through the driver's side window. They locked onto each other, like two bulls locking horns. Sellers didn't recognize him, but he knew the man wasn't after Ben or the hag downstairs.

Had Ginny's lawyer hired someone to get something on him? What good would it do her? The divorce papers already said he was guilty of being cruel. He and Ginny didn't own a lot of stuff anyhow. Hiring somebody would be a waste of money.

It could be the insurance company spying on him, hoping to get something on him so they wouldn't have to pay his claim. But why now? He'd filed it more than six months earlier. It wasn't that much money.

Only one other thing came to mind. His father's death. And if that was it, it sure had taken them a long time to make a connection to him. Sellers' stomach turned over. He recalled the night his father had died, as he liked to call it. The night his father had died. An image of his old man standing over him with his fists doubled up flashed into his mind.

"You son of a bitch," his father had shouted.

Alan had yelled back, "You ought to know. You married her."

Now, his chest grew tight, and his breath was hard to get. It had been a couple of days since he'd gone outside. He needed some fresh air. He needed to talk to his personal-injury lawyer. And he needed to see if his Firebird's air-conditioner had been fixed.

Slipping his fillet knife in one of his back pockets and his wallet into the other, Sellers grabbed his keys and slammed the front door behind him on his way to the Cadillac. He started the car and let all the windows down to cool it off, the sweet scent of honeysuckle that covered the wire fence filling the air. Easing up near to the Lexus, he looked the guy dead in the eye and spun the steering wheel so the car did a U-turn.

Up close, Sellers was even more positive. He didn't know him. Though the man had dark hair and dark eyes, he didn't look like a Mexican. He looked like an Anglo, in his thirties, plain and nondescript, someone who could easily get lost in a crowd.

Keeping under the speed limit all the way down Market Street to Twenty-fifth, Sellers eye-balled his rearview mirror to see if the guy followed him. The Lexus stayed a block away. Sellers turned onto Harborside Drive and headed west. He drove past cruise ship parking lots, the shambles of the gray, exploded grain elevator, then the new operable one and more cruise ship parking lots, all the way down the north side of the island. The man stayed behind him across the Causeway Bridge and into Texas City, a town supported by oil and chemical refineries.

By the time Sellers got to his lawyer's office in a strip mall, though, the Lexus had disappeared. He emerged into the merciless heat an hour later armed with the knowledge that the man couldn't be anyone from the insurance company. His case had settled. His lawyer had the money in his trust account where he would hold it so Ginny couldn't get it in the divorce.

The identity of the man really bugged Sellers, now. If it wasn't his wife, and it wasn't the insurance company...his hand shook as he inserted the key into the ignition. He must be wrong. No one knew about his involvement in his father's death. It had to be something else.

In La Marque, he had lunch at a little Mexican food cafe he'd been going to since he was a kid. His father used to take him there. He ordered his favorite bean and beef burrito and a Corona and watched the door, hoping the man didn't show up there.

When he got back outside, Sellers turned on the air-conditioning full blast and headed back to the island. The sun's glare made it difficult to make out details of the boats motoring around the Causeway Bridge. He drove to the repair shop to check on his Firebird and found the air-conditioner had been fixed. He paid for it and arranged for one of the young mechanics to drive it to Sellers' apartment after work.

When he arrived home, there was no sign of the Lexus. Relieved, Sellers checked his mail, still hoping to find out something about his mother. There was nothing but junk mail, so he went inside, and lay down. He awoke later to pounding on his front door. The guy from the car dealership stood there, keys in hand.

"I'll run you back," Sellers said. "Where to, man?" The Lexus wasn't anywhere around. Maybe the guy had seen what he came for. His Firebird was parked several houses down. He would have to store the Cadillac again soon. He sure hated giving it up.

Twenty-five minutes later, Sellers had paid the guy, dropped him at his car, and cruised down the seawall. He was half-tempted to go by Mary's house just to see if he could catch a glimpse of Ginny, thinking it would creep her out a little, but decided not to risk it. If he did enough stuff, Ginny's lawyer would be happy to get his ass thrown in jail. No, he'd wait and watch from a distance. Let her think she was safe. Let her get her own place. Let her relax and drop her guard. Then, wham.

After buying some fried chicken, Sellers went home and settled on his couch with a beer, his sack of chicken, and the remote control. Except for the weird guy, he'd had a good day. He'd gotten his Firebird back. He had money waiting for him after the divorce. He still had enough money to get by for a while, even if he sent Ginny a couple of checks.

After he finished eating, Sellers kicked back on the sofa and watched TV for a couple of hours. The summer sun had not set when he took out the garbage and spotted the Lexus parked way down the street like the guy didn't think Alan could see that far.

He felt jittery, like being called to the principal's office in high school, except worse. What if it was the cops? Did they think they finally had something on him? But why didn't they just come out and arrest him? Asshole.

The car had a regular Texas license plate, not like a cop car. It could be a drug car, like the ones they confiscated in a bust, except what drug dealer would drive a Lexus, even a late model Lexus? Puke. That wasn't their style.

Finally, he decided not to put up with the man's shit anymore. He would front him out once and for all. As soon as it got good and dark, he'd teach the creep a lesson. Every few minutes, he peeked through the kitchen blinds. After eleven o'clock, he flipped on the porch light, shuffled down the stairs so the guy had plenty of time to see him, and got into the Cadillac. Easing into the street, he headed for the seawall. He wanted to be sure to be far away from his apartment so Nurse Nosy wouldn't call the landlord and try to get him evicted again.

Cruising all the way up to the beachfront, he turned toward Cherry Hill, the easternmost point of the island. Sellers' father had told him that during World War II the army had a fort there. Big guns had lined the insides of concrete bunkers along the seawall in case of a submarine invasion. In the fifties and sixties, so many kids had crashed into the bunkers while drag racing that the powers that be busted up the bunkers and pushed them over the side onto the beach.

He sped up close to the end where people liked to watch the ships in the channel. The Lexus kept up with him. If the man knew the island at all, he had to know where Sellers was leading him.

No cars were at the point. It was too late at night. Too dangerous.

The Lexus followed. This time Sellers knew there was no mistake. He slowed. Eased to a stop. The Lexus pulled parallel to him. Sellers got out and dashed around to the driver's side. The man opened his door and put a foot out just as Sellers approached. Sellers grabbed him by his shirt lapels and jerked him the rest of the way out, throwing him against the side of the car. The man was much taller, but years of working on the wharves had made Sellers stronger.

He rammed his forearm across the man's throat and held his fillet knife to the man's jugular. "All right, Jerkoff, you'd better tell me what this is about and quick, or I'm going to make fish bait out of you."

The man didn't try to defend himself. "I want to hire you to do a job for me."

A knot formed in Sellers' stomach. He pressed the tip of the fillet knife into the man's skin and stared into his eyes. "Just what kind of a job offer would require you to trail me around for two days?"

The man's jaw muscles flexed as he tried to swallow. "I want you to terminate my wife."

Chapter Nineteen

MARTIN

"Martin, you and Mary treat me like a baby," Ginny said, stomping to the sofa and throwing herself on it.

Martin chuckled at the irritation in her voice. She still acted like such a baby sometimes. When he'd arrived, she'd been fixing her dinner before dressing for work. She wore a Minnie Mouse tee shirt and boxer shorts and nothing else. She could have passed for twelve, except for the slight bulge that caused her abdomen to pooch out.

Over her protests, he was installing a deadbolt in the front door of her new apartment. "You are a baby as far as we're concerned. We worry about your safety."

"What, about Alan? I told you. He doesn't give a damn about me any more." She crossed her arms and glared at her brother.

"Fat chance," Martin said, glancing over his shoulder at her. "I hope you don't go out like that."

"Give me a break, will you? I'm in my own apartment getting ready to go to work. Do you want me to dress like a nun or something?" Ginny picked up her plate from the table and ate, standing over her brother as he worked. "You're invading my privacy."

"Some people would say girls who dress like that are asking for it."

"First of all, that's sexist. Secondly, it's only a tee shirt and boxers. Get off it." She stuffed a forkful of food into her mouth. "Anyway, the only place I'd wear this besides around here is if I had to run to the store or something. You know that. What's the matter with you?"

He brushed at the perspiration on his forehead. The apartment was getting hot, what with his having to hold the door open while he installed the lock. "You haven't heard hide nor hair from Sellers?"

Ginny swallowed another mouthful of spaghetti and shook her head. "Not for several days." She snorted, and Martin recognized how much like him she was sometimes.

She said, "That's a record for him. The last time was just about getting my stuff from the apartment, that's all. He wasn't ugly to me or anything."

"You didn't tell him where you're working?"

"I wouldn't do that. Not that it would be too hard for him to figure out." She sighed and put the plate down again. "I can't wait until this divorce is over. Mary calls me every day and now you, with your deadbolt."

"You haven't seen him around the parking lot?" Martin raised his right eyebrow like an evil villain.

Ginny shook her head. "No. I swear. I would have told you."

Putting the key in the new lock from the outside, he worked the bolt back and forth a couple of times before pushing the door closed and trying it from the inside. He was pleased with himself and perched on the arm of the sofa. "I got an extra key for the manager, one for your roommate, when you get one, and there's one for you. Don't give any keys to anyone else." He handed her three keys, not confessing that he'd kept a fourth one for himself.

"I'm not stupid."

Martin patted her on the shoulder. "I didn't say you were, Sis. It's just better if keys to your apartment aren't all over town. Did you put that dowel in the track of your sliding back door like I told you?"

"Yes, Brother Dear. You want to check?"

Martin went into her bedroom and returned a few moments later. "That'll work."

"Are you happy now?"

"What do you do all the time now that you're working nights?"

"Why?" She thought she knew what was coming.

"You aren't seeing someone else, are you? Another guy?"

"What if I am?"

"Do you think that's a good idea? You haven't even decided what to do with the baby yet."

"Have you been following me? All this time I've been feeling like it was Alan following me, but it was my own brother. How can you manage that when you're supposed to be at work?"

"Don't you think Sellers will get angry if he thinks you're seeing someone else?"

Ginny backed toward the kitchen with her plate. "If he's already angry, what difference will it make?"

"So what are you going to do about the baby?" He sounded like a broken record, but he couldn't help it. She needed to make a final decision.

Ginny turned from the sink and stared up at her brother. "I don't know. Maybe I'll get rid of it."

"You mean it? I can find a clinic for you."

"I've been discussing it with my counselor, Martin. And if I need a clinic, I already know where some are." She wore a big frown. "Just let me alone, and I'll tell you when I've decided what to do." She rinsed her plate and silverware off and put them into the dishwasher, not looking at him. She scraped the leftovers into a small plastic container and put the pot in the sink, turning on the water to fill it up. When she faced her brother, who was leaning on the doorjamb watching her, her face had turned pink.

Her look unsettled him. He wished he could do more to protect her without smothering her. He'd like to lock her up somewhere until Alan Sellers became a nonissue, whenever that would be. "You're still scared, aren't you?" He crossed his arms, the screwdriver still in one hand.

"I wish if he was going to try something, he'd go ahead and do it." She pushed past him and walked back into the living room. "I've really got to get ready for work now."

Martin followed her. "I know you're tired of me playing big brother, but I just want you to know I'm worried. I'm doing all I can to get out on the street to protect you." He hadn't told her he'd asked to go back to sergeant. The decision wasn't completely about her anyway, and he didn't want her to think it was. Still, he'd feel better if he could get out there fast. He might hear something, and he could keep a better eye on Sellers.

She hugged him. "Quit worrying. I'm being as careful as I can."

"I'm not trying to scare you, but I've had a couple of the guys drive by his apartment several times. They haven't seen any sign of him or anyone else. I think he's up to something. I just don't know what."

"Maybe he's gone back to work and just isn't around like he used to be." She snorted with contempt, like she didn't believe her own words.

"Sellers?"

"I don't know. But if you can help me go get my stuff, maybe we can find out. Listen, I've got to get dressed. Thanks for the new lock. Really." She stood on her tiptoes and kissed her brother on the cheek, then pulled him by the arm toward the door, opening it.

Stepping out onto the porch, he held onto the door. "You'll call me if you see anything suspicious."

Ginny gave him an exaggerated nod. "Yes. I promise. But I'm sure everything's going to be okay. 'Bye."

She held up the new keys and jingled them when he reached his car and gave her a backward glance. "Thanks again, Bro," she called and closed the door.

Chapter Twenty

DENA

On Saturday morning, Dena, Meredith, and Dena's best friend, Ellen, a high school drama teacher, drove to the warehouse to attack Dena's father's closed legal files. Juliet took the kids for the day. Zack was still out of town.

Dena had promised Luke she'd have all her side of the family's stuff cleaned out by the end of the summer. The property would be listed for sale in the early fall, if they couldn't make a deal with the folks who were already interested. The idea of having the money to put her plans into motion had energized her.

She parked in the alley next to an old hotel that needed to be bought and refurbished. The temperature was in the nineties, and the humidity was so bad Dena started perspiring before she could even get inside the door. Heavy, dark clouds bore evidence a rainstorm might be on the way. As far as she was concerned, it couldn't get there fast enough.

"You're a good friend to help me with this," Dena told Ellen as each of them, armed with a flashlight, traipsed up the back alley stairs.

"What about me? Don't I get any credit for being here?" Meredith turned the key in the lock and swung the door wide, revealing a cavern of darkness, but for an occasional crack of light filtering in through a broken window.

"You're being paid and, anyway, you owe me for ratting me out to Lucas. Put that cigarette out before you go in there," Dena said. "I don't want you burning the place down just when I'm about to get some extra money."

Meredith didn't respond to Dena's comment but threw her cigarette over the side of the stairs into the alley. "Happy?" She hoisted her backpack onto one shoulder and stepped ahead of them.

Ellen stopped and dug in her purse for a moment. "What's that about?" she whispered, pulling out a scrunchy and gathering her long red hair into it. "You and Meredith at odds over something?"

"Divided loyalties," Dena whispered back. "She acts like she's my friend half the time and the other, a spy for Lucas. He and she go back a lot further than she and I do, so what can I expect?"

"I don't understand. Why would Lucas need her to spy on you?" She tucked her purse under her arm as they skirted broken furniture.

"We're having a feud over what kind of law I can practice. He doesn't want me doing family law, and I don't want him telling me what to do." Dena fanned herself with her hand. "It sure is oppressive in here."

Ellen pulled her tee shirt up over her stomach and tied it in a knot. "Some of this old furniture might be worth something."

Dena glanced at some of the pieces. "We'll have someone come in and appraise it later. Today we're going to start shredding files, which I know must be around here somewhere." She shined her flashlight over the area to their right, trying to see what her father had stored there.

"Don't you think in time Lucas will get over whatever he's worried about? After all, you haven't been practicing with him that long."

"I don't know. Seems like there's something else going on. It's more a feeling than anything else. Like today, he didn't want me coming without Meredith. He lined up the shredder rental himself." She shrugged. "It could be just that he's a control freak, which he is."

"Hmm, is there something dangerous here? I mean, rotten boards or something like that?" Ellen shined her flashlight around the area to her left.

"I don't think so. Surely he would have mentioned it if things were that bad."

Dena grasped the back of what, in the dim light, appeared to be an overstuffed chair. A dust cloud mushroomed from it. They both coughed.

"Something he doesn't want you to know about then," Ellen said after the coughing fit passed and then a sneeze. "Are you sure he isn't into anything illegal? Drugs? Gambling? Gun running? Receiving stolen property?"

Dena blew out a gust of air. "Lucas? Are you nuts? You know how straight he is."

"Maybe he's just being overprotective." Ellen pushed a cardboard box aside with her foot. It left a long scrape in the dusty floor.

Dena said, "He's been too much like that lately as it is. We may be fixing to butt heads again." She called out, "Meredith, we can't see you. Shine your light or something."

"I'm over here, Mrs. Armstrong, can't you guys keep up?" A light appeared on the far side of the storage area.

"I really appreciate your helping, Ellen," Dena said. "Sorry it's such a filthy task. I'll pay you back somehow."

They dodged a lot of junk and several interesting looking pieces of furniture until they found an area that contained mostly stacked Permafile boxes gray with dirt and age.

Ellen shook her head. "You'd do the same for me. Besides, we haven't had much time together lately. It'll give us an opportunity to catch up while we work."

Dena set her purse down and searched the walls for light switches. The ones she found only lit up the back half of the area with small, bald bulbs. The rest seemed to be inoperable. At least they had enough to see the boxes that needed to be sorted through.

Ellen began tugging on boxes, lining them up, so the identifying marks all faced the same way. There was a tiny scraping sound and then a sudden squeal, which sent them running toward each other. Dena flashed her light across the floor. "I think it's a mouse," she said as she spotted the tail of a tiny, furry creature disappearing behind a broken table leg. She shivered. "I feel like Nancy Drew investigating a crime with her friend George."

"I'm George? Thanks a lot." Ellen's laugh was high-pitched. "I can see why Lucas didn't want you here alone."

"George was a girl. Let's look for some more lights. I don't want to stick my hand into anything even in the semi-dark, do you?"

"Heck, no. You go back over to that far wall where you were, and I'll cover this one. There's got to be another set of switches somewhere. Oh, this makes my flesh crawl."

"Mine, too."

"Meredith!" Ellen called. "Why don't you come help us find some lights?"

"Yeah," Dena said in a loud voice. "What are you doing, anyway?" She strode over to the corner and started working her way across the long dim wall. Their progress was relatively slow since they each had to climb over boxes and other stuff. God, she didn't know her father had been such a pack rat. Yuck. The very thought of mice and bugs. She shook her head and hurried to find more lights.

"I'm coming," Meredith yelled. "I just found some of the neatest things. A collection of stuff from the old Jack Tar Hotel."

"That was a million years ago," Dena said.

Thunder rumbled in the distance.

"Oh, great," Ellen called. "All we need is a thunderstorm. I hope the roof of this joint doesn't leak."

"At least it'll be cooler."

Large overhead fluorescent lights sputtered and came on.

"Is that better?" Meredith hollered.

"Where were you five minutes ago?" Dena was relieved they'd be able to see their way around.

"Did you hear what I said?" Meredith strode back toward them. "I wonder who owns the Jack Tar stuff?"

"It depends on whether the antique mall folks are using any of the storage space up here or not. Lucas said they weren't supposed to be. If they're not, it's either Lucas or me. Or both. C'mon, let's get started." Dena switched off her flashlight and set it and her shoulder bag on top of an old barrister's bookcase. She'd like to be able to acquire the bookcase for herself. She would discuss it with Lucas later.

Ellen sneezed again. "Anybody got a tissue?"

Dena pulled one from her purse and handed it to her. She untied the blue ropes from the end of the box with the lowest numbers marked on the outside. "I guess this is as good a place to begin as any." Opening the flaps, she glanced down at dozens of manila folders. For the love of God, why couldn't Lucas agree to hire a shredding company? He was so tight.

Ellen looked over Dena's shoulder and groaned. "I'm not sure I knew what I was getting into, but I'm here, so just tell me what you're looking for."

Meredith headed back toward the door through which they'd come. "I'll go check on the shredder, and I'm going to ask those guys downstairs if they have any kind of fan we can borrow."

"It'll stir up the dust, but maybe they could point it up so we at least have some air circulating," Dena said.

"Ellen, pull out the metal brads, then look for any other heavy stuff that might jam the shredder, like those huge paper clips. Other than that, watch for formal documents like wills and codicils or anything else that looks too important to shred. Most of it will be outdated stuff, but let me check 'em if you have any doubts."

"I vote we drag up a couple of chairs. I think it's going to be a long day."

After they were seated, Meredith returned from the opposite direction with a man pushing a large shredder. "There's an elevator on that side," she said. Behind the first man, another man carried large standing fan. Meredith had the men plug them both into an extension cord she had carried from downstairs. "Thanks, guys," she said, beaming.

As they walked away, Ellen turned to Dena and said, "Oh, to be twenty again."

Meredith made a face. "I'm twenty-two." They formed an assembly line. Ellen pulled the metal pieces out of each file, Dena examined the contents, and Meredith fed it to the shredder.

The thunder grew closer for a while. A few raindrops pattered on the roof. A slight breeze blew in every few minutes from the direction of the stairwell and the alley door, which they had propped open. Otherwise, except for the grating noise of the shredder, everything was still and quiet. Before long all of them were covered with a layer of grit.

"Remind me next time to bring a radio," Meredith said later that afternoon after they'd been back from lunch for a while. "By the way, Olympia Grill was a good choice. I love their Greek salad."

"Remind me next time to try harder to talk Lucas into hiring a service for this," Dena said. "What was he thinking? And what about his father's files and his own? What is he doing about them?

Here's another thought. Couldn't we have had a big bonfire of this stuff at the beach?"

"He's really anal, you know, Mrs. A.," Meredith said. "His father was the same way. There are no files. They were destroyed every year after the first five years of Mr. Barlow Senior's practice, Lucas told me, and he does his own each year. You didn't know?"

"And so he what, after Mitchell died, came over here and shredded all Mitchell's old files?"

"Eventually, after that artificial five-year time limitation you lawyers pulled out of the air from some place."

"Weird," Ellen said. "I didn't think anyone was that compulsive."

"Yeah, well, Mr. Barlow is," Meredith said. "And he's a Virgo to boot."

"What's that mean?" Ellen said.

Meredith's laugh turned into a cough. "They're persnickety. Nitpickers. You know."

"Wait," Ellen whispered, holding up her hand. "I think I hear someone."

"That's not even funny."

"Shhh," Ellen said. "Turn off the machine."

The hairs stood up on the back of Dena's neck.

Meredith whispered. "They'd have to be legitimate to be heard over the shredder. What stalker would make that much noise? It's probably one of the guys who carried that stuff up."

Everything was quiet.

"Anyone down there?" Meredith called out. She jogged toward the stairwell.

"Meredith." Ellen frowned and grabbed Dena's arm.

"What's your problem?" Dena patted Ellen's hand. "No one's out there."

"All clear," Meredith called from the stairs.

Ellen shook her head. "I just have the creeps, I guess."

"This place is enough to give them to you. Why don't we quit for today? We've done three big boxes."

"You don't mind?" Ellen stood up and stretched.

"Nah," she said and looked at her watch. "It's nearly four, anyway. Let me just find old lady Heslep's file, and we'll call it a day."

"Remind me who that is?" Ellen asked.

"An old client of my dad's. I'm preparing a codicil to her will. Her daughter called and said since she was coming into the office, she wanted everything from her old files, notes and all." She shrugged. "I don't know what it's about. People are just weird sometimes."

Meredith returned and helped Dena sort through some boxes until they found the appropriate one. It dated back to before Dena was born. Ellen filled the empty boxes with file folders and the hardware they'd thrown on the floor.

"Boy, I didn't know Mrs. H. was that old," Meredith said, thumbing through the folders. She stopped, hovering over them, glancing past her shoulder at Dena.

"What're you doing?" Dena asked.

Meredith combed past several folders at one time.

"What's that? What are you hiding?" She reached around Meredith and pushed her arm away. Digging out an armful of files, she stood and thumbed through them. What Meredith had tried to conceal were files with REBECCA written across them in large, bold, faded red letters. Rebecca had been Dena's mother's name. She wiped away the dust to make out anything else written on the folder. Yellowed, peeling plastic tape that had once sealed the files fell away under her probing fingers.

"You find Mrs. H.'s file?" Meredith asked.

"Don't try to buffalo me," Dena said. "This is my mother's, isn't it? You knew it was here, didn't you?"

Meredith took the other files out of Dena's hands. "I guess."

Ellen walked over and looked at the files Dena clutched in both hands. "What's going on?"

"Is there some reason my mother has files here? What's in them, her will? What else, something Lucas doesn't want me to see? Is that why he suggested you help out today?" Dena opened the top folder to look through it.

A door slammed in the distance. "You hear that?" Ellen's voice was unnaturally loud.

A tremor snaked through Dena's body. She glanced at Meredith. "It's nothing." There was no other lettering on the folders. She looked back in the Permafile box and found a letter-sized paper box sealed shut with silver duct tape. The name REBECCA stood out in large letters. Why would her father have a box with her mother's name on it in the law office? If it was her mother.

Meredith stood with the other files in her hands, staring down at the box.

"Let's get out of here, Dena," Ellen said, shaking her arm. "You can take that home with you and look at it later. I'm going to go ahead and take this box of trash down to the dumpster."

Just finding something unexpected with her mother's name emblazoned on it unnerved Dena. She didn't answer Ellen.

"You want to see if you can find Mrs. Heslep's file, Meredith?"

Meredith nodded. She dug through the files in the rest of the box. "Here they are."

"Let's go then," Dena said. She felt drained.

"Mrs. Armstrong," Meredith said. "I'm sorry."

Dena shook her head. "Get the shredder, will you?"

"I was just doing what Mr. Barlow asked me to."

"Okay. Can you just get the shredder? Roll it to the door where those men can find it easily when they come to get it."

Ellen was already by the entrance. "Dena?"

"I'm coming." She put the Rebecca file and box and her purse into one of the larger empty boxes with the Heslep file and headed for the stairs. Though stunned, a sense of anticipation, a pleasurable sensation swirled in her stomach. When she got a minute to herself, she'd see what she'd found. Even if the files contained just her mother's will and some other old papers, they would be a nice addition to the small collection of things she had to remember her mother by.

"I was just doing what Mr. Barlow asked." Meredith's voice was full of apology.

"I heard you the first time. Don't forget the shredder." Dena couldn't think of anything else to say to the younger woman without yelling. "We'll talk about it some other time."

Chapter Twenty-One

ALAN SELLERS

*T*he Monday after he agreed to do the job, Sellers broke into the lawyer's house. Feeling stifled by the humidity, he was in a bad mood before ever starting out. As soon as he got the whole thing over with, he could go on with his life. He might move out of Galveston. He wanted to get away from the Gulf coast. Maybe he'd move down to Mexico, hang out on the beach at Puerta Vallerta.

The husband had filled him in on some important details—like their address and how to get into the house and that she had a gun and where she kept it. At approximately 9:30 a.m., he left the Cadillac two blocks away on a street similar to theirs, a suburban area where most everyone was at work during the day.

By the time he reached their house, he had long ago broken a sweat. He strolled right up to the door, poked the doorbell, and waited. There shouldn't be anyone home, but he had to be sure. If anyone spotted him as they drove by, he would look like he had business there. He rang the doorbell a second time. No one answered.

He twisted the front door knob. Locked, as expected. A car approached, so he pushed the doorbell again. After the car passed, he ran to the rear of the house and through the gate of the high cedar fence. He pulled on his gloves and approached a narrow, chest-high window with a small outdoor serving bar next to the back door. It had no blinds. There were plants on the windowsill behind the sink. The refrigerator and stove were opposite. The window gave way. Relief poured out of him.

The husband had offered him a key, but no way would he get caught with a key. First of all, he didn't plan on getting caught. Secondly, if he was going to make it look like a burglary gone bad, then he had to case the place and figure out a way to get in. The husband had told him about the crappy windows that needed replacing, and that the kitchen one was broke. Usually, a dowel was in the track, but the husband would remove it.

Unable to boost himself through the window, Sellers spotted a picnic table near the fence, which he could climb on. He ran over, grabbed one end of it, and heard a growl. Hair rose on the back of his neck. The husband hadn't said anything about a dog.

Dropping the table, he eased around. Nothing was there. There was another low growl followed by a loud bark from the other side of the fence. Laughing with relief, Sellers dragged the picnic table across the backyard and climbed through the window, dropping to the floor on the other side of the sink. He stood for a moment listening for the sound of a person. The cool air in the house felt good after the summer heat. The only sound was the whirr of the refrigerator.

To his right stood a small dining area with a table, six chairs, and a glassed-in cabinet. Between the kitchen and the dining area, a door with a square window in it led to the garage. He opened it, examining the locking mechanisms: a deadbolt and a push-button. Inside the garage, he found the washer and dryer, some boxes piled on a floor-to-ceiling shelf against one wall, and a large closet stuffed with tools and tool boxes stacked one on top of another. He had found his hiding place.

He'd slip into the garage when the door was open and no one was around. He'd hide in the tool room until everyone went to bed and then walk right into the house. The deadbolt lock would be his only problem, the other lock he could open with a credit card or a screwdriver. He'd definitely bring a screwdriver.

He hoped they never used the deadbolt. Most people with an electric garage door opener thought they were safe. Spotting the controls just inside the entrance to the garage, he nodded. The Armstrongs were like most people.

All he needed to do now was locate the jewelry to take with him the night he finished her off so it would look like a burglary. Soon, very soon, the bitch would get what she deserved, and he'd get a lot of money.

There was some felt-wrapped silverware in the china cabinet, but the bedroom was where the good stuff would be. He would have to remember to bring a bag to put the stuff in.

Now, about his way out. How should he leave that night, go back through the kitchen window like he would do today or go out through the garage? The garage. He could hit the control box on his way out and jump over the sensors and no one would ever be sure how he left.

He checked out the living room and the den. There was a wedding picture sitting on top of a big screen television. The lawyer and her *loving* husband. Next to it was another, an older framed photograph. A man, a woman, and a little girl standing against a fake backdrop. The girl could have been the lawyer when she was little. He picked up the third photograph, an eight-by-ten color close-up of two kids. The little boy as a toddler held a baby on his lap. Something about the boy seemed familiar. A shadow crossed over him and left as quickly as it came.

He surveyed the remainder of the room. A corner wet bar. A painting of a shrimp boat and some seagulls. A small built-in bookcase held a wooden box with some fabric and flowers glued it, a letter, and an old photograph behind glass. A sofa, easy chair, and an ancient-looking rocker.

He opened two doors in the hall and discovered a small bathroom and a coat closet.

Their bedroom smelled like the lawyer—was it vanilla? Her perfume bottles lined the dresser. A queen-size bed and night tables with lamps on them stood against the far wall. In one corner, a flat screen TV sat on a stand next to a chest of drawers and on the other side, a chair and a lamp sat on a table in one corner. What would it be like to be that rich?

In one closet were suits, pants, and shoes, lined up like in a department store. In fact, it gave off the feeling of being in a clothing store, almost too neat and orderly. He should have asked for more money.

Feeling sorry for himself, he closed the door and opened the other, an even deeper walk-in with women's clothes, just as full as her husband's, but not so neat. His mouth settled into a grim line. It wasn't right. It wasn't fair. They had so much. Why'd the husband want her out of the way? Not that Sellers gave a shit. He'd been hired to do it. He would do it for pleasure, for himself, if not for other people who didn't have so much. He didn't give a shit about other people either. But they had so much. What else could the husband want?

He closed the door and turned out the light. Feeling panicky—a fluttering in his stomach—he forced out a breath. No one would be home any time soon. He had until the afternoon.

On the dresser stood the large jewelry box the husband had told him about. Fumbling with its tiny drawers, he opened them one-by-one, finding rows of earrings, among them a pair of pearls, a pair that looked like tiny diamonds, and some black heart-shaped ones. The second drawer held something wrapped in tissue. Unwrapping it, he found baby teeth. What a joke. The next drawer held some high school and college rings, one with a small diamond. He opened a little glass door and found a string of pearls, two heavy gold chains, and three strands of colored beads. In a drawer on the bottom, behind some costume jewelry, he found what the husband had told him to look for. A heavy gold cuff bracelet, a large solitaire diamond ring, a diamond tennis bracelet, diamond earrings of at least a carat each, and a key. Bingo.

In one of the bedside tables, Sellers found some books, old pay stubs, a dead outmoded cell phone, and other junk. In the small notebook he always carried, Sellers jotted down the husband's work address from the pay stubs, for insurance, in case he ever had to get into contact with him. In case he needed more information on the husband.

Skirting around the end of the bed, he reached the other bedside table and the locked top drawer the husband had told him about. He fit the key into it. Within easy reach lay a handgun, a small black revolver with a brown grip. Even though he'd been told about it, a jolt of electricity ran up his arm when he picked it up. "Son-of-a-bitch." Everything was beginning to feel real. He opened the gun's cylinder. A five shot, loaded with four rounds.

Why would she have a gun? The husband had told him about it, but now that he saw it and touched it and examined it, he couldn't help but wonder if something else was going on that he didn't, and probably wouldn't, know about.

All he had to do was get into the house while no one was home and get that key out of her jewelry box, and he'd be home free. Only if she had some reason to open the drawer would she know something was wrong.

He was ready to clear out. He had to get away, had to think. Moving fast, he wiped off the gun's grip, relocked the drawer, and put the key back. He checked out the remainder of the house, memorizing which were the kids' rooms, then hurried to the kitchen. He climbed through the window and leaned back in to run the water in the sink to flush away his footprint. He put the plants back in place and closed the window. Dragging the picnic table back near the fence started the neighbors' dog barking again. Stuffing his gloves into his back pocket, he peered around the side of the house and, not seeing anyone, crept up to the front of the house and walked casually back to his father's car.

Chapter Twenty-Two

DENA

arefoot and dressed in short, white cotton shorts and an old tee shirt, Dena stood peeling potatoes at the kitchen sink when Zack arrived home. Things had been going smoothly recently, at least when he'd been home, which wasn't often. No harsh words, but a pat on the arm here and there. The hint of the possibility of more in the future. Did she want that? She thought she'd made up her mind, but when he touched her kindly, when he didn't give her the evil eye or speak meanly to her, she felt ambivalent.

Now he came through the garage and into the kitchen, standing close behind her, slipping an arm around her waist. Feeling an adrenaline spike, Dena laughed and turned off the faucet, turning to look at him. They hadn't made love in eons. Was he leading up to that?

"To what do I owe this sudden display of affection?" She dried her hands.

"I've got some news."

He was so close she could feel the warmth of his body. "Really? What's up?"

"You remember that three-week trip to Japan I told you about that I said I might not have to go on? I'm going to have to go, but not for the whole three weeks." He leaned back against the stove and picked up the dishtowel she'd used to dry her hands and began twisting it. "I'll only be gone for a few days, a week at the longest. Henry has to go to a conference in California and, as soon as it's over, he'll fly to Japan and take my place." Dena tried to act like she was pleased. She had wanted to use that time for her own plans, things like getting the cleancut of the warehouse finished. Their prospects had made an offer on the building. She and Lucas had accepted. All they had to do was clean out the building and ink the deal.

"Well, that's great, I guess. Unless you were looking forward to seeing Japan."

"I thought you'd be happy about it."

"Sure, and the kids will be really excited. They miss you so much when you're gone."

"I've got some other news, as well."

"There's more?" Now she was feeling apprehensive. She hadn't shared with him that she was going to open up her own law office. And she hadn't shared with Luke that she'd been planning on filing for divorce. Even though the two men weren't crazy about each other, they did talk every once in a while. She hoped whatever Zack had to tell her wouldn't mess up her plans.

"The company is hiring a new guy. He'll start next month. It's going to be his job to do most of the traveling."

"That's wonderful. So you won't be gone anymore?" She wasn't sure how she felt about that. But at least with his being gone for a few days to Japan, she'd have time to think about what she really wanted to do where he was concerned.

"I won't have to travel very often. Once or twice a year at the most."

"The kids will be tickled to death." She wondered whether he thought they could mend their relationship if he were home more. Did she want that?

"I'm happy about it, too. I was getting tired of being gone all the time. This trip to Japan will be the last one for a long time," he said. "Want a drink?" He started for the bar.

She shook her head. "What made old Dillman decide to hire someone to travel?"

"I made the suggestion a few months ago at an office conference. I proposed he hire a single person and make it clear it would be the new hire's job to go on all the trips that required only one person." He poured himself three fingers of bourbon and took a swallow. "After I suggested it, some of the other guys, Henry and them, chimed in. I'm really surprised that Dillman even seriously considered it."

"Me, too, after all this time. He never seemed to think you guys had much of a life outside of the company."

"Yeah, I thought so, too." He kissed her on the cheek.

She tried not to breathe the same air lest she feel nauseated by the smell. "Let me finish the potatoes and get dinner ready." She turned on the water and picked up the potato peeler again.

"I'm going to go work in the yard," he said and then yelled for the kids.

Dena's stomach churned. Zack and the kids went out into the back yard where they pulled weeds and picked some vegetables for a salad. Seeing the three of them together made her think about how hard it would be to split them up. He glanced her way and caught her watching him and waved. She was about to take the wooden dowel out of the window track and ask him if he wanted anything when she noticed it lying on the sill parallel to the window. That was odd. Why would someone have removed it and not put it back? Shrugging, she slid the window open. "You guys need anything out there?"

"A bottle of water," he said.

"Hi, Mama," Paul called. Melissa waved at her.

Later, at dinner, Zack said, "I've been thinking I'll fix up the house a little this summer."

"Can me help, Daddy?" Paul looked up at his father with his big round eyes.

"*May I* help," Dena corrected him. "What brought that on?"

Zack reached out and rumpled the little boy's bushy hair and answered Dena. "I just thought it was high time I did some of the things I've been putting off, like patching the leak in the hose and fixing the lock on the kitchen window so you can take that stick out of there. You know, things like that."

"Great," Dena said. "Can we paper the kids' bathroom while we're at it? I saw some beautiful wallpaper with zoo animals on it the other day."

"Sure." Zack's smile was like the ones he had shown her back when they were dating. "We'll make it a summer project." He looked at Paul and then Melissa. "And the kids can help."

"Oh, goody, Daddy," Paul said, his face lighting up.

"We can all work together fixing up the house. Maybe over Labor Day Weekend we could have some people over." Zack looked at Dena as if for approval. "The kids could invite their friends, and we could too, and we could have a barbecue or fish fry."

"Yea, yea, yea." Paul hollered and clapped his hands. "We'll have a party." He clapped his hands again. "Want to have a party, 'Lissa?"

"We could have ice cream and hamburgers? Would you like that, Melissa?"

"And hot dogs," Melissa said. "I like hot dogs."

"And a piñata?" Paul looked from one parent to another.

Zack and Dena both laughed, but Dena's face flushed with guilt. They might not be a family by then.

"Yeah, we can have hamburgers, and hot dogs, and ice cream and whatever you want, okay?" Zack said.

"Yea." Paul clapped his hands together again.

"But it's going to be a lot of work, Paul," Zack said.

"I work hard, Daddy. I like ice cream."

Melissa shrieked and, sliding down from her booster seat, did a little dance.

"I've been remiss in a lot of things," Zack said.

Dena looked at him but didn't say anything. Surely there was no way he knew what her plans were. And if he did, wouldn't he confront her? Or was this his way to get her to change her mind before it was too late?

"Did Mommy tell you kids that I won't be going out of town much anymore? One more short trip, and then I won't have to go for a long time."

"Yea." Paul clapped his hands again.

"That's what I say, Paul," Zack said. "Everything will be different when I get back. Yea."

Chapter Twenty-Three

DENA

"I remember how happy your father was when he and your mother were married," Anita Heslep said as her daughter, Vera, helped her walk to Dena's desk to sign her codicil. A wisp of a smile graced the old woman's face.

Dena reared back in surprise. Mrs. Heslep would be ninety years old the following week. She still had all her faculties though walking was difficult sometimes, depending on what her arthritis decided to do that day. Her words.

Mrs. Heslep hadn't said anything of a personal nature until then. Was she really all right mentally? Dena leaned down and peered into old, milky eyes. The woman smelled like mothballs. "What made you think of that?" The two younger women seated Mrs. Heslep in Dena's chair and rolled her close to the desk where she would be able to sign the codicil.

Mrs. Heslep picked up the pen with her bony, brown-spotted hand and leaned over the paper. "Oh, I looked across this desk at you and saw a glimpse of your mother in your face. Your parents would have been very proud of you. I knew your mother." She raised her head and winked at Dena, a sparkle in her eyes. "Sign on each page?"

Dena stepped closer. "I didn't know you'd ever met my mother, Mrs. Heslep. I knew you were a client of my father's, of course. Here, let me show you again," Dena said. "Go ahead and initial the short lines on each page until Meredith comes back with Lucas and the lady from down the hall to be witnesses."

Dena pointed to the line on the bottom right corner of the first page. Mrs. Heslep's hand trembled as she placed her initials on that page, then the following three pages when Dena turned them for her. Vera sat in a chair against the wall.

Mrs. Heslep adjusted her glasses and relaxed in the chair while they waited for the others. "Your mother sometimes helped out in the office until you were born."

"Really? I didn't know that, either. My father never wanted to discuss her much with me." A note in Mrs. Heslep's voice made Dena feel weepy.

Mrs. Heslep folded her hands in her lap and smiled an I've-got-a-secret smile. "Oh, yes. I happened to have an appointment with your father the day your mother came from the doctor's office with the news she was expecting. You never saw a more delighted gentleman than your father when he came out of his office with your mother on his arm." She stared off into space and shook her head as if picturing them in her mind. "Oh, your father … he loved your mother so. You could see it in his eyes. And your mother…she had such a hard life."

Voices came toward them. Meredith and the secretary from the psychologist's office down the hall walked in. The woman frequently witnessed documents since most things required two witnesses and a notary. "Hi, Allison. Thanks for coming," Dena said.

Meredith said, "Let me get Mr. Barlow." She stepped out and was back a minute later with her notary stamp and Lucas behind her.

"This is Allison King, Mrs. Heslep. She's going to be a witness to your codicil. And here comes Lucas and you know Meredith." Dena nodded at everyone. She wanted to hurry and get it over with, hoping Mrs. Heslep might stay and tell her anything else she could remember. "Are we all ready?" She turned the codicil back to the first page and checked Mrs. Heslep's initials on each page until she came to the signature page. "Okay, here we go."

"Mrs. Heslep, by signing this document you acknowledge you have read over this codicil to your will, and that it contains the changes you wish to make." Dena placed her finger on a line halfway down the next to the last page. "Go ahead and sign here." She watched as Mrs. Heslep signed in a wavering hand. Flipping to the last page, except for the blueback, she again pointed to a line. "And here."

Mrs. Heslep's hand shook a little as she signed her full name again. When she was finished, she smiled up at Dena. Dena patted her shoulder. "That's great, all done." She took the codicil and handed it to Meredith who laid it out on the front of Dena's desk, opened it to the witnesses' lines, and handed Allison King a pen.

While the others were signing, Dena said, "We retrieved your old files for you last Saturday. Would you like me to give them to Vera to carry for you? They're in a plastic bag."

"Thank you, my dear. You're just as sweet as your father always knew you would be."

Dena shivered. Meredith gave the zipper bag to Vera. The room was quiet while everyone finished signing and Meredith notarized the codicil. She handed it back to Dena for a last look. Dena reviewed it and glanced at the faces of the people standing around her office. The moments in will and codicil executions were always awkward because people couldn't help but think about the inevitable.

"Thanks, y'all," Dena said. "Mrs. Heslep, you want Vera to take your codicil, too?" The others left, and it was just the three of them again.

"No, I do not, thank you. I'll just place it here in my handbag if you'll give it to me. But Vera has your check for what I owe you."

"All right. Vera, you can take that out to Meredith, and I'll help your mother out."

"That'll be fine," Vera said and, gathering her things and her mother's bag, went out to Meredith's desk.

Dena sat down across from Mrs. Heslep who was still sitting in her chair behind the desk. "I wonder if you can tell me anything else about my parents. About when my mother was alive, I mean."

"Oh, well, I really didn't know them socially, dear. But I enjoyed visiting with your mother when she was here. And I saw them occasionally downtown at lunch. Your father used to take her to Mabry's Cafeteria sometimes. They'd meet here or at the courthouse. I used to work at the courthouse, in the county clerk's office, you know."

"I remember you mentioning that. You were there what, forty years?"

"They gave me a party at Mabry's when I retired." She seemed really pleased.

"Sounds like it was a popular place. Where was that? I don't know it."

"You wouldn't. It's been gone, I should think, since the late seventies. But it was around by the old Star Drug Store."

"That's still there. Sometimes I eat lunch there."

"Downtown has changed several times since my day, though many storefronts are still the same."

"Yes, Ma'am."

"Well, you don't want to listen to a lot of prattle. Help me up if you would."

Dena held Mrs. Heslep's cane in one hand and gripped the old lady's arm while she pushed herself up out of her chair. "That's good. Hand me my cane."

Dena handed her the cane and waited for her to hobble around the desk. Mrs. Heslep hung her handbag over her left arm and bore her weight on the cane. She was quite a bit shorter than Dena, which made her quite tiny, and hunched over, her shoulders sloped. Dena walked with her to the door. Whispering, Mrs. Heslep said, "I was very sorry when I heard about your mother, Dear. Your father didn't come to the courthouse for weeks after her death. Her suicide was the talk of the courthouse, and I suppose he knew it."

Dena gasped, feeling as if someone had dropped a bomb on her head, and put her hand to her queasy stomach. "No. She died in a car accident. A freak accident when her car went over the side of the seawall in a rainstorm."

Mrs. Heslep reached for Dena's forearm. "Oh, no, my dear. I'm so sorry. You didn't know? I have such a mouth."

"What ... what did you hear, Mrs. Heslep?" She stared down at her, almost afraid to find out, but she had to know. "Tell me what they said."

The old lady studied Dena's face for a moment. "I suppose you have a right. What does it matter now, it was so long ago?" She released Dena's arm and braced herself on the doorjamb. "She ran her car into the end of the seawall on Cherry Hill."

Tears gathered at the edge of Dena's eyes. It couldn't be true. Her mother, a suicide? She bit her lip so she wouldn't break down. Her breath was hard to get.

"I'm so sorry. I was sure you knew that. Your father was devastated. He wasn't the same for years and years. Well," she muttered under her breath, "I really let the cat out of the bag."

Dena pursed her lips. "It's all right. Doesn't matter." She forced a bit of a smile. "Let's get you out to Vera." She patted her on the arm. "Thank you for telling me, and don't worry. I'm a big girl."

As soon as the two ladies left, Dena hurried into her office and closed the door, leaning against it, doubled over and gripping her stomach. She fought to keep her lunch down.

Once she felt normal, she stalked to Lucas' office and slammed the door. Lucas pushed back from his desk.

"Lucas. I want to talk to you." Standing over him with her hands on both hips, Dena glared at her cousin. She felt like crying but couldn't let herself go. "Did my mother commit suicide?"

He threw his glasses down and folded his hands across his big belly. "Sit down, Dena."

"No, just tell me. She did, didn't she?"

Lucas started to get out of his chair, but when Dena didn't back off, he sank back down. He sighed long and loud. "Yes."

All the energy drained out of Dena. "Why didn't anyone ever tell me?"

"Your father, and mine for that matter, felt it best to protect you. I was a kid, but you were a tot when it happened."

"You have to tell me what you know." She picked up the files from one of his desk chairs and plopped down.

"You haven't read those files you found Saturday, have you?"

"I stuck them in my closet until I could get to them. Is something in there about it?"

"You go home and review the contents of that box and the files. When you get through, if you have any unanswered questions, I'll try to answer them. I'm really sorry."

Dena's head pounded. A knot had formed at the base of her skull. "All right. But as soon as I get through, I'll be back. I can't believe you kept this from me."

Chapter Twenty-Four

ALAN SELLERS

They had agreed to meet on the mainland at a topless bar on Tuesday night if Sellers decided to go along with the deal. Sellers had. He sat at a table in the middle of the room so he wouldn't stand out too much. He'd already watched one table dance where the girl started out on the stage and the runway and took most everything off. She had worked her way from the runway to his table, her tits shaking in his face, her ass busting out of its G-string. He'd practically been forced to slide a few bills under the string on her hip. She'd been in his face so long he figured it was the only way to get rid of her.

The husband was late. Sellers didn't like spending his cash on naked dancers unless it was his idea, and he wasn't in the mood for it right then. Maybe later, after he got his money, all of his money, he'd be able to relax, suck down some drinks and not care how he spent a few bucks. But it wouldn't be in that joint. It wouldn't be anywhere in Galveston County. He'd already decided that. Right now, he wanted to get his money and get out of there. He had a lot of stuff to do, and it didn't include wasting his time looking at some bitch he would have to pay to get.

"Hey, Buddy," a voice said close to his ear.

Sellers flinched.

The husband pulled up a chair next to him.

"Hey, Man," Sellers said. "You're late. They made me have two drinks." He tried not to look the guy in the eye. He didn't want too much to do with him.

The husband shrugged. "I'll pay them, don't worry. So what do you think?"

"Yeah, I can do it."

The husband nodded. "So no problems, huh, Buddy?"

Sellers cut his eyes at him. He didn't like being called Buddy. He didn't like to have to meet the guy there. He couldn't hear well behind all that loud music, not that he felt like having any long drawn out conversations with the husband anyhow. "I said I can do it. When do you want it done?"

"Wednesday after next. I'll be out of the country."

"Yeah? Why Wednesday? Why not Tuesday or Thursday?" Sellers wondered if there was some catch. He hated being pinned down to one day.

"That's my business. You want the job or not?"

"Okay. I don't give a flip. Just give me my money."

"Meet me in the parking lot in a minute. I'm going to the head and take care of your tab." The husband walked toward the men's room.

Sellers watched the man's back. His shirt and pants probably cost more than a longshoreman could make in a couple of days working on the wharves. Well, no more of that for Alan Sellers. After a few minutes, he got up to leave as another girl showed up on the runway, a redhead who looked way younger than even Ginny. He threw a couple of bucks on the table and headed to the parking lot.

He'd brought the Caddy. So far as he knew, the husband didn't know about the Firebird. He might need a second ride sometime, so he didn't want the man to know. After unlocking the car, he got in and started it, turning the air conditioner on full blast. Even in the evenings, it was hotter outside than those women were inside.

The husband slid in on the passenger side and tossed a wrinkled lunch bag at Sellers. Sellers glanced inside and saw a pile of hundred dollar bills. He didn't count it. He figured the guy wouldn't cheat him, at least he wouldn't try to stiff him yet. He didn't trust him around the corner.

"It's all there if you want to check it out."

"Hey, Man, I know you wouldn't rip me off. I know what you're up to. I saw that little piece who works at your house."

"What are you talking about?"

Sellers forced a laugh. "I said I know why you want me to do your wife. I followed that sweet little girl who takes care of your kids."

"When? When did you follow Juliet?"

"Juliet? I knew you were bangin' that bitch. Hey, man, I don't blame you. She's real pretty. And if you don't screw me on my money, your girlfriend will get to stay that way."

"Boy, have you got things wrong. She's not my girlfriend. She's just our *au pair*."

"Yeah, right. Whatever that is."

"You think I'd mess around with a girl who is practically a teenager? Yeah, she's cute but too young. I've got me a …"

The man stiffened in the middle of the sentence. What a dumb ass. "So what do you have, Mister?"

"None of your damn business. You're hired to do a job. Just do it, and keep your nose out of my life." He jerked the door handle and put one foot outside the door.

"That's good for me. I don't like you. You don't like me either. Just tell me what you're going to do about the rest of my money."

"You got any bright ideas?"

"Yeah, send me a package care of general delivery in Mason, Texas."

"You going to be living there?"

"Mind your own business. Just send it. And if you don't I'll be back. Now get out of my car, and don't ever come near me again."

The husband halfway saluted Sellers as he got out and slammed the door.

Sellers pulled onto South Forty-five and drove back toward Galveston. Now he was committed. Now he had the money. He would have to do her. Week after next. He almost wished he didn't have to wait that long. Too bad he didn't have the … what did he call her, well, that girl, for security. But he didn't really need her. He knew the guy's name. There were kids. No way that fool would double-cross him. At least, he'd better not, or he'd be really sorry.

All the way home Sellers thought about needing an extra insurance policy in case the husband tried to double-cross him. By the time he got to his apartment, he had an idea. He got out his notebook to check. He had what he needed right there.

Chapter Twenty-Five

DENA

ena found a will in the papers she'd brought home from the warehouse. She'd had to wait until Juliet left and she'd put the kids to bed. Zack called to say he'd be late. Some work had to get done in anticipation of the Japan trip. The timing couldn't have been better.

She had tucked the box and file folder away in her closet, with things she rarely disturbed but couldn't bear to get rid of, a scrapbook from the first years of their marriage, an old stamp collection of her father's, her bronzed baby shoes.

Laying the dusty folder and box on an old towel on top of the duvet, Dena surveyed her find, her palms sweating. The risk that she'd discover something she'd be better off not knowing had already passed with Old Lady Heslep letting the secret out. Now it was just a matter of the details.

She sat cross-legged on the bed, sewing scissors in hand. Why she hesitated, she didn't know. Was she afraid her few memories of her mother would be tarnished? Once the contents were revealed, she'd be unable to return to her childish view of her parents as two people whose lives orbited around her, their only child. She would have to see them as individuals with separate lives and examine their relationship to each other, and their relationship to her, albeit posthumously. It was time for her to do that, time for her to put away her childlike ideals and assume the role of the adult in her relationship with her parents.

Drawing a deep breath, Dena attacked the box almost viciously. She cut and tore the duct tape away and balled it up, pitching it at a wastebasket across the room. Her heart palpitated when she lifted the top from the box and set it aside. There were several nine-by-twelve envelopes. Dena laid them on the bed and tossed the box to the floor. Opening the file folder, she found a tissue copy of the will, the type lawyers used before copiers. There were also a few notes in her father's handwriting on a faded yellow legal pad. Funny, she had never thought to check with the county clerk's office to see if her mother's will had been filed. It never mattered before.

Dena read through the will first. It was a simple document and of no real consequence. Her mother had left everything to her father. If her father predeceased her, then to Dena, in trust. In that event, it appointed Dena's now-deceased uncle, James Barlow, as guardian of Dena's person and estate, in other words, to raise her. That was something Dena had not known, but it came as no real surprise.

The first envelope contained yellowed, brittle newspaper clippings folded into waxed paper. The top one read:

GALVESTON-An unidentified person died a fiery death when a blue Mustang convertible slammed into the barricade at the East End of the seawall Saturday night. Witnesses reported that rather than braking on the approach, the lone occupant accelerated and could have been driving as fast as 80 mph. Two nearby fishermen said debris landed adjacent to

their car on Boddecker Drive. The fireball could be seen as far away as
the 14th Street rock groin.

No wonder her father hadn't wanted her to know how her mother died. The next clipping bore a large headline, "Prominent Attorney's Wife Apparent Suicide." It gave details of Rebecca Barlow's fiery death, her social activities since her marriage to Dena's father, information about the Barlow and Barlow law firm, and the surviving two-year-old Dena. The obituary followed and contained a photograph of Dena's mother that Dena had never seen before, her hair long, thick, and wavy, wide-eyed, and a modest smile. What a stranger that person in the obituary was to her. Her mother appeared younger in that photograph than Dena's present age.

The next envelope contained mental health commitment documents listing Rebecca Barlow as the patient. Stunned, she thumbed through the papers. The terms "danger to himself or others" jumped off the form pleadings. There was a commitment to the psychiatric ward of the hospital in Galveston, which back then, Dena knew, was the Graves Building.   The second month Dena had been a licensed attorney, the probate judge had appointed her to represent mental health patients who had been involuntarily committed to the hospital. She had heard horror stories about the shock treatments of patients in the years gone by. Had her own mother been subjected to them?

Why had her mother been committed to a mental hospital? What was wrong with her? Rebecca Jean Lowell had been a number of years younger than Horace Benjamin Barlow, who, as an already established attorney, had a lot more to lose by marrying someone with a mental illness than she did, him. What could have been so bad that her mother felt she had to take her own life? A little piece of Dena wasn't sure she really wanted to know, but she had come this far, and she wasn't about to stop until she had concrete answers.

She steeled herself and turned to the third and last envelope. Inside she found another envelope, one about the size of a standard thank-you note, addressed to her in unfamiliar handwriting. A small cry escaped Dena and tears erupted down her face. She pulled out a folded sheet, the letterhead bore the engraved initials RJB.

My darling daughter,

Forgive me for leaving you. I know I will never be a good mother and you will be better off with your father as both father and mother to you than with me in your life. With any luck, he will remarry a wonderful woman, which he deserves.

I love you with all my heart. Please know that. I would not be leaving you otherwise. Please forgive me.

I hope your father will honor my request and give you this letter when you are grown. There is so much I want to tell you, so much that I know he will keep from you, to protect you as he protected me, saved me, and is still trying to protect me.

If a man ever comes to you and claims he is your brother, you must believe him. I had a baby by another man before I married your father and gave birth to you. I lost all rights to my baby after I tried to escape from my husband and flee Houston with my son. Your father saved my life.

I will always love you, no matter what, and pray you have a wonderful life.

Love always,

Your Mama, Becky Barlow

Dena dropped the letter onto the bed and stared into space, horrified at the thought she had an older brother she'd never known about. She had thought Lucas and his family were her only living relatives, besides her own children, of course.

A slow burn built in her at her father. How could he have kept those awful things from her? Had he been worried she would commit suicide, too? Preposterous. He'd gone to his grave without ever even telling her that her own flesh and blood was out there somewhere. He had known her mother left a letter for her but had concealed it. What paternalistic gall.

She scanned her mother's letter until she came to the part about fleeing Houston. Fleeing, why? Fleeing whom? Fleeing what? She entertained the idea of going to Houston and trying to find some answers but realized the impossibility of her situation. Zack would think she was nuts. Lucas would really discourage her. Ellen might lend some moral support, but wouldn't be of any help with her search. Where would she begin?

Grabbing her purse off the floor beside the bed, Dena dug around inside until she came to the information she had been searching for. She punched numbers into her cell and waited through five long rings. She began having wild thoughts about the man who was her brother. What if his father was a criminal, a gang member like Mafia, and had raised him to be a criminal? What if her brother was deformed or mentally retarded? He could be African-American or Asian or a Latino, but why would that matter? About the time she was ready to hang up, Martin Richardson answered.

"This is Dena Armstrong. I have a favor to ask of you."

The deep voice at the other end of the line said, "Anything for you, Dena. How can I help?"

He sounded self-assured, something she wasn't feeling too much of at that moment. "I need to get into contact with someone who can do some confidential research for me, probably mostly in Houston, no questions asked." She added, "And money is not a problem."

"Is it something I could do for you, Ma'am?"

"No, I'd rather not. I hope you don't mind. It's very personal."

"You would tell me if it involved your safety."

"Yes. And no, it doesn't. I just didn't know who else to ask."

"I understand. Got a pen handy?"

"Yes." Dena nodded, as if he could see her. She wrote down the information he gave her. "Thanks a million. This will be strictly between us, won't it?"

"Yes, Ma'am. No problem there."

"Goodbye." As soon as she hung up, she scrambled off the bed and scooped everything back into the box. She didn't want to share any of it with Zack right then and maybe ever. After she put it away, Dena made the phone call to the person Martin had suggested. Now she had to wait until the answers came back. She hoped it wouldn't be more than a few days.

Chapter Twenty-Six

ALAN SELLERS

"**H**ello, Dena? This is Alan Sellers. When is Ginny coming to get her stuff?" He lay on the sofa with "Law And Order" reruns turned down very low on the television. Ready to put his plan into action, the first step was to line up the return of Ginny's property. He hoped she'd be lulled into a false sense of security when he gave everything he still had back. She couldn't think too badly of him if some of the stuff he'd said was damaged really wasn't. He'd just say he'd told her that because he was angry. Which was no lie.

"Okay, Mr. Sellers, which stuff are you speaking of?"

"Anything she wants, Dena. She can have it all. She just needs to call me and tell me when she's coming."

"I'll certainly try to get that message to her."

"Could you do that soon, Dena? Could you do it maybe this week? Her stuff is in my way. I'd like her to get it right away."

"I said I would try to get a message to her. That's about all I can do."

"You want to give me her work number? I could call her at work myself and make arrangements with her." That would get her goat.

"I can't do that."

"Aw, gee, Dena, see I'm not calling her on her cell, right?" Ginny didn't answer the phone anymore, but he wasn't going to tell Dena that. "You could give me her work number. I'm not going to hurt her or anything. I'm under a protective order, right?"

"I'm glad you aren't going to hurt her, but I'm still not giving you her work number. I'll call her today, though, and ask her to call you and make arrangements to get over there as soon as possible and get her *stuff*."

"You think I'm still sore at her, don't you, Dena? You think I'm still mad enough that I would do something to her. All I want is for her to come get her stuff, and then we could get the divorce. By the way, when can we get the divorce, Dena? You think we could get it this week?"

"There'll be no divorce until Ginny gets her personal property, and then I still have to draw up the decree and get you both to look it over and sign it and then we have to go to court. Just as a point of information, let's say I do get the decree drawn up this week, when could you come sign it?"

He almost laughed out loud. She sounded so uptight. He must make her nervous. She sure had acted like it when they were in court. He liked it that way. If she was nervous now, what would she be like when he showed up at her house? He cleared his throat. "Well, I think I could probably come sign the papers any day this week. You just let me know, Dena, and I'll be right over. By the way, is your office still at the same place you put on them papers from a couple of months ago?"

"Yes. Okay, so I'll call Ginny and get back to you about the decree."

"All righty, Dena. I look forward to hearing from you. By the way, did I tell you I have a new girlfriend? Her name is Wendy. As soon as I get divorced, we're going to Las Vegas for the weekend. I might even marry her. Won't that be great?"

When she sighed really loud into the phone, he knew he was getting to her.

"I'm sure that will be very nice. I'm hanging up now."

"Okey-dokey, Dena. Talk to you later." He pressed the end button and burst out laughing. He wished he could see that lady's face about now. She was probably having a fit.

At eleven, Sellers was dressed and out the door. Instead of the Cadillac, he drove the Firebird to Armstrong's office where he parked and played his waiting game again. He was getting good at parking and waiting. Maybe he should be a private dick, with the amount of time he spent spying on people. Too bad he never heard of one who got paid what the husband had offered him to do his wife. Too bad, because he could get used to it even though when he first started sitting around waiting he couldn't stand it. Now he kind of liked it. It was better to sit and think all day than have to mess with a bunch of stupid people who yammered at you all the time. If he had to spend all day doing something, he'd rather be by himself. The worst thing about it was the heat.

Lunchtime came at the husband's office. A dozen people poured outside, climbed into cars, and drove away. Armstrong was not one of them. Sellers choked down a cheese sandwich and a Coke. Thirty minutes later, two more men came down the stairs. Neither of them was the husband either. He wasn't about to give up. During the hottest part of the day, he ran his tank of gas down considerably by running his engine so he could have air-conditioning. He didn't care. His wanted to find out who the husband was screwing and what made her so special he'd be willing to risk everything for her. He was sure that was what was going on.

In the middle of the afternoon, the husband arrived at his office in his Lexus. The man walked so quickly, he practically ran inside. About thirty minutes later, the husband left the building and instead of getting into his Lexus, he drove away in a recent model black convertible Corvette with darkly tinted windows. Sellers took a swig from his bottle of water and set it in the console before he followed. There was more to this man than he thought.

He cruised a couple of car lengths behind the husband. The man headed east toward the ferry to the Bolivar Peninsula when he veered off Harborside Drive headed toward the Yacht Basin. Sellers sped up, drove past the guard at the entrance to the condos like he knew where he was going, and barely made it in time to see the Corvette park inside a garage beside another Lexus, a silver sedan. The garage door descended behind it.

Circling, Sellers parked in a visitor lot and ambled to the front of the condo unit to get a number and see if whoever was inside was dumb enough to display their name. No such luck. The mailboxes were by number, not names. He'd just have to play the waiting game again. At least the temperature was dropping as the day wound down.

Ninety minutes later, he was still waiting. He didn't have to guess what they were doing. He knew. He could leave, but he wanted to catch a look at the woman and maybe get her license number. Couldn't the husband have gone for a quickie so Alan could get back home into his air-conditioned apartment? Asshole.

At dusk, the man finally came out. How did guys like him get away with it? How could they get off work so much? And how could he afford a Corvette on top of the Lexus? Sellers had thought it was the wife who had the money, not the husband. Maybe that was the real key to the thing. Maybe he needed her money for something. Maybe the husband had his wife heavily insured. He needed to cash in to pay for that car, the other woman, and God knew what else. Just like in the movies.

He should have known. The stupid jerk getting himself in a fix like that in the first place.

As the husband backed out of the garage, his headlights lit the rear of the Lexus just long enough for Sellers to see a partial number. What's more, before the garage door started down, Sellers caught sight of a slender, black-headed woman backing through a doorway as she waved goodbye.

Chapter Twenty-Seven

DENA

Dena didn't like bringing work home with her, but if she didn't discuss Alan Sellers with someone, she would wake up in the middle of the night worrying about everything and not be able to get back to sleep. Since that phone call earlier in the day, she just couldn't stop thinking about him. There was something decidedly strange about a person who would act so weird.

Zack disturbed her reverie when he moved into the chair next to her after dinner and shook her arm. "You haven't been with us all night. What's on your mind?"

Her shoulders hunched up around her neck. "It's just that Sellers divorce case. Sorry."

"More threats?"

"No." She wiped at her face and balled up her napkin. "I just can't figure out what's going on in his mind. He acts so weird."

"Like what?"

"One day he's screaming angry, and the next he's as sweet as pie. It's strange. But never mind." She rose from the table and picked up her plate.

"You're not still worried about him attacking you, are you?"

"Not really. I think he just likes to annoy people."

Zack nodded and squeezed her arm. "I'll be in the den."

After she had cleaned up the kitchen and put the children to bed, she walked into the den, where Zack watched television.

"I got my ticket to Japan today," he said when she sat on the other end of the sofa.

"So you know definitely when you're leaving and when you're coming back?"

"Yes. Leaving on Friday and returning the following Friday night." He turned sideways to face her. "It's a little bit longer than I thought, but if Henry gets there earlier, I can always change my reservations."

"Don't worry about us. You go and stay as long as you want. You won't even get to see what the place is like if you're just there for a couple of days."

"It's okay. I really don't mind. The way I figure it, it takes a day to a day-and-a-half just to get there, depending on connecting flights. The reason I'm leaving so early on Friday is that if I left any later, I wouldn't get there until after the welcoming cocktail party Sunday night. Don't forget there's a big time difference. With all the stopovers, it can take twenty to thirty hours just to get there."

"You have to do the preparations, too, don't you? You're going to be so pressed for time."

"I've made allowances for that."

"I've forgotten. Is it next weekend you're leaving?"

Zack cocked his head and looked her over. "Yes, Sweetheart. I said next Friday. I'll only be gone a week. Five days if you don't count the day I leave or the day I come back. And then we can make some plans. A weekend alone or with Bob and Ellen."

Sweetheart? Every day he seemed to grow warmer toward her. She slid down onto the carpet and clasped her arms around her bent knees, her focus on the TV. A trip alone or with Bob and Ellen? She didn't know if she wanted that.

Zack scooted over and ran his fingers through her hair, scratching her head.

He used to do that all the time when they were first together. Now it had been quite a while since he'd been that close to her.

"A weekend away from the kids would be good for us."

She looked over her shoulder at him. Next, he'd want to have sex. She wasn't sure that was such a good idea though some couples got divorced and still had sex, both before and after the divorce. "Think I'll go to bed."

"You go ahead. I want to catch the news."

Relief swept over her. She left him and went to take a hot shower to help her sleep. Afterward, she pulled on her favorite white cotton nightgown and climbed under the covers. When Zack came in, she was still wide-awake. He turned on the light in his closet and undressed just inside it.

"Zack," she said, staring at the ceiling in the dark.

"Hmmm?"

"I still have the strangest feeling about this divorce case."

"Why's that?"

"Well, what would you think about someone who suddenly became agreeable after acting so mean in the beginning?"

"Like what?"

"Like saying he'll give his wife whatever she wants after saying before that someone broke into his house and stole her stuff?"

"Maybe he just wanted to give her a hard time. I wouldn't worry about it."

"That's what I was thinking. Otherwise, it doesn't make sense."

"It'll work out, you'll see. Go to sleep now."

He walked into the bathroom and closed the door behind himself.

Dena turned over and faced the window. He was probably right. She focused on her breathing and closed her eyes.

Chapter Twenty-Eight

MARTIN

"Richardson, the chief wants you." Boyd stuck his head in Martin's office, hollered, and took off before Martin could quit writing on his clipboard and get out of his chair.

"What does she want?" Martin called after the cap's departing back, but Boyd didn't respond. Just like the cap to leave him in suspense.

Pulling his leg off his desk, Martin rose to his feet. When the chief wanted someone, she didn't like to be kept waiting. He yanked his blazer off the back of his chair and shrugged it on as he hustled to her office. When he got there, her door was closed, and nobody sat behind the desk outside, a bad sign. He didn't know if he should knock, sit down and wait, or what. When he heard the chief yelling at someone, he decided to sit and wait.

He hoped she wasn't yelling on his account. It'd been several weeks since he'd talked to Captain Boyd so the chief would have had time to get over being angry with him. At least he hoped so.

He wanted to stick his head closer to the door to hear what she was yelling about, but no way was he going to be caught in that position, and that would be just his luck. So he waited. Five minutes. Ten. He could have finished making his notes for his report if he'd known it would be that long.

The door jerked open and a red-faced juvenile cop rushed past Martin, exchanged looks, but otherwise didn't acknowledge him. Martin glanced past the man and saw the chief popping the top on a can of diet Dr Pepper. Her eyes swept over him.

"Come in, Richardson, and close the door behind you."

He didn't like her tone, but he shut the door and sat in a chair across from the chief's. A sweet smell hung in the air. A fat candle burned by the window. Things had changed a lot since he'd come on the force.

The chief smiled, showing her big, horse-like teeth. It was easy to tell when she was happy and when she wasn't. Her black hair was twirled up at the back of her head.

Her blue eyes, the color of the Gulf of Mexico on one of its calmer days, penetrated all the way to a person's backbone. She was known for not mincing words. Martin waited, anticipating the unexpected.

She took a swallow from a can of Dr Pepper. "How's it going, Richardson?" Standing up behind her desk, she looked every bit the two hundred pounds it was rumored she weighed, but she was nearly as tall as Martin and didn't have an ounce of fat on her.

"Fine." He waited for the ax to fall.

"Let me show you something." She walked to a chart on an easel in the back corner behind her desk. "You gave me a really good idea. Boyd tell you?"

"No, Ma'am. He didn't tell me anything." The captain had said nothing to him since the day Martin had been in his office. Even if he'd said something, Martin wouldn't have told the chief until the cap said it was okay. He knew how things worked. Following her to the chart, he waited to hear what she would say.

"You know what this is?" She pointed to the chart with her forefinger, the soda can still in her hand.

"Looks like a duty roster."

"That's exactly what it is. Since Captain Boyd reported to me that you were unhappy being stuck in an office, I got this brilliant idea for us all to go back out on the street. Hell, Richardson, I miss the action, too."

"Yes, Ma'am." The tension eased out of his body.

"So I asked some of the other officers. Most of them agreed with me. They'd all like to get out on the street once in a while. The ones who said no, well, I guess they're probably the ones who need to be in touch with the community even more than the rest of us."

He hoped she hadn't told them it was his idea. "So if everyone goes back out on the street, who'll be riding the desks?"

"You thought you would have to do both, right? No, I still don't have a decent overtime budget. Here's the deal." She pointed at the chart again. "You'll ride shotgun for one week a month on the evening shift for ninety days. You'll be paired with a man in the downtown area, so if there's any emergency, you'll be close by. After ninety days, you'll ride shotgun on the midnight shift, then days, and so on."

Martin thought the idea stunk, but he only nodded at the chief. The least he could do was hear her out. "So every month I get to be out on the street for a week?"

"Yeah. See, the captain will be on the week after you and then me. Each shift will rotate their officers for a week." She turned and grinned at him, obviously very pleased with herself. "This chart shows how it will work for a full year and who you'll be paired with."

Martin was afraid to look and see whom she would stick him with. "What about months that have five weeks?"

She glanced at the chart. "Oh, well, we'll just work our usual office duty. So what do you think?"

Martin adjusted his shoulder holster and his jacket and shifted his eyes to the chart in an effort to avoid answering. Finding his name in the first group, he could see she'd paired him with a rookie who had barely made it past the entrance requirements. She probably thought Martin could help the guy. It wasn't what he'd had in mind at all.

"If it's all the same with you, I'd just like to go back to being sergeant and get my old partner back."

"Well, it's not all the same to me, damn it." Her eyes flared. "You know how many hours I've spent trying to work all this out? You know how much a lot of those men out there look up to you, getting all shot up, having that bum leg, and refusing disability? What are they going to think if you take a demotion?

Hell, they'll probably think it's my fault. Morale will go down." She pitched her soda can in the trash and stalked back to her desk. Shaking her finger at him, she continued her tirade for a few more minutes before she finally dropped into her chair. "What's the matter with you anyway, Richardson? Most men would give their left *cojone* to be lieutenant."

Sweat had beaded on his forehead. He sat back down. "I just want to be back on the street for a while."

"Does this have something to do with your sister?"

Flexing his jaw muscle to keep himself calm, he waited a moment before responding. "Not you, too."

"What? Am I deaf, dumb, and blind? You think I don't know what goes on in this town that affects my men? You think because I'm a woman, I'm not as good a chief, that I don't have my finger on the pulse of the department?"

Martin fought to keep the edge out of his voice. "It has nothing to do with you being a female, Chief. Have I ever treated you like that? I think you're doing a good job, I swear. I just don't like my business being flaunted in front of everyone, that's all."

"Then you ought to tell your sister not to come up here with her problems. Okay, okay. So level with me, Richardson. What's going on?"

He studied her face a moment. What did he have to lose? She wasn't going to give him what he wanted unless he was square with her. "All right. It isn't just about my sister, but she's getting ready to get this divorce. The guy is off his rocker. I think he's going to go for her, and I'm stuck in here all day every day."

"So you want on the street so you can look after her."

"Yeah, that's a big part of it."

"Missing Morales, your old partner…"

Martin nodded. "I worked hard to get where I am, but I don't like it. It's lonely."

"How do you think I feel?"

"Probably the same, but I'm asking you. Let me partner with Joe."

"You've been divorced a couple of years, am I right?"

"Yes, Ma'am."

She nodded. "Seeing anyone else?"

Martin shrugged. "Nope."

"So you're lonely. Morales is fixing to go on the evening shift."

"I don't care. I could run this guy down and see what he's up to during the day when my sister is working days, and then look out for her after she gets off, and vice versa."

"You mean drive by."

"Yeah, whatever it takes. Look, I don't mean to make you angry, but not everybody has the balls you have."

She laughed. "And what's that supposed to mean?"

"You don't mind chewing on a guy's ass even if he used to be your old partner. Me, I don't like it. I don't like the politics. I don't like the city council members even knowing my name." He hiked his right ankle over his other knee and leaned back in his chair. "Hell, if you want to know the truth, Chief, I just want to do my job and find me a lady and have some kids. That's all I want."

The chief propped her chin on her fist. "I can understand that, Richardson. Tell you what I'm thinking. Maybe you made lieutenant too young, maybe not. The point is, if you're not happy, you're not going to be a very good lieutenant or anything else."

"Hey, I'm doing my job."

"I'm not saying you aren't. You've got some personal business to take care of. Fine. I'm going to stick you out there for ninety days." She stood up. "On evenings with Morales. No demotion right now. Then I'm going to yank your sorry ass back in here, and we'll see what's up."

Martin stood and stuck out his hand. He wanted to hug her, but he knew that wasn't permissible.

"On two conditions."

Martin dropped his hand. Here it comes.

"You let it be known it was your idea, not mine. I'm not going to have a bunch of gossip and union meetings over this." She rounded her desk and walked toward the door. "And you got to realize that if I need you back in the office for a few days over some emergency or something, I'll jerk you back in here in a New York minute."

"Thank you."

She held the door open for him. Before he could get past her, she said, "You didn't really think my idea was all that bad, did you?"

Martin grabbed her hand and shook it hard. It was the most he could get away with, her being chief. "It certainly has some merit, Ma'am. I think it could use some close examination by all the other officers." He smiled when he wanted to cheer. All he could think about was getting out there and kicking Sellers' ass if he went anywhere near Ginny.

Chapter Twenty-Nine

ALAN SELLERS

*L*ate Thursday morning, Sellers received the call from Ginny. He was dozing in bed, having decided he wouldn't leave his apartment until he heard from her. He dragged himself to his cell phone, half asleep, fumbling around in a daze until he found where he'd left it.

"Hello, Alan? My lawyer told me to call you and set up a time to get my things."

"Hey, Doll, I've been waiting to hear from you. How're you doing?" He grabbed a Coke from the fridge and sprawled out on the bed.

"Fine. I've got a new job."

"Oh, yeah? Well, glad to hear that, Babe."

"Look, I'm on evening shift this week again. I can't come until Saturday, but I've definitely lined up a truck for the morning."

"Hey, I'm easy. I'll go along with whatever you say." The carbonation from the Coke woke him up and made his nostrils flare. He belched and his stomach growled. It was getting near lunchtime. He couldn't remember breakfast. All the days seemed the same lately.

"You're not playing games? You'll be there?"

"Definitely. No problem. You tell me the time...no, it don't matter. I'll just stay home all day. Come any time."

"Are you sure? Are you telling the truth? Because if you're playing games, I don't want to bother coming."

"Hey. Like I told Mrs. Armstrong, I'm through with games. I mean it. Really. You come down on Saturday, and I'll give you your stuff. Then we can sign the papers next week, okay?"

"I don't know whether I can trust you or not, but I'll be there around ten if everything works out."

"You can trust me. Really. I'll see you then, okay?"

"Your new girlfriend will be there, too?"

"What? Oh, I don't think so. It'll just be you and me and the truck you get, okay?"

"Okay. See you on Saturday."

Sellers started his mental countdown. Saturday, Ginny would get her stuff. He'd follow her home and find out where she had moved. Sunday, he'd begin watching her to see what she did all day, figure out her schedule. Monday, he'd call the lawyer again and arrange a day to sign the papers. During the week, Ginny would sign the papers and get the divorce. The following weekend, it would be all over for Ginny. He hadn't quite worked that out yet, but he would.

After Ginny, it would be the lawyer's turn. The next Monday, her husband would be out of town. That morning, he'd break into her house, get the key to the jewelry box, and hide in the garage. Monday night, it would be all over for the lawyer. He knew her husband said Wednesday, but he didn't give a shit. Monday worked best.

He needed an alibi. Or did he? What if instead of cutting Ginny he just ran her down on the street like a dog? But he couldn't do it in his old man's car. And he didn't want to do it in the Firebird. Maybe he could steal a car. Maybe he could catch her out on the street over the weekend and run her down and dump the car and high tail it to Houston, go out to the bars, and make sure he was seen. He could still have his fun with the lady lawyer.

His plan for the lawyer was a good one. A burglary. That covered his butt pretty good. He could show up at Marlo's Club afterwards. Everybody he knew would probably be so drunk they wouldn't know what time he got there. He'd have to remember to take a change of clothes in case he got blood on the other ones. What could he do with the first set? Dump them. Dump them far away from the lawyer's house, and far away from Marlo's, and far away from where he threw the stuff into the bayou. He could swing through the downtown area and throw them into an alley dumpster. Yeah, like on Postoffice Street or The Strand. He could go to the Salvation Army and buy some old clothes. He could change into his regular ones and throw the old ones out. Yeah. It was all coming together.

The only thing that bothered him was the possibility that the lawyer might find out about Ginny before Monday night. Would she suspect something? She probably wouldn't if it were a hit-and-run. But she would if he cut Ginny. He'd have to think about that. Maybe he should wait a while on Ginny.

What if the lawyer got killed in a routine burglary? Would Ginny find out? And if she found out, would she suspect him? She probably wouldn't if it was known to be a burglary. Then later, if he kept tabs on Ginny, he could grab her off the street one day. Or he could run her down. Or he could get into her apartment.

But he had already made his plans and didn't want to change them. He didn't want to wait. He wanted to kill Ginny and wished he could do it now. Man, he hated her. Bad enough he'd have to wait until the divorce was over. He knew he had to wait that long. If he did it any sooner, Martin would be on his ass.

He had to go through the divorce peaceably. He'd just have to try to hide Ginny's body so they wouldn't find it until after Monday. By then it would be too late. He'd have to find a way to do it on Sunday. He wandered into the kitchen where he dug around in the cabinets until he found some chocolate chip cookies. He stuffed them in his mouth on his way back to the bedroom, the sweet, strong flavor of chocolate filling his mouth and nose. He lay on the bed and devoured the cookies, not caring where the crumbs fell. Afterward, feeling content and happy, he fell back asleep.

Chapter Thirty

ALAN SELLERS

aturday morning, a sharp horn blast woke Sellers up. He rolled out of bed and looked through the living room window. When he opened the blinds, his pupils shrank from the sun's glare. He could almost feel the heat rising from the pavement. Ginny sat in a truck's passenger side in front of his apartment. Sellers' excitement at the prospect of his plan falling into place caused him to smile.

He ran back into the bedroom and was pulling on his jeans when someone rapped on the door. Hollering for her to wait, Sellers put on a tee shirt and some tennis shoes, combed his hair, and yanked the door open.

A jolt hit him like a smack in the face.

Martin stood there, looking like he was itching for a fight. Sweat beaded on his upper lip. Patches of sweat marred the underarms of a gray muscle shirt. No question Martin wanted him to see the size of his biceps.

Sellers backed up a step.

"You ready, Fella?" Martin clenched and unclenched his fists.

Sellers forced a smile, acting like Martin's unexpected appearance didn't faze him. He was one man Sellers didn't want to tackle from the front.

"Hey, Martin." He held out his hand. "What'cha know good?"

Martin looked down at Sellers' hand, back at his face, and then into the house. "You got her stuff ready?"

Sellers dropped his hand. The son-of-a-bitch wasn't even going to attempt to be friendly. "Yeah, but she can come in and look around. She can have anything else in the place she wants."

Martin pointed at Sellers' chest. "You wait here." He took the stairs down two at a time.

Sellers shut the door. He wanted to hit something. Breathing deeply to calm himself, he went into the kitchen to start coffee. He couldn't follow her home if Martin was with her. Martin was no dummy.

There was another knock. Sellers resumed his smile and took another lengthy breath before opening the door, his shaking hands down at his sides. "Hi, Gin," he said when he saw her framed in the doorway, her long blond hair tied back in a ponytail. She'd gotten fat. She wore a tee shirt stretched over her jeans, her moving clothes, but it didn't hide her muffin top.

"Hi," Ginny said, her eyes looking past him into the apartment.

"Come on in and look around. I've boxed up a bunch of stuff, but whatever else you want, it's yours. I'm making coffee, want some?" She looked pretty good, even if she had put on the weight.

He didn't want to run her down even in his mind. He wanted one last piece of her.

"No, thanks." Ginny brushed past him, careful not to let their bodies touch. He caught a whiff of her flowery perfume.

Martin stood in the doorway.

"You want a cup of coffee?"

"No, I just want to get this over with. Sis, check those boxes first. When you get through, look around and see if there's anything else you want while I'm putting them in the truck."

"Okay." Ginny crouched down, examining the boxes in the pile next to the TV.

Sellers forced a smile. "So how you been?"

Martin looked sideways at him, a scowl on his face.

"So I'm going to get some coffee," Sellers said, his neck feeling warm. "Sure you don't want some?"

"Look, Fella," Martin said, his eyes like slits, "we're not friends, okay? I don't want your stinking coffee. I'm getting my sister in and out of here, that's all."

"Okay. Okay. Just trying to be sociable." Sellers backed into the kitchen. He would be cool. He poured himself a cup and sat at the table.

"This box can go down," Ginny said, showing the top one to Martin. Opening the second one, she glanced at the books inside and then closed it again. "And this one."

Martin stacked them and carried them out. Ginny checked the others. Sellers watched her but said nothing.

"Take these, Martin," she said when her brother appeared again. "I'll look around for a few other things." She disappeared into the bedroom. Sellers sipped his coffee and continued to sit at the same place.

A few minutes later, Ginny came out with an armful of sheets, pillowcases, and towels. "This is half the linens, okay? I counted them out."

"Fine. Whatever you want."

She looked at her brother. "Get some empty boxes out of the truck, will you?" She dumped the linens on the sofa.

Martin glared at Sellers before he went out again as if he expected Sellers to do something each time he was gone loading the truck.

Sellers watched Ginny as she looked into the kitchen cabinets. He continued to sip his coffee. Memories flooded him. It would be a shame to waste her, but she couldn't get away with treating him like a dog.

"Can I have this set of glassware?"

He glanced at her face. Her blue eyes flickered around the room like a fly, not resting for very long in one place. He liked seeing she was still afraid of him.

"Which set?" He couldn't see from where he sat. He stood to see what she was talking about just as Martin returned.

"What are you doing?" Martin bellowed, dropping the empty boxes and coming at him.

Sellers shrank back. "Nothing, Man."

Ginny got between them. "I was just asking him about a set of glassware. He wasn't doing anything." She pushed her brother back, separating the two men.

"Are you sure?" Martin glared over her head.

"Go sit," Ginny said. "It's okay. Alan doesn't mean me any harm," she said turning to Alan. "Do you?"

"No, Man. I wasn't doing anything." He backed up to his chair at the end of the table. Fire raged inside him. His brain screamed harsh words. In spite of Martin's leg injury, his very size alone had always left Sellers feeling defenseless.

"Just so you know," Martin pointed his finger at him. "I don't trust you. I don't trust you for one minute alone with my sister." He moved into the living room.

Sellers' hands went up in front of himself, as if to show he wouldn't touch anything. "I was just going to see what glasses she was talking about. Shit. I wasn't going to hurt her."

"I don't like you using that kind of language around her either," Martin said, looking like a thunder cloud.

"You two stop it." Ginny cried, looking from one to the other. "Stop it right now. I just want to get my stuff. Stop it, Martin. Sit down."

"Just so he understands what I'm going to do to him if he ever lays a hand on you."

"He knows that," Ginny said. "Please, go sit in the living room."

Martin glowered in Sellers' direction one more time as he pushed the linens aside and sat on the couch.

Ginny turned to Alan and shrugged. "I'm sorry it had to be like this."

Sellers looked into the other room at Martin. He was almost afraid to say anything to her. There wasn't a damn thing he'd do around Martin. That was for sure. But when he did what he was going to do, Martin wouldn't ever be able to prove it was him. He'd make sure of that. He shrugged back at her, glad she couldn't read his mind. He could barely contain the frustration and anger boiling inside of him.

"Come over here, and tell me what I can have out of this cabinet," she whispered.

Sellers got back out of his chair, cast a glance at Martin, and crossed to the kitchen cabinet. There were two complete sets of glasses and a lot of mismatched ones they had somehow accumulated during their short time together.

"Take whatever you want," he said, friendly as could be.

"I want to be fair about it."

"Then just take half of everything, like you did the sheets. I don't care," he said.

"You're sure?"

"I'm sure."

"Okay. Thanks for being a good sport." Her smile reminded him of how young she was. She was such a little girl. Still a bitch, though.

"Yeah … you bring some newspaper or something to wrap this stuff in? I'll help you." He had to hurry up and get them out of there before he did something he'd regret. He couldn't take much more of her fake friendliness.

When the boxes were all stacked up, Ginny asked Martin to load them into the truck. While he was gone, she said to Sellers, "I'm sorry things didn't work out for us."

Sellers leaned against the doorjamb and stared outside. He didn't think she should get all that stuff since she had taken his money out of that account. He wasn't going to need it where he was going, though, and he didn't want to listen to her try to sweet-talk him. He just wanted her to get the hell away from him and take her brother with her. He had to concentrate on remaining calm when what he wanted was to reach out and punch her in that baby face. He reached out and gripped the doorknob instead, his knuckles turning white.

"Did you ever go to counseling?"

"Didn't see any need to." He couldn't look at her.

She put her hands in her pockets, her small breasts jutting out. "Are you okay?"

"Sure, why shouldn't I be?"

She rubbed her forearms. "No reason, I guess."

"You going to call your lawyer on Monday and give her the go-ahead on the paperwork?"

"Yes," she said.

"When?"

"If she can get it done, probably early in the week. I want Martin to look over the decree with me."

That son of a bitch Martin was going to ruin his plans again. "And the divorce?"

"Probably Thursday or Friday morning if she can do it then."

"Well, if you look over the papers on Monday or Tuesday, I'll go in on Wednesday and sign them so I don't have to go to court."

"Okay, I'll tell her."

"Anything else I need to do?" He raised his eyebrows.

"I guess not." She looked out at Martin who stood next to the truck. "See you."

Sellers stared after them and breathed a long sigh of relief when they pulled away. He ambled down to the Firebird and pulled his notepad from the glove box where he'd stashed it when he found out Ginny would be coming that morning. He flipped through the pages until he came to the timetable he'd made. He crossed off the line that read "Delivery of Property." He made an adjustment to the date he would follow her home.

"What are you looking at?" he said to Miss Bitch who lived downstairs and stood watching him from her doorway.

She slammed her door.

He slipped the notebook into his back pocket and climbed back up the stairs to his apartment. Now that Ginny had gotten what she wanted, he would pack up the rest. Before long, he'd be pulling up stakes and moving on. He slammed the front door as hard as he could when he got inside, hoping Miss Bitch would be annoyed. He felt a little better.

Chapter Thirty-One

DENA

"I'm ready to get divorced," Ginny told Dena Monday afternoon when she phoned.

The call was a welcome break. Dena had been researching a legal point for another case. Her aching neck told her she'd been hunched over the computer for too long. "You got everything you wanted out of the apartment?" She picked up a pen and started doodling on her desk pad.

"Everything I wanted that was still there." Ginny giggled. "I'm so excited to be getting this over with. Print out the decree and get me divorced before he changes his mind."

Hard to believe Alan Sellers let Ginny just waltz in there and take whatever she wanted. His behavior didn't pass the sniff test. "Don't you think it's weird he was actually home when you went this weekend?"

"Can you believe it?"

"No," Dena said. She drew a stick figure with horns on her pad. "He didn't try anything?"

"He didn't give me any trouble. He just let me come in and pick out what I wanted."

"Anyone go with you?"

"Martin, why?"

"Why, that explains it. What could he do with Martin there?"

"I don't think he would have done anything to me anyway. He acted almost like he did when we first met and was really rather sweet," Ginny said, her voice sounding tearful.

Ginny was so naïve. No wonder Martin worried about her. "You said almost."

"He was distant. Like he was hurt, you know? But he didn't act at all like he did on the phone those times. He even tried to shake Martin's hand when we first got there."

"What do you mean tried?"

"Martin hates him. He wouldn't touch him. But that's Martin, he never forgives and forgets." Ginny made a smacking sound, like she was chewing gum.

"I can't say as I blame him. He feels responsible for you."

"I know, but he can be so hateful when it's not necessary. And suspicious, even over little things."

"Humpf. Beating you up was not a little thing. I would think you'd be at least a little bit suspicious, yourself."

Ginny didn't respond for several moments. Finally, she said, "But if he really has a girlfriend then it makes sense. It's been two months since all this started. I just think he's tired of playing games."

Dena scratched her head with the pen. She knew she had been too trusting of people in the past, too, but it only took a little experience in family law to open her eyes. The world was full of devious people, and Alan Sellers was one of them.

"You want to know what he told me?"

"When he called you? What?" There was a hopeful tone in Ginny's voice.

"That he might get married again real soon." Dena stuck the pen behind her ear and turned back to her computer. She hit print and sent the information she'd found to the printer.

"Oh?" Was that regret in her voice?

"You're not having second thoughts, are you?"

"I guess not, not really. Whoever the girl is, she can have him."

"Did you see any signs of a woman staying there?"

"I wasn't looking for any," Ginny said.

"What about perfume or makeup on the dresser or in the bathroom?"

"I didn't see any. Not even mine that I didn't take."

"You see why I don't believe him?"

"He did tell me in a phone call once that a girl was staying there or spending the night or something," Ginny said.

"Then there should have been evidence of it."

"Well, I don't know if there was anything around or not. I really just wanted to get my stuff and leave. Besides, it doesn't matter anymore, anyway."

Annoyance tugged at Dena. "I'm just saying—"

"Don't worry, Mrs. Armstrong. Martin has already lectured me on not going anywhere at night and looking over my shoulder every time I go outside."

Dena pulled her calendar up on her computer to see when she could get Ginny in to look over the decree. "How about you come on Wednesday to review the decree?"

"That would be okay. Martin wants to come with me."

Dena wouldn't mind seeing Martin, herself. There was something reassuring about him. "How about three o'clock?"

"Too late. Did he tell you he's back out on the streets again? He's on three to eleven."

Why did Ginny think Martin would have told her that? She looked at her calendar. She could bring her lunch that day and see them earlier. "How about one?"

"Okay. Then will you call Alan to come in and sign it on Thursday, so he won't have to go to court on Friday?"

Dena clicked on Thursday on the calendar. "I can't. I'll be in court all day. I'm afraid he'll have to come in on Friday, and we'll have to get you divorced on Monday. I'm sorry."

"I guess that'll be okay." Ginny sounded disappointed.

"Why wouldn't it be?" Dena thought there must be something going on they hadn't told her about. "Is there something going on next Monday? Can you get off work? If not, we can do it later next week."

"It's not that."

"What, then?"

"I think Alan had something he wanted to do, and I told him I thought I'd go to court on Friday."

"I just don't see how I can do it any sooner. I could see you after five on Tuesday if you could come without Martin, and then him on Wednesday, but I really don't want to." She leaned her elbow on the desk, her cheek on her hand. She didn't want to stay late that week with Zack going out of town on Friday. Things had been going pretty smoothly, and she should be home in the evenings as much as possible.

"He'll just have to tough it out." Ginny was back to giggling. "Serves him right for being such a meanie in the beginning."

"Who cares what Alan Sellers wants anyway? Listen, I need to go…"

"Okay. I'll call Martin and tell him when we have to be there, and we'll see you Wednesday at one."

After they disconnected, Dena pulled Ginny's file and took it to Meredith, who had her face right up next to the computer screen, her stringy hair hanging down like a veil. The ashtray was out of the desk drawer and on the desk, a burning cigarette sitting in it. Dena coughed. She wished she could hold her breath, but she had to have a conversation with the secretary. She wasn't even going to complain about what Meredith was doing. It was only a matter of time now before she opened her own office and wouldn't have to deal with Meredith anymore. "Good news."

Meredith slung her arm over the back of her chair and pushed her hair behind her ears. "I could use some good news the way this day is going." She stubbed out her cigarette and took the file from Dena.

Dena waved the smoke away. "Well, this will brighten your day. You can print out the Sellers' decree. Ginny's coming to review it on Wednesday afternoon."

"Terrific," Meredith said. "I'm jumping for joy."

"What's the matter? I thought you'd be happy. Alan Sellers will be out of our hair after Friday," Dena said.

"I am. I am, except I have to assemble it all over again. Doesn't matter. I'll do it gladly."

"I thought it was all ready."

"I was working on it when Mr. Barlow came back here this morning to get my scissors and tripped over all the wires." She looked at the tangle of plugs and extension cords on the floor. "He knocked my coffee over and while we were trying to get everything dried off and straightened out, the computer came unplugged, and I hadn't saved it, so I have to start all over again."

If Lucas wasn't so tight, they could have gotten an electrician in there to put in some new outlets, so the other ones wouldn't be overloaded. But Lucas didn't want to spend the money, another reason Dena wanted her own office. When Meredith stopped venting and turned her attention to Dena, Dena said, "I'm sorry, but you'll have plenty of time to redo it. They're not coming until Wednesday at one."

"It wouldn't be so bad if Mr. Barlow would just stay out from behind here. He's so impatient. If he could have waited one minute while I finished what I was doing, I could have gotten the scissors. That's the second time he's done that. Luckily the first time he only disconnected the printer while I was printing an order."

"I can see why it's been a bad day for you." Dena started inching back toward her office.

"It doesn't exactly put me in a good mood to have to do it over," Meredith said, her voice low and grumbling.

"It can wait until tomorrow." Dena would do it herself, if she had time. They shared the software, and sometimes she did do her own pleadings. Sometimes it was just faster.

"That's good, 'cause it's the pits typing out that list of property and doodads and everything."

"You don't have to do that again. Ginny went over there on Saturday and got everything. All we need now is a decree that says they each keep the property in his or her possession, except for describing the cars and the vehicle identification numbers." Dena paused in her doorway, ready to get back to other cases. "I know how you love typing numbers. Be sure to put in that he agrees to the divorce, and that he didn't appear in court."

"If that's all I have to do, no sweat. That other one was pages and pages of little stuff. Even with all the software we have now, it still takes a long time."

Annoyance tugged at Dena. Would Meredith ever just do something without having to complain? "Just one more thing. Will you call Sellers and set up an appointment for him to come in on Friday to read and sign the decree, and tell him we'll do the divorce on Monday?"

Meredith frowned and made a face. "If I have to."

Dena smiled back. "I'll be in my office if you have any questions." She closed the door behind her and breathed a long sigh of relief. She didn't know why she was so impatient lately. She just was. Maybe it was that she just wanted to get the show— her life—on the road. Get all the details settled, get the break with Lucas and the break with Zach done. She wanted a fresh start all the way around. Only a little longer, she told herself. In the not too distant future, her life would take a big turn.

Chapter Thirty-Two

ALAN SELLERS

e paced back and forth from the living room to the kitchen. The veins in his forehead throbbed as if they were about to burst. He clenched his jaw and his fists. All his plans were screwed.

Kicking over a chair in the kitchen, he bellowed at the four walls and pounded on them. How could things have gone so wrong?

It was all that lawyer's fault. He had worked it out so carefully, and she had to throw a wrench into his plans. Man, would she be sorry, but he wasn't going to give up yet. She hadn't beaten him.

He had to pull himself together. Had to think things out. He'd just have to come up with a new plan for Ginny, that's all. Or he'd have to put off taking out the lawyer until a day or so later. Or both. His new plan would have to work around the changes she'd made.

Damn her anyway.

He got his notebook out of the bedroom and flipped through it to find a blank page and then pulled a joint out of a drawer. He went back into the living room where he stretched out on the sofa and lit the joint, taking a long drag.

He had to concentrate, had to relax. He took another drag and closed his eyes. A plan, a plan, he must design a new plan.

Fact one, he was stuck with a Monday divorce date. He had to accept it.

Fact two, he had to find out where Ginny lived.

Therefore, he had to follow Ginny on Monday.

He stubbed out the joint, saving the butt. His mind drifted. He dozed. He awoke.

Too bad the secretary hadn't told him when Ginny was reviewing the divorce decree. He could have followed her then. He could hang around the lawyer's office on Tuesday and Wednesday. No. He needed a firm plan, not one based on possibilities. He also needed to get those old clothes.

Fact three, the husband would be gone for a week.

Fact four, if he killed Ginny on Monday or Tuesday and hid her body before anyone found it, he could then get the lawyer when the husband wanted him to.

He breathed a sigh of relief and reached for his pen. It was all coming together again, just like he knew it would.

"Nothing has changed, You Bitches, except you might get to live a few days longer. Until Tuesday, Ginny. Until Wednesday, Mrs. Armstrong, Ma'am." He laughed, his voice hoarse from the pot.

Chapter Thirty-Three

DENA

Meredith had barely finished printing out the divorce decree when Ginny and Martin arrived at precisely one o'clock Wednesday afternoon. Meredith fluttered around like a nervous little bird, except she was hardly bird-like. Dena hoped Martin wouldn't notice Meredith's admiring glances. She liked to think that as small as their firm was, Barlow and Barlow had a professional persona. Of course, cigarette smoke wafting in the air didn't help.

Ginny came in wearing a cotton tunic with white daisies on it over a pair of washed out jeans and sandals. She looked like a pregnant adolescent.

Martin wore slacks, a nice shirt, a loose tie, and a blazer. He looked much like the detectives on television cop shows.

When he shook Dena's hand, she again felt a connection. His grip was warm and gentle, like a living, breathing teddy bear's.

"It's nice to see you again."

"Nice to see you again, too. Everything going all right?"

"Fine." She cleared her throat and turned to Meredith who was practically gawking. "You remember our legal secretary, Meredith?"

"Hello, Ma'am," Martin said.

If he'd been wearing a cowboy hat, he probably would have tipped it. That would have cinched Meredith's crush on him.

"Hi, Lieutenant." She handed the paperwork to Dena on top of Ginny's file, her eyes never leaving Martin.

"Let's go into my office," Dena said, nodding in that direction. She gave Meredith her reprimand look before she followed them inside.

"Guess what, Mrs. Armstrong?" Ginny said after Dena closed the door. "I've decided to go ahead with the abortion."

Dena stopped halfway into her chair. "What finally caused you to make that decision?"

"Last Saturday." She glanced at Martin who had his arms crossed. "I tried to talk to Alan, but he seemed so distant. I don't know. I just think it's for the best."

Dena glanced from her to Martin. Did he and Mary finally succeed in pressuring her to do it, or was it her own decision? "Your counselor know about it?"

"I talked it over with her at my last appointment. The thing is, Mrs. Armstrong, I can get in next Monday if I go right when they open."

"Where will you go?"

"The clinic is in Austin. I'm hoping to fly up on Saturday." She rested a hand on her stomach. "I can stay with a girlfriend. We'd go to church on Sunday. Get to visit. She'd drive me to the clinic on Monday and take care of me after."

"So you want to be divorced before you go." Dena glanced from Ginny to Martin. She frowned as she thought of all the other cases she had on her docket already.

Ginny leaned forward in her chair, her small face wrinkled up in a hopeful expression. "If you can swing it. I know you're busy, but now that I've made my decision, I don't want to put it off."

Dena opened the calendar on her computer. Why not? The girl had been through a lot, and if there was a way to finalize the divorce before she left, Ginny could put it all behind her and get off to a fresh start when she returned. Dena could understand her feeling that way.

"Let me think a minute." She clicked through the calendar. It was already Wednesday. They'd have to get Sellers into the office that very afternoon, unless she wanted to have him come to the courthouse and meet her during a break the next day, which she didn't. She reached for the phone, pushing the intercom button.

"Meredith, call Sellers and ask him if he can come late this afternoon to sign the decree. Tell him something's come up, and I have to do the divorce on Friday. Tell him there's no way he can come tomorrow, so it will have to be today. Okay?"

"Okay, Mrs. A. Will you want me to stay late today then?"

"Depends on what time he comes. I don't want to be here alone with him." Her eyes met Martin's. He inclined his head.

She'd started to say *I don't want to be alone with the creepy, scary guy*, but that would be wrong to admit on several levels.

"Thanks, Dena," Martin said, a small smile tugging at the corner of his lips.

"You're a doll," Ginny said.

"I know it." Dena took her glasses off and rubbed her eyes. She'd be swamped the next few days but was glad she'd make at least one person happy. "Remember me in your will."

"You don't know what this means to us," Martin said, "to know that bastard will be out of our lives forever."

"I can make a wild guess." She flashed her eyes at him and handed each of them a copy of the decree. "Why don't you go over the decree while I check with Meredith to see if she's gotten hold of Mr. Sellers. Since you already retrieved your property, we didn't put that in, but everything else should be what we discussed. Of course, there's no mention of any baby." Dena left them turning pages while she went out to talk to Meredith. If Sellers was going to come in that afternoon, they really didn't have a lot of extra time for visiting. Besides, like most of her clients, she was sure Ginny didn't want to pay her hourly rate for chitchat.

Dena closed her office door behind her. "Did you get Sellers on the phone?"

Meredith glanced up from the computer. "God, have you ever seen a more beautiful man in your life?"

"I know you aren't talking about Alan Sellers."

"Ha. Ha. Very funny. That Martin Richardson. I could hardly take my eyes off him, but he could hardly take his eyes off you. What's that about?"

Dena's face grew warm. She had thought what she felt between herself and Martin was her imagination, but if Meredith had noticed something, maybe not. Good thing she wouldn't be seeing him any more except in passing at the courthouse. She had enough problems without another man in her life. "I don't know what you're talking about, Meredith. Did you get hold of Sellers or not?"

"Oh, yeah. Alan Sellers. He sounded agitated but said he'd be here. He wanted to know why the sudden rush."

"What did you tell him?"

"That I didn't know."

"We'll discuss it later. Right now, I've got to get back in there and get them out of here before he shows up."

"He said he could come at two o'clock." She looked at her watch. "You know it's one-thirty now?"

"We'll be through in a minute," Dena said. "Let me check and see if they're finished reading over it yet." She patted Meredith on the shoulder. "Thanks."

When she walked back into her office, Dena asked, "Did you understand everything?"

"Yes, it seems simple enough, Mrs. Armstrong, but you left out a couple of things," Ginny said.

"What?" Dena picked up her copy.

"You didn't put who gets what property," Ginny said.

"I just told you why. It's not necessary since you already have what you wanted. We put your car in there," Dena said.

Susan P. Baker

"What if he comes around later claiming some of the stuff is his?"

"Call the police. He's not supposed to come around at all. That's what the permanent injunction's for," Dena said. "The protective order is only good for two years, but the permanent injunction is good forever."

"I don't see in here where it says that," Martin said, flipping through the pages.

"It should be toward the end." Dena turned to the next to the last page of her copy and read it. The injunction wasn't there. What was Meredith thinking? She glanced at Ginny and then at Martin.

"I'm so sorry. We had an accident with the computer, and Meredith had to do it over." She felt like an idiot for not proofing it before they got there. "I guess she misunderstood my instructions." Feeling guilty, she looked from one to the other. "I'm sorry," she repeated.

Martin cleared his throat. "Can you put it in before you go to court?"

"Sure," Dena said, if you can wait a few minutes, we need to add those pages now. Meredith's pretty fast."

Ginny said, "You don't mind?"

"Of course not, Ginny. It's my mistake. We have to have it because of the protective order expiring, and we have to put it in anyway before Alan signs it." Dena glanced at her watch. "Shoot, he'll be here at two so we'd better hurry. You'll wait?"

"We'll wait," Martin said.

"Okay." Dena stood. "You want a Coke or coffee?"

They both shook their heads.

"Stay right here," she said, and then felt like a moron. Where else would they go? "Meredith," Dena said loudly as she went through the doorway.

Meredith flinched. She was pulling a page from the printer. "What?"

"What are you so jumpy about?"

"Alan Sellers. I'm still scared he's going to come up here and do something crazy. What's the matter now?"

Dena frowned. That was the least of their worries at this point. "We screwed up. We left out the permanent injunction."

"You said I could leave out all that stuff."

"I know what I said. I didn't mean the injunctive relief. I keep forgetting you can't read my mind. I should have looked at it before they got here. The important thing is, we need to have it in there and have this signed and get them out of here before Sellers gets here. Can you add it real quick?"

"Show me which sections," Meredith said, turning her chair in an about-face so she could work at the computer. She pulled up the forms and paged to the correct section.

Dena said, "From here where it says all the stuff about not coming into contact with her at her home or elsewhere, including the sections about not calling her, and add the part about her family and place of employment."

"Okay. I'll insert it into the decree that's on here and reprint the last few pages with the changes. It's going to take me a couple of minutes."

"Just do it as fast as you can." Dena stood behind Meredith.

"If you don't stand here looking over my shoulder, I'll get it done a lot sooner."

"Okay, sorry. I'm going back in there. Holler when you're through."

"Right." Meredith started pushing buttons.

Dena went back into her office, leaving the door open in case Meredith needed her for anything. What a mess. She felt like crawling under her desk and hiding. Still, it could have been worse. They could have failed to see the omission until the day of court, or, heaven forbid, after the divorce was final. Martin's face was grim, his lips clamped together in a thin line. Ginny wrung her hands and kept glancing his way.

"So what time are you leaving on Saturday, Ginny?" Dena drummed her fingers on her desk.

"Early in the morning, around eight I think."

"My husband's going out of town on Friday." She didn't know why she mentioned that. Just making conversation in the awkward minutes.

"Where's he going?" Martin asked.

"Japan, but it's a quick trip. He's practically flying there and then turning around and flying back again. Said he might be back as early as Wednesday."

"Wow. I'd love to go there," Ginny said.

"Me, too," Dena said. She looked at Martin. "Are you taking Ginny to the airport?"

"No, she's going to take her car so we won't have to pick her up when she gets back. Coming home she'll be getting in after I start my shift," Martin said, standing up and moving around the room. "It'll be several days, anyway. Until she's feeling good enough to come home."

"I don't take Zack either. He flies out of Intercontinental. It's too far away." Dena said.

The printer started up. Dena rose and rounded her desk. "We may get you out of here before Mr. Sellers gets here yet," she said to Ginny. "Can I have your copies back so I can switch them out?"

They handed her their copies, and Dena went out to Meredith's office. Her stomach churned. She hated to be rushed, and she hated to make mistakes.

Meredith pulled the staples out of the first copies and as the new pages came out, added them and stapled them together. Dena handed them over to Ginny and Martin who had moved to the doorway and stood there waiting.

Ginny read over it and signed it and folded up her copy, putting it in her shoulder bag. Dena told her what time to be at the courthouse on Friday, said goodbye, and ushered them out of her office at two on the dot. Her whole body felt jittery. She was pacing back and forth next to Meredith's desk bemoaning the fact they'd almost screwed up when footsteps approached in the hall. Dena flashed a look at Meredith and hurried into her office just as the door opened.

"May I help you?" Meredith's voice came out very loud, like she wanted Dena to hear everything that was said.

"It's me, Alan Sellers, in the flesh, here to sign my divorce decree."

"If you'll have a seat, Mr. Sellers, I'll tell Mrs. Armstrong you're here," Meredith said. She went into Dena's office, closing the door behind her and leaning up against it.

"He's here, quote 'in the flesh,'" Meredith said, puffing her cheeks out like she wanted to vomit.

"I heard him. Yuck." Dena felt some trepidation at the thought of being alone with him even in her private office.

"He's kind of creepy. Hurry up, and let's get him out of here."

"I'm ready. Tell him to come in." She pulled her shoulders back, putting on a brave front while wishing Lucas wasn't out of the office. "Don't be afraid. We'll be all right. Be sure to leave the door open."

"Where's your cousin when we need him?"

"Just get Sellers in here. I don't want him to get impatient and leave."

Meredith opened the door and said, "Mrs. Armstrong will see you now."

Sellers carried a magazine into Dena's office and tossed it onto one client chair and sat in the other. His dirty blond locks had fallen over his forehead, partly covering his eyes. He brushed at his hair with his fingers.

"Hey, Dena," he said.

"Hello, Mr. Sellers," she said. "This shouldn't take long." She forced herself to smile. He looked harmless enough. For a moment, she was skeptical again about everything Ginny's family had said. Still, he seemed to radiate some negative energy.

"I saw Ginny and Martin as I drove up. Almost hit them with my daddy's white Caddy," he said, as if to impress her.

"I didn't know you had a Cadillac, Mr. Sellers. Is it something we should put into the decree?"

He stiffened. "Why would you do that?" He scooted up to the edge of the chair.

"It's yours, isn't it? Your father is deceased I understand?"

"Yeah. So it's not in this here paperwork?"

"No. But give me a moment, and I'll write it in next to your Firebird." She flipped the decree back to that page. "Year and model? And do you have the VIN number?"

"Yeah. Hang on a minute." Sellers thumbed through his wallet.

If Martin and Ginny had seen him, had they spoken? She wouldn't ask him. It didn't really matter. She honestly felt relatively calm around him. No longer afraid as she had been shortly after that courtroom episode.

He handed her the cards with the data on them. When she was through interlineating the information, she handed the decree to him. "For you to read over."

He glanced at the top page. "No, that's okay. I trust you to put all the right stuff in it." His sigh sounded melodramatic. "You got a pen?"

"I can't let you sign it without going over it with you if you aren't going to read it."

"Mrs. Armstrong, I just want to get this over with," he said, his eyes moving around her office, taking everything in.

Dena's stomach got a strange feeling in it. She reminded herself again of who he was and what he'd done. She looked back into his eyes and found herself feeling sorry for him. There was something about him. She explained what she felt her obligations were. "I understand how you must feel, Mr. Sellers," she said as she watched him, "but even though I'm not your lawyer, my conscience wouldn't allow me to let you sign something when you don't know what it says. It'll only take a few minutes for me to go over these pages."

"Yes, Ma'am." He stared at her, his eyes unwavering.

"Thank you." She picked up one of the copies, wanting to get through as quickly as possible. She dreaded coming to the part where she would have to tell him about the permanent injunction. What if he wanted to argue about it? Most men would hotly contest it.

She started with the first paragraph, reading through each portion and stopping to explain what it meant in layman's terms. She went through it page by page, explaining the terminology and all the things the injunction prohibited him from doing. She glanced at him as she read the part that said he was permanently enjoined from intentionally, knowingly, or recklessly coming into contact with Ginny. He didn't so much as glance back at her.

She read through the part about his being enjoined from calling her, or threatening her, or calling or threatening her family. Her eyes went to his face again. He was still staring down at the typed pages.

She finished reading and explaining the terms, and he never interrupted her. When she looked up again, he was watching her.

"Do you have any questions?"

"No, Ma'am. Do you have a pen?"

Dena handed him a pen and watched while he signed his name. He handed the original to her. She gave him a copy.

"If you wait about two weeks, you can get a certified copy at the district clerk's office. I appreciate your being so cooperative in signing this, Mr. Sellers, and coming over here today on such short notice." Dena stood.

"That's okay, Dena. The sooner the better," he replied, standing up also.

"Yes, I guess so, if you've got plans with another woman." Dena forced a smile. "I'll be sure and ask the judge to waive that thirty-day waiting period." She reached out to him to shake hands, even though she cringed inwardly at the thought. "Good luck to you," she said.

Sellers took her hand, and he smiled, too. "Thank you. I'll need it," he said. "Is that it?"

"Yes." She pulled her hand away and walked him to the door.

"Well, I'll be seeing you," he said over his shoulder as he went out.

Dena watched his back as he departed. She closed the door, and when she turned back, Meredith was holding out a bottle of hand sanitizer. She squeezed a large dollop into Dena's hand.

Dena might not have liked his limp, fishy handshake, but clearly the man was perfectly harmless. She made a silent vow never to get so worked up over a case again.

Chapter Thirty-Four

ALAN SELLERS

arly Friday morning, Sellers sat in his father's Cadillac in the front parking lot, as far from the county Justice Center's main entrance as he could get. He had arrived early so he could get a parking space where he could see everyone coming and going. He focused his binoculars cn the entrance until Ginny arrived and then on the exit until she left.

He'd packed some sandwiches, cookies, water, and sodas in a throw-away cooler he picked up at the grocery store. He was prepared for everything except taking a piss. For that, he'd have to leave. Hopefully, it wouldn't come to that, but he had drunk a Coke as soon as he arrived so he knew it would.

As if in response to his thoughts, Ginny came out, alone, and hurried to her car. He could barely make out the smile on her face. His knuckles whitened as he gripped the steering wheel, prepared to tail her. He knew he could hold it now.

She pulled out into traffic on Broadway and, to his surprise, she drove toward the Causeway. All the way across the Causeway

Bridge, he tailed his now ex-wife, staying so far back that at times he could hardly make out her car. Interstate Forty-five was always busy, crowded with cars and trucks, many of them driving over the speed limit. Adjusting the radio, he settled back behind the wheel and sang along with the music on a Houston country station. He felt good, the air-conditioning in the car had revived him, and his plan was progressing on schedule. What else could he want? Just after they entered Harris County, he caught sight of Ginny taking the Baybrook Mall exit. She must be working retail again.

He stopped at the first gas station he could find near the mall and relieved himself. Zipping up, he wiped his hands on his khakis and got back in the Caddy, driving to the part of the lot Ginny used to park in. Her car was already there. He drove past and found a tree to park under on the edge of the parking lot and prepared to spend the day.

A little past six o'clock, she came out. Again he followed her, this time, to an apartment complex on Bay Area Boulevard.

At first, he stayed in the car, studying the apartment layout and planning his next move. There were several multistoried building units. Parking was below the apartments in numbered spaces. He wanted to wait until it got dark and then slip unseen into her apartment. After a while, he walked around the complex, checking it out.

All of the apartments on each level opened out onto one long balcony with an overhang to shield the tenants from the weather. There were no private entrances, though each apartment had its own small balcony on the opposite side, most likely, he figured, off the bedroom. A sliding glass door led out to the balcony.

After his walk-through, Sellers knew where to park to be in view of Ginny's apartment and still be close enough to get out quickly. He moved the car to the spot he'd picked out and sat watching and figuring he could get up to her balcony. Once up there, he would pop the lock with his pocketknife.

Waiting for the dark of night and for traffic to slow down before he left the car, he spent the next two hours observing the residents. He had known it would be like this, but it was hard to be patient. He had an urge to run up the stairs, barge in, and get it over with. As he watched, a man approached her door and knocked. Ginny answered the door, swinging it wide to let the man enter. The man kissed her. Sellers didn't recognize him. He slammed his palm on the steering wheel.

Bitch. She didn't even wait until the ink was dry. Damn her. How many men had she screwed since she moved out? He gripped the edge of the front seat, the veins standing out on his forehead as he struggled for control.

Several hours passed. He squirmed around in the car, trying to get comfortable. The apartment lights finally went out and stayed out. He held his head in his hands. His anger had given him a headache, the pounding incessant. He must overcome it. He had to let the anger go. He needed another plan.

Finally, he made up his mind. He'd frame the boyfriend. He set his watch alarm for six the next morning and relieved himself at a gas station one last time. He picked up a hamburger and a single beer on the way back. He would stay and wait. When the man came out, no matter what time, he would go in, and that man's fingerprints, not his, would be found all over the place.

Chapter Thirty-Five

DENA

*G*roggy with sleep, Dena groped across the bed, but Zack wasn't there. It was Saturday, and he was gone. She scooted over to his side of the bed and buried her face in his pillow, breathing deeply through her nose, trying to hold on to him by his scent on the bedclothes. Her thoughts went to the previous morning when they had said goodbye and to what they had done the night before that.

She had been awakened Friday morning by his repeatedly calling her name. Feeling a hand on her shoulder, she pulled the covers around her naked body and tried to turn over. He stopped her with a kiss on the forehead. Peeking through one eyelid, she had focused on him sitting fully clothed on the edge of the bed. He leaned over her and looked into her face. She had the feeling he'd been there for some time. It was still dark outside. The hall light cast shadows in the room.

"I have to leave now," he'd whispered. His breath smelled of coffee.

SUSAN P. BAKER

She stared at him, memorizing the lines in his face, remembering the lovemaking of the night before, embarrassed at having engaged in it.

"I hated to wake you up," he said. "You were sleeping so peacefully. I just wanted to tell you goodbye."

Dena pulled her arms out from under the covers and reached for him, pulling him down to her. She held him for a few moments before he drew back and kissed her gently on the mouth.

"I wish you didn't have to go," she said.

"I'll be back soon," he said. "It's still early, so you don't have to get up yet. I'll lower the garage door when I go out." He cupped her cheek in his large hand. The muscles in his jaws flexed. His nostrils flared. "Farewell, my sleepyhead."

"I love you, Zachary Armstrong," she had murmured. And she wondered why she had said that. They'd had sex, sure. But did that mean they were still in love?

"You're going to have to let go of me so I can leave."

"I don't want you to go," Dena said. She couldn't have explained it, but a hint of sadness had crept into her soul.

"I know you don't."

"I'll miss you."

"Let go. I have to leave now."

"Be careful."

"I will."

Dena pulled herself up and hugged him close to her, feeling his freshly shaved cheek against hers.

"Kiss the kids for me," he whispered.

"I will." She touched his cheek one last time.

"You go back to sleep."

"Okay." Dena lay down on the pillow, watching him through her eyelashes as he stood up. "'Bye."

Her eyes had followed him as he went through the bedroom door and pulled it closed. She smoothed the covers around her again. In the early years, every time he went someplace, she'd had a feeling deep down that she might not ever see him again, that something unknown would prevent him from returning. That feeling had faded over the years, until recently she couldn't wait for him to be gone. But then lately.... As she lay there, she heard car noises in the garage. Then he was gone.

Now, rolling onto her side, she turned her thoughts to other things. What could she do with the children all weekend? She could bake their favorite cookies and play games with them. After they were in bed, she could catch up on her emails.

She kept telling herself to go back to sleep, but it was no use. She had looked at the clock. It was seven. Paul would be up and at the cartoons any minute. Her mind started working on the day's schedule. She thought of all the things in store for her, things she had to do that day or the next. Why had she looked at the time?

She rolled over the other way, trying to sleep, thinking of pleasant things. Like Christmas morning when she was a child. Like weddings. Like the births of the children. Like how good the sex had been.

She thought of Ginny Sellers, oops ... Richardson. Ginny would be on her way to get her abortion in a few minutes. She had felt sorry for the girl, but it was probably for the best. This way Ginny could start a whole new life. It had been a difficult decision, but it had been her own decision.

Ginny had positively glowed when they'd met at the courthouse. After the judge pronounced her divorced, she had hugged Dena long and hard. They'd stopped on the first floor for a few minutes for soft drinks before Ginny pressed a check for the balance due into Dena's hand, thanking her profusely, and left to go to work.

Now, Dena yawned and stretched. She heard little footsteps in the hall and then the TV came on. Time to be Mommy.

Chapter Thirty-Six

ALAN SELLERS

The electronic beeping of his cell phone dragged him out of the deep sleep he was enjoying in the back seat of the Cadillac. When he switched off the alarm, he remembered where he was. The time had come for an accounting. The man his wife had slept with should be leaving any time.

He sat up in the car to resume his vigil. The urge to urinate was unbearable. The sky had not yet grown bright, so he got out on the passenger side and, shielded from view by the dimness, urinated into the ditch by the side of the road. As he started to climb back into the car and take up his surveillance again, the lights came on in Ginny's apartment.

Grabbing his fillet knife from the back shelf of the car, he slipped it and his wallet into his rear pockets. He put his keys, pocketknife, and change into his front pockets. Now, he was ready. After crossing the street, he walked to the rear of Ginny's building where he could see her car and the stairs that led down from her floor.

He didn't know which car was her boyfriend's. He hid behind the dumpster and waited. It stank like what it was, but at least he could see the guest parking area. He was ready to climb up as soon as the man drove away.

Seven o'clock approached. He touched his front pants pocket, feeling for his pocketknife. Checked his back pocket again. The fillet knife was in place. He crouched down and watched the stairs and the parking lot, hoping that someone glancing from a window wouldn't notice him.

His chest grew tight. His stomach knotted up. He swallowed several times. He wished he had drunk something before he crossed the street. Something to eat would be great, too. But that could wait. After he did Ginny, he would get one of those breakfast specials like at Denny's with pancakes, sausage, two scrambled eggs, and orange juice. Later, he would sack out at home and sleep all day.

He was having a hard time waiting. A muscle jumped in his leg. His hands shook. Remembering the man upstairs, he grew angry for a moment. And calmed himself with inner talk. They better have enjoyed themselves. It was their last time together.

Footsteps and voices came from upstairs. The man shuffled down the stairs. The time had come. He lugged a small suitcase. Wait...Ginny came down behind him. She held her overnight bag. Had the man been living there?

He stayed where he was and watched. The man walked Ginny to her car. She opened the trunk. He put the suitcase inside, then the overnight bag. Were they going off someplace together? Sellers' vision blurred momentarily. He wanted to run at them. He wanted to scream at both of them to stop. If he'd had a gun, he'd have shot them dead where they stood. But he didn't have a gun. He hadn't prepared for this. He could do nothing but watch.

They went around to the driver's side of her car. The car beeped and Ginny opened the door. The man put his arms around her and kissed her. She hugged him and got into the car.

The man walked backwards a few steps before turning and walking to his own car. Ginny started up and backed out. The man started his car and followed Ginny into the street. Ginny turned to the right. So did the man.

Running across to the Cadillac, Sellers hopped in, started it, and pulled a quick U-turn to go after them. They weren't getting away from him that easily. A block down the road, the man turned off. Sellers floored the accelerator and sped after Ginny. He didn't know where she was going, but wherever it was, he'd catch her alone, and that would be it.

She pulled out onto Interstate Forty-five North. He followed. After ten minutes, fifteen, in weekend traffic, which wasn't as bad as weekday traffic, Ginny exited onto Airport Boulevard in Houston. A hand gripped Alan's insides and twisted his stomach. He followed her as she drove down the feeder road and as she turned left onto Airport. When she turned right into a long term parking lot, he continued on his way. Bitch! His head grew hot and throbbed. He hammered the steering wheel, knowing he'd made a useless trip. A shuttle would pick her up and drop her at the curb at Hobby Airport. There would be totally no way to get at her without getting caught.

Breathe, he told himself. Calm down. He clenched his fist and released it. Same with his teeth. Finally, driving back out to Interstate forty-five, he aimed the car back toward Galveston. She might be going out of town now, but she'd be back. He knew she would. She never put much distance between herself and Martin and Mary.

His timetable would have to change, but not his goals. She hadn't beaten him yet.

Chapter Thirty-Seven

DENA

"Hello," Dena said into her cell after she'd fumbled it a few times early Sunday morning, the middle of the night as far as she was concerned.

"Good news," Zack said. "I'm for sure coming home late Wednesday night." There was a hollow sound after he spoke.

Still half-asleep, Dena struggled to sit up.

"Dena. Are you there?" Zack's voice sounded stilted.

"Yes. That's great."

"You have to wait a bit before you speak and talk slowly. Because of the distance there's some lag time. Do you understand?"

Dena waited for the hollow tone to go away, then said, "Yes."

"Henry was able to get here a little sooner, like I'd hoped, so I'll definitely be there Wednesday night."

"That's great. How's everything going?"

"Fine. How are the kids?"

"They're okay. We played games and baked cookies yesterday. We're going to go to church this morning. Can you believe it?"

Zack laughed. "No. What prompted you to do that?"

Waiting a beat, Dena said, "Melissa came home from one of her friends' houses yesterday wanting to know why we never went to church like they did."

"Is she even old enough to know what church is?"

"Well, really she asked about Sunday school. She said she wanted to go to school on Sundays like her friend."

"Maybe we can get back into going regularly from now on."

"I think I'd like that," Dena said. "The kids would enjoy Sunday school."

"I have to hang up. They're having the cocktail party in a few minutes. I'm expected to be there."

"I bet you're tired," Dena said.

"I only have to go for a little while, then I have to get ready to leave."

"I'll see you Wednesday," Dena said and yawned.

"Listen, don't wait up. It'll be very late when I get there. Go ahead and go to bed, and I'll make sure to wake you up when I get in."

"Okay. No problem."

"I have to hang up now."

"Okay, see you soon."

"Hug the kids for me."

"I will. 'Bye."

There was silence. The phone clicked in her ear. She sat on the side of the bed, thinking of the things she'd planned to get done while he was gone. She would get up and accomplish everything she could in the next few days so she'd have time for Zack when he returned. She had a feeling they would have a lot to talk about when he came home. Like figuring out what their future as a couple would be.

Chapter Thirty-Eight

ALAN SELLERS

nger and frustration gnawed at his gut as he slipped
through the Armstrong's gate for what he hoped was the
last time. He hadn't been able to take care of Ginny
because she'd been a moving target. The Armstrong woman, on
the other hand, was not a moving target. He already considered
taking her out as a mission accomplished. There was always time
for Ginny later.

No one had been around the street. If his luck held, he'd get
in and out real quick. He just had to get that key. He jogged to
the picnic table and dragged it across the backyard, placing it
under the kitchen window like he'd done the last time. The
neighbor's dog barked again, like the last time. He climbed up on
the table and gave the window a little tug expecting it to open
wide. It didn't budge. He put both hands on it, pulling on the
aluminum rim. The window moved about half an inch and then
nothing. He tried slipping the lock with his pocketknife, but the
window still wouldn't open.

He wasn't going to let a woman beat him. He had to find a
way to get into that house. In the back corner stood the shed with
the tools he'd checked out the last time. The door opened toward
the back fence. He walked around it and yanked it open. Surely
there'd be something he could use inside. He found a shovel, a
rusting rake, a heavy pickax, a push-type lawn mower, and some
small gardening tools, nothing that could help him get inside the
house.

He closed the door and leaned against the outside. The day
had started out so smoothly, not like the Saturday before. He'd
gone to the charity store and gotten his old clothes. He'd slept all
day the day before, resting up. It was that lawyer's fault
everything was getting messed up. He wasn't going to let it stop
him. Nothing would stop him. He'd have to think of another way
to get in and get the key. He had until late Wednesday. Her old
man would be arriving on the scene expecting to find her dead by
then.

He walked back to the house and went from window to
window, tugging and pulling. None of them opened. He dragged
the picnic table back across the yard to where he'd found it. He
let himself out of the gate. He hid behind a bush until he had
checked the street to make sure no one was there and walked to
his car.

***

Tuesday morning, Sellers hid in the hedges at the side of the
lawyer's house. It was very early when he arrived, still very dark.
He would sneak into the garage as she drove away, before the
door came all the way down. If it worked, he could get the key,
hide out in the garage all day, and kill her that night.

He was very proud of himself. It had taken him just a couple
of hours of thinking the whole thing over to come up with the

idea. He'd thought about the layout of the house, about coming back with a bigger knife and trying to slip the lock, but he hadn't wanted to waste a lot of time and energy or risk being caught. He'd started thinking about waiting until the maid got there and possibly getting inside a day early and spending the night in there, but who wanted to sleep in a garage? It was then that the idea came to him. If the lawyer was like most people, she would push on her garage door controls as she drove off, never watching to see whether the door closed or not.

His idea was brilliant. She'd be tending to her kids and watching the street, and he would roll under the door and be out of sight in seconds. He could get the key, hide in the garage, and wait. After she went to sleep, he would sneak inside and cut her throat with his fillet knife, just as he would a big fish, except he wouldn't gut her like he would a fish or maybe he would, depending on how things were going.

If he couldn't get inside that morning, he would try that afternoon after the maid got there and opened the garage door. He didn't want to do that. Too many people might be around. Crossing his fingers, he waited, again. Seemed to him like that was all he did lately.

The bushes scratched his arms. The humidity must be a hundred and fifty per cent. Mosquitoes buzzed in his ears. He swatted them off the back of his neck. Finally, the sun rose. Checking his watch, he saw it was seven-thirty. A few minutes later, the garage door groaned as it rose. His hands shook. Crouching down, he tried to make himself as small as possible.

The children chattered. The car doors opened and closed. She cranked the car. It wouldn't start. Again she cranked it. Again. Exhaust fumes billowed into his face. He covered his mouth and nose so he wouldn't cough.

He could run up to her right then, fling open the door of her car, and slit her throat. He considered it for a few milliseconds. But he had promised the husband he wouldn't do anything in front of the kids. He could have done it if he had moved right then. She cranked the car again. The engine sputtered to life. Black smoke rolled out from underneath. As she revved the engine, he coughed uncontrollably and pressed his hand hard against his mouth.

Through his tearing eyes, he watched as she backed into the street. The door descended as she drove away. He sprang forward and dove under it, rolling inside. The door stopped and started going back up, but he was fast as he ran to the controls and punched them so it would continue its descent.

He was in. He coughed a few times to clear his lungs. He listened for any sounds of her return. The street was quiet. He cheered himself.

Walking toward the light coming through the window in the door from the kitchen, he mentally patted himself on the back. Few people in this world were as creative as he was. Few people would have thought out a plan so carefully. Most people would have been caught.

He found the door unlocked and went inside. There were two cereal bowls and a single coffee cup in the sink. It only confirmed what he already knew, the husband was on his trip. He saw what the problem had been with the window, too. A long stick had been placed in the window track. No wonder he couldn't slide it open.

He ambled into the bedroom first thing to get the key from her jewelry box, careful to wipe away his fingerprints. After pocketing the key, he opened the refrigerator and, rummaging through the fruit bin, found an apple. In the den, he bit into the apple and turned on the TV. Propping his feet on a footstool, he made himself at home.

Chapter Thirty-Nine

DENA

"I'm just calling to confirm tonight," Dena said on Tuesday afternoon before tackling a pile of mail.

"We wouldn't miss it for the world," Ellen said. "Are you sure you want to do this, though? I have a feeling it was Zack's idea for you to have us over for dinner while he was gone."

"I'm positive. In fact, I'm looking forward to it. The kids are excited, too. They haven't seen y'all in such a long time."

"Great. And I'm eager to see them. Bob just wants to eat a home-cooked meal. He's sick of eating in restaurants." She chuckled.

"I hope he likes lasagna and stuffed cabbage."

"He loves your stuffed cabbage. But why fix both? That's an awful lot of work just for us."

"The kids. They hate my stuffed cabbage."

Ellen laughed again. "Little monsters. They don't know what they're missing."

"Yes, but don't tell them. I like to eat the leftovers."

"So what can we bring? Some wine?"

"If you want. I have some white, but no red. I was going to stop off on the way home and pick some up."

"Let me get it. What about dessert? Want me to pick up something that'll go with the wine?"

"No, that's okay. I've made a chocolate pie." Dena's mouth watered at the thought of putting a forkful of chocolate meringue pie into her mouth.

"You have got to be kidding. I swear you're trying to steal Bob from me, Dena Armstrong. When did you do all this?"

Dena liked it when Ellen teased her about Bob even though they both knew he was devoted to Ellen. "Last night. Ever since Zack called on Sunday, I haven't been able to sit still. Besides, I made the pie as a bribe for Bob."

"For what, may I ask?"

"I thought maybe he'd look at the car. I've been having trouble starting it, and it seems to be getting worse. This morning I didn't think it was going to start at all. Zack took his car to the airport, or I wouldn't ask, but I'm afraid tomorrow I might be stuck."

"Why didn't you call him before? You know he doesn't mind."

"I thought it would be okay until this morning. I thought Zack could look at it when he got back," Dena said. "But tomorrow morning I have early court. I don't want to be late if it breaks down."

"You shouldn't have waited this long. You could have been stranded at home this morning, or the kid's camp, or—"

"All right. All right. I hear you. Stop scolding me." Dena laughed louder than she intended. She hoped Ellen wouldn't think something was wrong with her.

"Okay. I'll make sure Bob brings a change of clothes so he can fix it tonight."

"You don't think he'll mind?"

"Of course not. You know how he is. In fact, do you want him to come to the office this evening to make sure you can get home?"

"Lucas promised to stick around in case I have a problem."

After they hung up, Dena sorted her mail. Receiving mail always made her feel good ever since she was a child. At the office, she enjoyed seeing how much money she brought in, even though she would take it back out to Meredith to record and make up the deposit. If it was a copy of a responsive pleading that had been filed, she always wanted to know about it right away anyway.

One particular envelope in Tuesday's mail had caught her eye. A thick manila envelope bore the return address of the private investigator she'd hired. Dena's heart beat in her throat. If her afternoon schedule was not so full, she'd rip into it right then and there. She had too much scheduled, though, to be distracted by its contents if it contained what she thought. She'd save it for the privacy of home. She stuffed it into her roller bag. Her whole world could very well be turned upside down in just a matter of a few days.

Chapter Forty

ALAN SELLERS

He awoke abruptly from having dozed off in the chair, an adrenaline spike hitting him until he looked at his watch and realized he had plenty of time. He cut off the TV, wiped the remote clean, and walked back into the kitchen. He wanted to find something to eat that she wouldn't miss. In the pantry he spotted a jar of peanut butter and a loaf of bread. He'd make a sandwich.

A bit later, leaning against the stove, he chewed and stared into the backyard. Besides the tool shed, there was a patch of garden. A tire swing hung from a large branch of the tree in the far back corner. He didn't know people still had tire swings. He'd never had one, but one of his friends had. Next to the tree, a kid's red, plastic wagon lay on its side.

What would it have been like to have a house and a yard and a place to play? And why couldn't he have been born to a family that had all that? Why did he get stuck with his father? Not that the Armstrong kids had such a better father. Their father wanted to kill their mother.

Alan didn't know what had happened to his own mother. Maybe his father took her out one day and drowned her like he had a bag of kittens once. He didn't think so, else why would his father get so mad when Alan had asked about her? But it could have happened. At least the Armstrong kids would know how their mother ended up.

Shaking himself out of his thoughts, he stuffed the remainder of the sandwich into his mouth and wiped his hands on his pants. He cleaned up and inspected the kitchen to make sure he was leaving things like he found them. Using a dishrag, he wiped the areas he had touched, congratulating himself for being so cautious, and put the rag back where he'd found it.

Back in the den, he considered watching more TV and had just settled down into the chair opposite the television when someone inserted a key in the front door lock. Alarm shot through his body. He ran through the living room and through the kitchen and jerked the garage door open at the same time as that someone closed the front door. He pulled the door closed as quietly as possible and crouched down, duckwalking around the corner to his hiding place in the tool room.

His scalp tingled and his heart drummed in his chest. No sounds came from the direction of the kitchen. He slowed his breathing and flexed his fingers to stop his hands from shaking. After he settled down, Alan glanced at his watch again. His watch said the same time as it had when he'd woken up. The damn thing had stopped.

Chapter Forty-One

DENA

"I'll get it," Melissa hollered to her mother in response to the door chime. The little girl ran to the door, yanking it open for Ellen and Bob. It was seven p.m.

"It's Aunt Ellen and Uncle Bob," Melissa called over her shoulder, throwing herself at them.

Dena greeted them and scolded Melissa for opening the door before knowing who was there.

"Come in, come in. I'm in the kitchen putting the finishing touches on everything."

"I'll help you," Ellen said, following her. "Juliet already gone?"

"She wanted to help, but I told her to leave a bit early for once," Dena said.

"Uncle Bob," Paul shrieked as he ran down the hall.

"Hi, Paul." Bob swung him up into his arms. "How're you doing?"

"Fine," Paul said grinning. "How you doing?"

"Fine," Bob said in the same tone of voice Paul had used. He carried the little boy into the kitchen where the women were wiping out wineglasses. Melissa wore a child-size apron tied around her waist. She carried a plate to the table and centered it in front of a chair before returning to the counter for the next one.

"I hear you've got car problems," Bob said as he put Paul down.

"I hate to bother you with it, but I'm having trouble getting it started. I thought it would make it until Zack got back, but this morning it gave me a real scare, though this afternoon it started right up."

"I could look at it now. How long until dinner?"

"About ten minutes. Do you mind?"

"Aren't you going to change first?" Ellen frowned in his direction.

Bob shrugged. "Tell you what, pour me a little glass of wine to get me motivated, and I'll just look under the hood before dinner. I'll change after dinner and try to fix it."

"You're my hero," Dena said.

"Yep. That's what they all say," Bob said, winking at Paul who had his nose above the counter, checking out the food that would be their evening meal.

Dena exchanged glances with Ellen. It was true. Luckily, Ellen had seen him first.

Ellen uncorked the red wine and filled a water glass half-full for Bob. She held it out to him. "How's this for motivation?"

"Great." He planted a kiss on her cheek. Taking the glass, he headed to the garage, Paul following behind him like his shadow. When Bob went through the door, he yelled to Dena, "I'm going to put the door up for what's left of the light, okay?"

"Sure," Dena yelled back and closed the door behind him.

Bob pressed the controls to the garage door opener. The heavy door groaned and began rising.

Chapter Forty-Two

ALAN SELLERS

A spike of adrenaline struck Sellers. He shivered. A man's voice. Who was that? His muscles tensed.

The garage door began opening, letting in a lot more light than just the overhead one from the garage door opener. He straightened up, making himself as small as he could, shrinking against the tool shelf, being quiet and careful he didn't bump into anything.

Someone's feet scraped on the concrete floor. A car door opened. The car's hood popped.

His heart pounded. Blood rushed in his ears.

Footsteps. The hood creaked. "Can I help, Uncle Bob?" a little voice said.

"Let me see if I can figure out what's wrong first, Paul."

Hair stood up on Sellers' arms and on the back of his neck. About two feet separated the front-end of the car and his hiding place. He pulled his knife from his back pocket.

A minute passed. Another. The boy asked some questions. Then it was quiet again. Sweat rolled down his forehead, burning into one eye. He didn't dare wipe it away. His back pressed into the shelves. Only his eyelids and eyes moved.

Another shiver ran across his shoulders and down his back. He listened for an indication the man was coming in his direction.

He couldn't just stand there and wait to be discovered. The time seemed to stretch from minutes to hours.

If the man came to the door, Sellers would have to jump him. He'd be forced to cut the man and run like hell.

More shuffling. Some scraping footsteps. A bit later, a door opened and an unfamiliar female voice called out. "Bob and Paul, dinner's ready. Come wash up."

More footsteps and Dena Armstrong's voice, "Did you figure out what's wrong?"

"Not yet," the man replied. "I think it's your carburetor. The float might be sticking or the choke adjustment is off. I'll have to take the air cleaner off after dinner. Zack's tools in there?"

"Yes, most of them. A few are in his trunk, which, of course, is at the airport, but the good ones are in there. Want me to show you?"

Another trickle of sweat ran down Sellers' face.

"I'll find them after dinner. Let's go in. Come on, Kid."

Another patter and scrape of footsteps.

"Did Ellen tell you I made a chocolate pie?" The door closed.

Sellers heard the murmur of voices behind the wall and relaxed a little. He moved away from the shelves. A pain stabbed between his shoulder blades. His head throbbed. That damn lawyer.

The man was coming back after dinner and was sure to catch him in the tool room. He had to get the hell away from there.

There was still plenty of daylight left. A glance at his watch told him it would be a long while until it got dark, but only half an hour until the man returned. That was too close.

He crouched down on his hands and knees, glad he'd worn the old clothes. Pushing the door open a little wider, he looked out, but didn't see anyone through the window to the kitchen. He edged his way out the door, closing it almost all the way like it had been when he was inside. Peeking around the car, he looked to see if anyone was watching through the window. He could see the tops of their heads. They must be sitting at the dinette table.

Crawling between the car and the storage shelves on the inside walls of the garage, he came to the back of the car and, craning his neck, peeked through the rear window. Still no one at the kitchen door. He crawled to the edge of the garage door and looked out. No one there either. He looked over his shoulder at the window again. All clear. Straightening up, he stepped out of the garage and casually strolled diagonally across the front yard to the street. It was all he could do to keep from running back to his car. And now he had another worry. What if she missed the key before tomorrow?

Chapter Forty-Three

ALAN SELLERS

*E*verything went down the same way on Wednesday morning as it had on Tuesday, except there were thundershowers on and off all day. Once again he heard her car pull into the driveway. He leaned as far back into the tool room as he could, his back rammed into the shelves like before. It was an involuntary reaction on his part. He knew she couldn't see him. The door was almost closed.

The car door opened and closed. He heard the little boy call her name. Then the little girl's voice. When they went inside, someone locked the kitchen door. He hoped it hadn't been dead-bolted.

The stifling air made it hard to breathe in the tool closet. The maid, or whatever they called her, had the clothes dryer running. Hot air blew into the garage. An occasional gust of wind blowing in through the open garage door saved him from feeling like he would suffocate.

The rain had come in handy. None of the neighborhood kids had been outside to see him slip from the bushes to the garage after the maid had opened the door. It was a snap, except his clothes were sopping wet. He had layered them, the old over the new. But all of them were wet. His skin itched. Chafed. Irritated.

Holding his wristwatch up to the crack in the doorway, he could see that it was just after six o'clock. Only a few more hours. His fingers searched his back pocket for the fillet knife and the flashlight. They were still there.

After he'd gotten home the night before, he'd honed the edge of his fillet knife until it was more than razor sharp. He was ready. As soon as he did her, he would hit the road and never look back. Unless he returned to do Ginny, but that, he'd decide on later.

Chapter Forty-Four

DENA

"Could I persuade you to make some hamburgers for the kids?" Dena had changed from her rain-dampened clothes into a comfortable old bathrobe. All she wanted was to relax for a while before dinner, which she could do if Juliet would take care of dinner.

"Sure," Juliet answered, looking up from the TV show she watched with the kids. "Are you feeling all right? You're already in your bedclothes, but Mr. Armstrong's due home tonight, isn't he?"

Dena nodded. "Some friends came over last night and stayed far too late. I thought I'd make a salad for myself and later take a short nap and maybe a shower before he comes home."

"Want me to make dinner for all of you? I can make a nice Caesar salad with all the trimmings," Juliet said.

"That would be great," Dena said, "if you don't mind."

"Why don't you let me cook more?" Juliet asked in her accented English, which had really improved since she'd started working for them. "I enjoy it so much. You do enough at the office. Now sit here in your rocker, read your evening paper, and let me mother you for a change."

That was all the persuasion Dena needed. Zack wasn't around to scold her for not cooking. She did as she was told. "You're a bit young to be my mother, but I'll try to pretend, Juliet. Thanks."

"No need to thank me. That's why you hired me. You said I'd be cooking along with everything else, but you hardly let me do it."

"It's just I feel guilty if I don't fix my family's dinner." What she meant was that Zack tried to make her feel guilty. She unrolled the newspaper.

"Nonsense," Juliet said. "I'm going to the kitchen now, and I want you to call me if you need anything. Don't even think about getting out of your chair."

"Yes, Juliet," Dena said, like a child. She unfolded the paper to the front page. Nothing but bad news. For once, couldn't the headlines boldly shout about something good? Propping her feet on the tiny footstool, Dena hoped she could make it through dinner without falling asleep.

Chapter Forty-Five

ALAN SELLERS

He held his breath when the kitchen door opened and the now familiar tapping of the maid's shoes struck the concrete garage floor. The dryer door hinges creaked when she opened it. The dryer came to a stop. She hummed an unfamiliar song.

The maid should be going home soon. She always left sometime between six and seven. He wondered whether she stayed at the house later when the husband was out of town. She hadn't the day before, but that didn't mean she wouldn't that night. Not that it mattered, so long as she didn't spend the night. He'd just try to relax. Breathe in. Breathe out. She would leave soon enough. He had all night to do what he'd come for.

The waiting would drive some men crazy. There was nothing to do but stand in the dark room, not like waiting in his car in the daylight, with food, with drinks. But he could tough it out. He wasn't like other men.

He did feel a little jumpy from almost getting caught the previous night. Now, after the sun went down or after they closed the garage door, he would at least be able to sit in the doorway. Until dark, he had to stay out of sight. The only thing he could do was think, and he was running out of things he wanted to think about.

Memories of the night his father had died kept flooding him. Not wanting to think about that night, or his father, Sellers kept promising himself the wait to get Mrs. Armstrong would be worth it. He needed to concentrate on that. Not his father. Not the night his father died. Not what he had done to his father.

Chapter Forty-Six

DENA

*D*ena and the kids had their dinner on TV trays in the den. Juliet had delivered them ceremoniously. She'd made French fries to go with the hamburgers. The kids were excited and pretended it was a picnic. The Caesar salad that Juliet brought Dena was enormous.

"This is just like the ones they make in the famous restaurants." Dena squeezed Juliet's arm in appreciation.

"I told you I was a good cook, Ma'am." She beamed at Dena. "You just have to let me do it more often. I don't think in all these years you have let me cook for your family more than ten times. And never my own country's specialties," she added.

"How did you learn to make the food look so good? Mine never turns out quite that appealing."

"I worked in a restaurant in my country when I was young." Juliet's expression as she put her hands on her hips and looked down at Dena was classic. "Don't you remember?"

As if Juliet wasn't still young. "You've been with us so long, I really don't. I guess I was just anxious at the time to find someone who would be good with a baby that I didn't pay attention to anything else."

"You children like my hamburgers?" Juliet asked in a voice louder than the TV.

"Yea," Paul cheered.

"What about you, Melissa?"

"It's good," Melissa confirmed Paul's comment without taking her eyes from the television.

"And what about my French fries?" Juliet leaned over the children's faces, getting between them and the TV.

"I like 'em really, really good," Paul said with his mouth full.

Juliet turned back to Dena. "And those are homemade, Mrs. Armstrong. Not those tasteless things you have in the freezer."

Dena had just forked a mouthful of salad into her mouth. She chewed and swallowed. "I'm convinced. You don't have to say another word. I'll let you do most of the cooking. In fact, I'm going to be making a lot of other changes around here." Her mind went to the sex the previous week with Zack. It had been good, but not enough of a reason to stay in a relationship that had run its course. And she didn't want to be friends with benefits, either. She'd just have to regard it as goodbye sex.

"Well, thank you, Ma'am. Anytime I don't have an evening class, I will gladly stay to cook. I'm going back to the kitchen. Call me when you're through, and I'll come get the plates and finish up in the kitchen before I go."

Dena reached over and took her hand. "You're a good girl, Juliet. If I haven't told you lately, I really appreciate you."

"Thank you very much." Juliet's face flushed.

Juliet had made her point. Dena was not superwoman. Yes, she needed Juliet, and any other help she could get. She would be taking it—taking care of herself and her children and her business. Alone. Without Zack and Lucas trying to control everything she did. Right now, she was going to eat, relax, be with the children awhile, and then get a nap. She might even begin the divorce discussion with Zack that night when he got home if he was up for it. If not, there was always tomorrow.

Chapter Forty-Seven

ALAN SELLERS

The light shining through the garage door cracks grew dim. The garage grew darker and would have been totally black but for the light from the kitchen. He had shifted his body so he could see out the tool room doorway. He'd nudged the door wider with the toe of his shoe after someone had put the garage door down. Time was growing short.

Whoever had put the garage door down had closed the door to the kitchen, but had not locked it or shot the bolt. Amazing how everything seemed to fall into place, though it seemed like he'd been in the garage for half a century. A car had driven away quite some time ago. The maid. Now the lawyer and the children were alone in the house with him.

He stroked the hilt of the knife in his back pocket. In his left front pocket, he carried a small flashlight with an extremely intense light. Patting his pocket, he reassured himself the flashlight was still there. Expelling a deep breath, Sellers brushed his damp hair back off his forehead. The heat had practically drained all the energy out of him. He knew he'd get his second wind the moment he made his move.

The double layer of clothes hadn't ever really dried from being in the rain that morning and now were damp, not only with rainwater but with sweat. The time couldn't pass fast enough. He wouldn't be any readier than right then. Too bad it was still so early.

Chapter Forty-Eight

DENA

fter Juliet left, Dena gave up the idea of a nap and stayed in the den with the children and watched television. Later, she went into the kitchen and set out a tray with Kool-Aid® for the kids and a water glass filled with Texas Hill Country wine for herself. She was about to return to the den when she remembered the Oreos. She added them and a pile of napkins to the tray. A little voice inside her head told her she didn't need to eat the Oreos, that she'd gained enough weight to last for the whole summer, that Zack wouldn't like it, and then she remembered that soon she wouldn't have to worry about what Zack would or wouldn't like.

Smiling like the proverbial cat, she walked back into the den and, setting the tray on the coffee table, sat down cross-legged on the floor between the kids. "I'm extending our picnic," she told them. "Look what I've got for a snack."

Paul leaned over her shoulder and looked at the table. "Cookies!"

"And Kool-Aid," Melissa said with a broad smile. "Can we drink it in here, Mommy?"

Dena looked from one to the other of them with mock seriousness and held up her fist. "Yes, but the first one to spill Kool-Aid on my carpet gets a knuckle sandwich. Okay?"

"A knuckle sandwich." Paul shrieked, laughing at his mother. "I don't want one of those."

"Me, neither," Melissa said. "We'll be really careful, won't we, Paul?"

"Yep, we'll be really, really careful, Mommy."

Dena scooted over to the coffee table and filled their glasses. "I know you will," she said, handing a half-full glass to Paul and a quarter-full one to Melissa. She tossed a napkin down in front of each of them, pulled the lid off the cookie canister and, scooting back to her place on the floor, set it down between them. "Have an Oreo," she said, grinning as she took one herself.

They sat like that for a while, munching on Oreos and drinking their drinks. Dena didn't worry about the effect of the sugary drinks or cookies, it being summertime, no school the next day. Just camp. She got up several times to refill her wineglass or go to the bathroom. Otherwise their time together was uninterrupted.

She found herself laughing with the kids. Whether it was the influence of the wine or not, she didn't know, but she was really enjoying herself. She tried not to think about how much of a headache she would have the following day.

At nine o'clock, she turned off the TV. There was nothing on but cops-and-robbers unless she wanted to search Netflix for more children's movies, which she didn't. "Time to get ready for bed," she announced, hoping the kids would go without a hassle.

Paul stood and threw his arms around her neck. "I like watching TV with you, Mommy." He put his little cheek up against hers. "I like to hear you laugh."

Dena hugged her son. "Oh, you little sweetheart, you." She drew back and looked at the red Kool-Aid® and cookie crumbs lining his mouth and put her mouth to his neck and blew on it.

Paul was giggling and struggling, and Melissa came up and wrapped her arms around her mother's back. "Do me, do me," Melissa hollered.

Dena laid Melissa down on the floor and pulled up her shirt, blowing on Melissa's tummy. Then she did Paul again, then Melissa. The house echoed with giggles and laughter.

The doorbell rang.

Dena straightened up. "Who could that be?" She looked at the kids. They looked back at her and shrugged their little shoulders. "Stay right here," she told them. "Mommy will see who it is."

Getting up from the floor, Dena straightened her bathrobe and staggered a bit on the way to the front door. She looked through the peephole. Martin Richardson, in a police uniform, stood on her front porch. What in the…Her first thought was that something had happened to Zack. Her heart pounded. No. Martin would have no way of knowing that.

She looked again and shook her head. The doorbell rang again. She'd better answer it and see what was going on. "Just a minute," she hollered, brushing the crumbs off her robe and running her fingers through her hair. She couldn't think of anything that would bring Martin all the way out to the west end of Galveston, especially on a rainy night.

She pulled the door open. "What on earth are you doing here?"

"I need to talk to you." He stood with his plastic-wrapped police hat in his hand, water dripping from a yellow slicker that said POLICE in large letters.

"Well, come in out of the rain." She was eager to shut the door when she saw lightning flash behind him. "Let's go into the den." She led him down the short hall and knocked the newspapers from Zack's chair. "Sit down."

"I can't stay long." Martin glanced at the kids, the cookie canister, and back at Dena.

The children stood next to one another, shoulders touching, frightened looks on their faces. Dena bent down to their level. "There's nothing to be worried about. This is my policeman friend, Lieutenant Martin Richardson. He's just come over to tell me something." She turned to Martin. "These are my children, Melissa and Paul Armstrong."

"Hello," Martin said to them.

"Hi," Melissa said, stepping behind Dena.

"Are you really, really a policeman?" Paul asked.

"Yes," Martin said, "a real policeman. I usually work in an office at headquarters, a few miles from here."

"I can't believe you drove all the way out here," Dena said. "Why didn't you just call?"

"I tried to several times, but I kept getting voice mail."

Dena scowled at Paul. "Have you been playing with my cell phone again?"

Paul's eyes grew wide. "I go fix it," he said and ran down the hall.

"Melissa, go with him."

"Okay, Mommy," Melissa said and followed her brother.

Dena tossed her head and turned to Martin. "I'm sorry. Paul likes to pretend it's his phone. He flips switches and punches buttons and plays games on it. Never mind. What is it you want to talk to me about?"

Martin's face wore an expression that was a cross between concern and amusement. "I feel better talking to you in person anyway. This way at least I know you're all right."

"What do you mean?" Dena studied his face, which was a bit of a blur. She'd left her glasses on the end table. "Why wouldn't I be all right?" She shuddered.

Martin twisted his cap. "I don't want to alarm you any more than necessary, but have you heard from Ginny?"

Chapter Forty-Nine

MARTIN

*M*artin stared down at Dena, waiting for her reply. If he hadn't been so worried about his sister, he would have appreciated the chocolate rim around her mouth, which he was sure came from eating the Oreos in the cookie canister, and the sweet wine scent on her breath. He would have really enjoyed the way her robe fell open showing the light top of a bare breast. As it was, those things hardly registered.

Her eyes had grown wide and round. She dropped into her chair. "What do you mean, 'Have I heard from Ginny?' She's in Austin, recovering from the procedure with her girlfriend."

"No, she's not. She hasn't touched base with me. I called to check on her. She had called her friend and told her she wasn't coming."

"Well, she probably decided to stay someplace else or something." The color had drained from her face.

"We've called some of the area hotels in her price range, but we've had no luck so far."

The children ran back into the room. "I fixed the phone," Paul said, breathing hard.

"No, he didn't," Melissa said. "I did."

"Okay, kids. It doesn't matter now. You've just got to learn to be more careful, Paul, or only play games on your iPad."

"I didn't mean to do it, Mommy." Paul cast his eyes at the floor.

"Never mind," Dena said. "Come over here and give Mommy a hug." She squeezed her son and kissed him on the head. "Go brush your teeth and wash your hands and face and get ready for bed. You, too, Melissa. I'll come tuck you in shortly."

"Okay. 'Night, Mr. Policeman," Paul said and ran off again.

"Nice to meet you," Melissa said, looking up at Dena for approval and then at him.

Melissa sounded very ladylike for someone so small. She was a lot like her mother. He leaned down and, with a small smile, shook her hand. "You, too. Goodnight."

"'Night." Melissa stepped back and then skipped down the hall.

Dena's eyes followed her children until they were out of sight. Turning her attention back to Martin, she said, "You think something is wrong with Ginny."

"Your husband's not home yet?"

"He's due back late tonight." Her eyes were glued to his face. "I hope she's okay. You want to sit down?"

"That's all right. My partner's waiting outside. Look, I'll be blunt. We're checking the hotels and Southwest Airlines, but, honestly, I don't think we're going to turn up anything. It's not like Ginny to change her plans and not tell anybody. Frankly, I do think something's happened to her." He could hardly stand to admit it to himself, but he had to tell this lady what he thought was going on.

"You can't know that." She was clutching her stomach and staring up at him.

"No, you're right, but my gut feeling is that Sellers has done something to her."

"Oh, for heaven's sake. I don't believe it." She shook her head and started rocking back and forth in her chair. "That man was perfectly normal when he was in my office last week, just his usual eccentric self, friendly as could be. She's probably just staying someplace else. She could even be on her way home by now. Have you checked her apartment lately?"

He dropped his hat and crouched down in front of her. The way she was rocking in her chair was almost manic. "Yes, we have." He put a hand on each arm of the chair and stopped it. "Ma'am, you don't know him. He's crazy. He can appear normal one minute, and go berserk the next. I suspected he was up to something when he let Ginny have all that stuff from their apartment, but I couldn't prove it."

Dena jumped up. "I'm sick of hearing how crazy Alan Sellers is." She fisted her hands down by her sides. "I'm sick of it. That's all anyone said the whole time the divorce was going on. Well, if he's so crazy, why hasn't he been locked up?"

He stood and picked up his hat. Anger flared in his chest. He was only trying to help her. "I didn't come over here to argue with you," he said, his hand resting on his sidearm. "I just came to warn you, that's all. I hope I'm wrong. God knows, I hope I'm wrong …"

"Look, I'm sorry for shouting at you." She grasped his raincoat sleeve. "I don't know what came over me … yes I do, you've scared me half to death, that's what. I'm sitting here playing with my children, drinking a little wine, and you come over to my house without a shred of proof and tell me you think Alan Sellers has gone berserk." Her eyes flared. She let go of his sleeve and turned away. After a few moments, she turned back and looked up into his face. "What you're really telling me is you think I'm next, is that it?"

He didn't say anything. He gritted his teeth and turned his hat over and over in his hands.

"Good God." She clutched a handful of his raincoat sleeve again. "You couldn't get me on my cell, so you came to see if I was still alive, didn't you? You think Alan Sellers killed Ginny, and he's coming for me." She continued to stare up into his face. "Don't you? Because that's what he threatened to do, isn't it?" She put her fingers to her temples and squeezed her eyes shut.

Martin thought she was going to faint, her face was so pale, the skin stretched tight across her bones. He grabbed her arm. "Yes," he said. "That's exactly what I think."

She put her head down in her hands and shivered. He stood watching her. He couldn't stay much longer. Joe was waiting outside. They had to get going if they were going to find Sellers. "Dena …"

She looked back up at him, her eyes red-rimmed. "Don't feel sorry for me. I always cry when I'm really angry." She wiped her nose on her sleeve. He pulled his handkerchief from under his slicker and gave it to her. She wiped her eyes and blew her nose. "At least I have a gun."

"You do? I'm glad, but what are you doing with a gun?"

She straightened up. "Last year a man followed me home when Zack was out of town. I didn't have any way to defend myself or the children."

"He must not have hurt you."

"No. I drove to a friend's and when I came back, he was gone. The next day I went to a pawn shop and bought a thirty-eight."

His eyebrows drew together in a scowl. "You were lucky. So do you know how to use it?"

"Yes," she said, her eyes contracting like she was poised to shoot. "You simply take aim and fire. And you keep firing until you're out of bullets. At least that's what I'm going to do if I see Alan Sellers around my house."

"Good girl," he said. "I hope I'm wrong about this whole thing, and if I am, I'll call and tell you, but you can't be too careful. In the meantime, I'm going out to look for him at all his usual hangouts. I have people calling around, looking for Ginny. If I find either of them, I'll let you know. May I search your house while you put your kids to bed?"

"That seems silly since I've been here all evening, but yes, please do," Dena said. "If you don't, I will."

She looked so small and vulnerable that Martin wanted to hug her, but he resisted the temptation. "Okay, let's start in the kids' bedrooms."

Dena led him to Paul's room where Paul was running his trains instead of getting into bed.

"Mind if I check out your closet?"

"Why do you want to look in there?"

Martin smiled down at him. "'Cause I want to know what a little boy's closet is supposed to look like for when I have a son."

"Oh, it's plenty big." Paul followed Martin to the closet.

Martin slid Paul's closet door open and peered around inside. Then he walked over to Paul's bed and sat on the floor next to it. "May I tuck you in?"

"Okay, if you want." Paul climbed into bed. "Is it fun to be a policeman?"

Martin pulled the covers over Paul, smiling at him. "Sometimes it is. When you get to help people." He reached a hand under Paul's bed and pulled out a toy truck. "Look what I found sticking out from under your bed."

Paul grinned at Martin. "That's my parking lot under there." He leaned over the edge of the bed and lifted up the covers. "See my cars and trucks?"

Martin looked under the bed. "My goodness, there are all kinds of vehicles under there."

"That's my parking lot," Paul said again as he scooted back under the covers. "Like it?"

Martin stood up. "Yeah, that's a really neat place to keep them." He leaned over and tousled the little boy's hair. "Well I've got to go now. See ya'."

"'Bye," Paul said.

Martin exchanged glances with Dena. She kissed Paul goodnight. Martin walked across to Melissa's room and searched it quickly before Melissa came out of the bathroom. He was through before Dena finished making a lame excuse to Paul about why he couldn't have a story read to him.

Martin walked into Dena's bedroom and did a quick search of her long closet, her bathroom, and under her bed. He pulled open Zack's closet and rummaged across the bottom of it, impressed with the man's clothing—lined up by color, length of shirt sleeves, and the shoes neatly hung on shoeracks. He searched the spare room, the hall closet, and the little bathroom near the front door. When Melissa came out of her bathroom, he searched it just to know that he did, while Dena tucked her in.

When Dena came out of Melissa's room, Martin was standing in the hallway. "Well, I've been through the back part of your house and didn't find anything. I didn't think I would, but I feel better anyway. Want to check out the kitchen with me?"

Dena nodded and walked with him through the living room and into the kitchen. He turned on the lights and searched the pantry. He switched on the light in the garage and walked inside.

"Martin, I really don't see how anyone could be hiding in the garage," she called to him. "Juliet, our *au pair*, was in and out of there all evening doing laundry."

Martin looked back at Dena. "You're probably right. I'm just being cautious." He glanced inside the car and then toward what looked like a closet with the door standing partially open. "What's behind that door?"

"Zack's tools. It's packed so tightly that no one could fit inside."

He couldn't squeeze entirely between the front of the car and the clothes dryer. Leaning sideways over the bumper, he flashed his light into the crack. He could see toolboxes stacked up on the floor and upon a shelf. He snapped off the light and backed out. "Why don't you deadbolt this door just to be on the safe side? People have been known to rig up gadgets to electronically open garage doors."

Her mouth formed a grim line. "Okay. I will after you leave."

"Be sure you do." He sounded like a stern father, but he didn't care. He wanted her to take him seriously.

"I will," Dena snapped. "You've scared me so badly that I'll probably check and recheck every door a dozen times before I go to bed."

"Good." He glared at her when what he wanted to do was wrap an arm around her and take care of her. At least she sounded like she would heed his warning. "Well, I've got to go. Be careful. Don't be afraid to call dispatch if you hear anything suspicious, and you have my cell number, too."

"You don't have to worry about that." They walked back toward the front of the house. "I probably won't sleep until Zack gets home anyway, so I'll be awake to hear the slightest sound. Will you call me if you find out anything about Ginny?"

Martin turned as he reached the door. "Look, I hope I'm wrong. I really do. If I hear anything at all, good or bad, I'll definitely let you know."

"Thanks. You be careful, too, okay? If he knows you're looking for him he might go after you."

"He doesn't have the guts." Martin yanked the front door open. He stepped onto the small concrete porch and glanced over his shoulder at her. "Be sure and lock this door. I'm going to search around your house before I leave, so if you hear anything in the next few minutes, it'll be me." He took one last look at her before putting on his hat and dashing out into the rain. Thunder rumbled overhead like cannon fire and a bolt of lightning flashed from the direction of the beach.

Chapter Fifty

ALAN SELLERS

S weat rolled down his body. When he heard Martin's voice in the garage, he had almost pissed in his pants. Martin's light had flashed on the toolboxes, missing the tops of his shoes by a hair. If he hadn't been standing up to stretch when he heard the kitchen door open, he wouldn't have been able get out of the way soon enough and would have been caught.

Damn, he hated that man almost as much as he had hated his own father. Martin had better not ruin things for him. Martin might be big, but Sellers wasn't afraid of him. Sellers' years on the waterfront had made him wiry and muscular. He wished he could do to Martin what he had done to his father when his father messed with him once too often.

His father had failed to realize that time hadn't stood still. As the years went by, his father had grown older and weaker. He'd underestimated Alan. He'd taken Alan's short stature as a sign of weak boyishness—a fatal mistake. The scales had finally tipped the other way. In Alan's favor, not his father's.

As for Martin, Alan probably couldn't take him face-to-face. Martin was huge and trained as a cop. He did have that bum leg, though. A bum leg would slow him down. That was something Alan would have to think about—how to use that bum leg to his advantage. Doing Martin would have to wait until after Ginny. First, Lawyer Armstrong. Then, Ginny, whenever she returned from wherever she went the other day. Finally, Martin. But only if Alan still felt like it. He might just take Armstrong's money and start over someplace else.

Right now, he needed to focus. How long would it take Martin to clear out? How long would it take Lawyer Armstrong to settle down? It was too dark to see what time it was. He wished he'd brought his cell so he see the time, but he'd been afraid it might ring or light up at a bad time.

He didn't know how long it had been since Martin had almost caught him. Seemed like only a moment ago and yet, hours. Time was meaningless in the dim closet where he couldn't see anything clearly. He could only hear thunder in the distance and the patter of light rain from the direction of the garage door. The smell of motor oil was close to suffocating him.

Chapter *Fifty-One*

MARTIN

artin walked out to the waiting patrol car and leaned over the driver's window. "She's okay, Joe. I talked to her and told her what's going on. I searched the house. Everything seems to be in order. Just give me a minute to look around out here."

Joe jerked the door open. "I'll help you. It's boring just sitting here." He rolled up the window and slammed the door as he got out, popping on his plastic-covered hat.

"Sorry," Martin said. "I didn't mean to take so long. I just didn't want to say anything in front of her kids. Any calls?" They jumped the leaves and water rushing in the gutter and headed for the back of the house.

"No, the radio's been quiet. Don't worry, if Ginny's in Austin, they'll find her."

Martin, being well the taller of the two, reached over the six-foot wooden gate to unhook it so they could get inside. It took a few moments to figure out the catch and, as they stood there, it began raining harder. Thunder rumbled out over the Gulf. Joe buttoned up his raincoat.

When Martin forced the latch and opened the gate, each man flipped on his flashlight. Martin unstrapped his forty-five, just in case. He almost hoped they would find Sellers hiding in the bushes, though as angry and worried as Martin felt, he knew he might not be able to resist shooting him.

They scoured the yard and the inside of the tool shed, finding no one. When they were through, they ran their lights around all the plants. The fullness of the oleander bushes made it difficult to be sure no one was hiding in them, so Martin stepped between them and the fence and pushed the branches aside, shining his flashlight in and out of the overgrown bushes.

"I guess we can go now," Joe said. "I think we've done a pretty thorough search."

Martin thought he heard a hint of gaiety in Joe's voice and glanced at his partner to see whether he wore a smile. "It's not funny, Morales," he said.

"Hey, I ain't laughing. You see me laughing?" Morales turned away from Martin and strode toward the gate. "You did look like you thought you were clearing a path in a jungle, though," he said in a low voice. "Let's get out of here."

Martin grimaced. He probably did look like a fool, but he didn't care. "I hate to leave her unprotected. I know what Sellers is capable of."

"Husband's not back in town yet?" They got into their car, Joe behind the wheel.

There were so many dark clouds in the sky that the deep blue of their unit appeared black in the rain. "No. He's due in late tonight."

Joe nodded and pulled out into the street.

Martin stared back at her house. The hard knot in his stomach made him feel like he'd eaten lead. "I hope she'll be okay. She's alone with those two little kids."

"Stop worrying," Joe said. "We just searched the place. If anyone was there, we would have found him."

"I know. I know. There wasn't any evidence of his being around, but it just makes me uneasy to think of her being there alone."

Joe drove across Stewart Road and up the slope to Seawall Boulevard. "I think there's more to this than you're saying, *Amigo*."

"Shut up, Morales." Martin stared out the window as they resumed their normal patrol route. He wasn't about to admit he had feelings for a married woman.

Chapter Fifty-Two

DENA

Dena turned the lock behind Martin and hurried to the back of the house. She dead-bolted the garage door and pushed the button on the doorknob as well. After she checked the lock on the back door and mopped up the puddles of water left by Martin's dripping raincoat, she looked in on the kids.

She had been right from the beginning. Zack had thought she was crazy about Sellers, but she was right. It would be funny if it weren't so horrible.

In the den, Dena picked up their cookie and drink mess and took it to the kitchen. Never in her life had she sobered up so fast. Her head pounded. She was afraid to look out the kitchen window and into the backyard for fear of what she'd see.

Forcing herself to peer out, she almost fainted when she saw two flashes of light in the yard. She knew it was Martin and his partner, just like she knew her body would be rushing with adrenaline all evening at the slightest sound, ordinary or not. God, she wished Zack would come home.

Remembering the wooden dowels she had placed in every window's track all those months before, Dena glanced at the bottom of the kitchen window. The dowel was still there.

She hurried from room to room and checked each window's track, more scared than the time the man had followed her home. All the dowels were in place. In the den, she peered through the plate-glass window's long mini-blinds, just as the police cruiser drove away, leaving the street empty, the pavement glistening from the rain as the clouds parted and revealed a bright moon. She noticed the streetlight in front of her neighbor's house across the street was not lit. Had it been out for days or... Dropping the blinds, she took the remote control and turned the news up very loud. She stared at the TV screen, not seeing, not hearing.

Sometime after the news ended, Dena turned off the TV and walked around the house again. She rechecked all the doors and windows. She looked in on the children again. They were sleeping peacefully. She straightened the covers where they had become a bit mussed.

"You can come home now, Zack," she said aloud when she started putting out the lights. It wasn't all that early. He could come home at any time.

In an effort to distract herself, she turned on the television in their bedroom, making the volume loud. She tried reading, but she couldn't process the words on the page. Her mind ran in several directions at once. Finally, she remembered the unopened envelope she had received from the private investigator Tuesday afternoon. That would give her something else to think about. She had tucked it carefully into her roller bag, away from prying eyes, and had been too distracted ever since to remember it.

Retrieving her roller bag from the kitchen, Dena got down the box with her mother's papers in it, too, and settled on the bed. The envelope was overstuffed. She didn't know whether her hands shook because she would know in a few moments the details of her mother's past, or because she was still afraid Alan Sellers was out there someplace planning to get her.

After tearing off the flap, Dena pulled out a wad of legal papers and unfolded them under the bedside lamp. Adjusting her glasses, she read the first few words, her voice a loud whisper. As if they were electrified, the pages flew from her hands. A stabbing pain shot through her gut. "No," she cried aloud. "It can't be." Squeezing her eyes shut, she rocked on the bed. At first dizzy, she felt like she floated above herself, like she was having an out-of-body experience.

Chapter Fifty-Three

ALAN SELLERS

*H*e forced himself to be patient. Give her time. Martin would want to search the yard. Give him time to do that. If she hadn't put the kids to bed, let her have time to do that. He kept telling himself it wouldn't be that much longer.

He liked the feeling of anticipation. She was afraid now. Martin had warned her. She probably had butterflies in her stomach. Her hands were probably shaking. Her knees, rubbery. That pleased him.

When the sound of the deadbolt being thrown accosted his ears, he didn't let it bother him. So what was one more obstacle? Look how far he'd come. It wouldn't be that much longer. No deadbolt would keep him out.

The kitchen lights went out, causing the small pool of light through the kitchen window to disappear. Almost complete blackness enveloped the garage. Time grew shorter. Let her try to relax. Take her shower. Put on her pajamas. Read one of those books he'd seen on her bedside table. Watch TV until she fell asleep.

She would probably wake up when he burst through the door. That would be okay. She would be groggy. He would catch her off guard. Surprise her. He wanted her to be awake enough though. He wanted to be sure, before she died, that she knew he was the one cutting her throat. No one treated him like she had in the courtroom and got away with it. He wanted to be sure she knew.

So, he could be patient. It wouldn't be that much longer. And afterward, after Ginny, maybe after Martin, he'd take his vacation. He wouldn't have to work again for a long, long while. It was worth being patient.

Chapter Fifty-Four

DENA

fter several moments, Dena wiped her face on her sleeve and reread the pleadings. IN THE MATTER OF THE MARRIAGE OF ALAN SELLERS, SR. AND REBECCA LOWELL SELLERS, AND IN THE INTEREST OF ALAN SELLERS, JR., A MINOR CHILD. Her breath was shallow. Her chest ached. Her mind skittered in many directions like a lost and frightened small animal. It would take more than a few minutes before she could read further.

After a while, she became aware of soft pattering of rain on her bedroom window. Her eyes burned, and she realized she must have been staring blankly, perhaps not blinking for some period of time. Her fingers still held the photocopied pages, some of the writing fainter in places and harder to make out, a testament to the age of the original documents. Drawing a deep breath, she thumbed through the papers. There was an Original Petition for Divorce, which included an affidavit and a request for a Temporary Restraining Order, the Temporary Restraining

Order itself, the Temporary Orders after a hearing, an Inventory of Property, and a Final Decree of Divorce.

She flipped to the second page and read about the child. It had to be the same person. Same age. Ginny's husband was a junior. This baby was a junior.

So Alan Sellers was her brother, her half-brother. Incredible as it seemed, she knew it to be true. There had always been something familiar about him. Not his demeanor. Certainly the man had been raised in a totally different environment and behaved erratically, not as someone from her own background would have. She hurried into the den and picked up the photograph of her mother, father, and herself. There was something in his face, his coloring, that was like her mother. She heaved a huge sigh as she walked back down the hall toward her bedroom. It was true.

Her cell phone rang, and she flinched. She scrambled into the den to answer it, hoping it was Martin.

"Dena, it's Martin. We've found Ginny."

Dena sank down on the edge of the bed. "Is she all right?" Please, God, don't have let Alan Sellers hurt her.

"Yes," Martin said. "You won't believe what she did."

"Thank God," Dena whispered. "Did she even go to Austin?" Pulling her legs under her, she suddenly felt tired and chilled. She covered up with the bedspread.

"She decided she didn't want the abortion, so she went to Austin, but she rented a car and drove out to the Hill Country to our cousin's."

"Oh, no." The baby. Dena had forgotten all about Ginny's baby. If Sellers was her brother, the baby would be her niece or nephew. The whole scenario was too much to digest. All she could do was carry on the conversation like things were normal, but they weren't and never would be now. She just wanted to turn out the light and go to sleep and not wake up for a long time. The Sellers case had been nothing but a nightmare from the start.

"You still there?"

"Yes. Why didn't she call somebody? Let you or Mary know where she was?"

"I don't know. She didn't want to argue with us, I guess. We would have tried to talk her into going through with the abortion. My cousin, realizing we'd be worried, called Mary a little while ago. She had argued with Ginny and insisted we be told where she was, that we were probably scared half to death."

"No kidding." Dena weighed whether she should tell Martin about her discovery and decided not to for the time being. It was late. She was tired. She wanted to finish reading all the paperwork herself and mull it over before she discussed it with anyone. "I'm glad she's okay."

"Me, too," Martin said. "I feel like an idiot for getting everyone all worked up."

"You didn't know."

"I guess I should have done more checking before I raised an alarm. I'm sorry I got you so upset."

"That's okay. Listen, I'm going to go to bed now. I'm very tired."

"I'm sorry. I wish I could make up for it."

"It isn't necessary. I'm going to take my shower and go to bed. Besides, Zack will be coming home anytime."

"Well … call the station if you need me for anything."

"That's sweet of you, but I'm exhausted and just want to get some sleep."

"Goodnight."

"Thanks for calling." Dena clicked off the phone and stretched out on the bed. She could crawl under the covers in a few minutes and actually close her eyes without worrying about living to see morning. The whole thing was so ridiculous. It was almost funny. Not that she felt like laughing. Unless with hysteria. It was like something from television. She still felt stunned that Alan Sellers was her brother, but at least he was just eccentric and not a murderer. She shivered. She'd worry about it all later, in the clear light of day. Zack would be home. She'd be rested. Totally sober. It would all work out. The papers went back into her roller bag. She zipped it up and dragged it next to her dresser.

She laughed at herself for having been so terrified earlier. Picking up the remote control, she flipped channels until she found a talk show. What she needed was some comedy.

She began thinking about Zack's return. It seemed like ages since she'd seen him. They were going to have to sit down and have a big discussion about what to do with their lives. He hadn't been happy either, she knew, and should be amenable to an uncontested divorce with liberal visitation with the kids. She wouldn't ask him for child support. That should pacify him.

She took a shower and pulled on her favorite nightgown. There was really no need to wait up for him. He had keys, and she was so tired, weary to her bones. She got under the covers and put out the light. No more reading that night.

Chapter Fifty-Five

MARTIN

Martin clicked off his cell.

"What'd she say? Was she mad?"

Martin shrugged at his partner as he brushed his hand through his hair. "She was all right about it. Kind of quiet, in fact. Me, I'd have been pissed." He looked through the rain-spotted window at the Gulf. The moonlight reflected off the small breakers, otherwise, the sky was pitch black over the water.

"She sounds like a pretty cool lady," Joe said. "I thought she'd cuss you out or something."

"Nah, she's not the type. She's first class. She said she just wanted to get some sleep. She's tired." He remembered how she'd looked when he'd been at her house. She'd been so frightened. He'd wanted to put his arms around her and pull her close. She was just a little thing. and even if she was a lawyer, she still needed protecting.

"Hey, you know what?" Joe said, as they circled around a bar parking lot and drove back up to the seawall. "I could use a drink. Our shift will be over by the time we get back downtown. You want to get a beer after we get through?"

"Yeah, sure. You pick the place." Martin was pleased that Joe asked. Their relationship was on the mend. He had known things would get better if he went back on the street. He wasn't ever riding that desk again. He didn't care what the chief did to him. He glanced at Joe and then out at the street, all shiny and wet, reflecting the restaurant and hotel lights. He liked it when the weather caused the traffic to be slow.

Martin thought of Dena again. She was a married woman. Why did the good ones have to be married? Her kids sure were cute. Paul had a cool car collection. Martin stroked his chin absent-mindedly and stared out at the water. If he had kids, he'd sit on the floor and play with them. He'd wrestle with his son. He'd read to them. Ride bicycles. Go to the beach. He wouldn't go off traveling the world like Dena's husband did. He'd never leave them alone that much. Dena. He liked her name. Not that it would get him anywhere. He sighed and rubbed his neck. He would just have to try to find someone as likable as she was.

"Great. Just a beer would be fine with me," Joe said.

Joe's words startled Martin momentarily, bringing him back to the present. "You know what scares the hell out of me?"

"What?"

"If I'd found Sellers, I probably would have killed him."

Chapter Fifty-Six

DENA

ena dozed for a few minutes, and then awoke abruptly. She plumped up her pillow. She turned off the TV and hunkered down.

She dozed again, and when her head rolled off to the side, she awoke again. All the excitement of the evening must be too much for her brain. She stared at the ceiling in the dark. The room was silent, but for the raindrops on the glass and a gust of wind trying to get through the crack of the windowsill. She laid her head upon her pillow, ready to accept sleep.

She drifted off and began to dream. She was falling and couldn't stop. She tried to grab something, anything, to save herself, but as she reached out, nothing was there. She was in a void. It was dark. There was no one to help her. She flailed her arms.

Turning over, she awakened, bolting up to a sitting position. She reached out to Zack's side of the bed. It was still empty. She looked at the glowing numerals on the clock. She had only been asleep a few minutes. What had awakened her? The dream? She must have rolled over.

Settling back down, she pulled the comforter around her. Zack really should be home any minute. She listened for his car, tuning into the sounds of the night. The refrigerator whirred when it cut on. Raindrops pinged on the windows. The neighbor's dog barked. The kitchen doorknob rattled.

Zack. Dena flipped on her bedside lamp and bounded out of bed. She'd be nice and let him in. She ran across the soft bedroom carpet, flinging open the door and running through the dark into the kitchen. She heard the doorknob again. Was he having trouble with his key?

"Zack." She grabbed the doorknob and yanked, but the door wouldn't budge. Damn. She forgot she'd dead-bolted it. Locked it from the inside. The kitchen being pitch black made it impossible to see his face in the window. "It's the upper lock, Zack," she said, as she flipped on the light and found herself face-to-face with Alan Sellers. Her vision was blurry without her glasses, but it was him.

His nose and cheek pressed up against the glass. His right hand, wrapped around a pointy knife, pushed up against the window. His hazel eyes penetrated hers.

Dena backed away from the door as she looked at the ugly expression of hatred in his eyes. She watched, spellbound, as he threw his body against the door, trying to break it open, his eyes never leaving hers. The door groaned and crackled when he threw himself against it.

As if in a trance, her eyes locked with his for several seconds before she snapped. The doorknob twisted and turned. When she looked back at his face, his eyes bored into hers as again he threw himself against the door like a mad dog, penned-in. When the doorframe cracked, Dena bolted and ran for her gun. She knew it would be only moments before the frame gave way.

Running into the bedroom, she rounded the bed to her night table, pulling on the drawer. It wouldn't open. Damn. Zack had put that lock in it. The wood splintered in the kitchen.

She hurried to her jewelry box and dug inside for the key. She couldn't put her fingers on it. She locked the bedroom door and went back to the jewelry box. Oh God, oh God. She dumped out the contents. She shook all over. Her hands scrabbled through the jewelry. The key wasn't there. It really wasn't there. The kitchen door cracked again and burst open, banging into the side of the cabinet.

Chapter Fifty-Seven

MARTIN

artin and Joe cruised down the rain-splattered seawall toward downtown Galveston, both of them quiet. Comfortable with each other, Martin thought, just like the old days.

"Something's nagging at me," Martin said. "Something's not quite right. It's like a little voice inside my head keeps talking to me."

"Stress," Joe said.

"No. It's more than that. I keep replaying the day in my mind, like viewing a movie. Calling Ginny's cell phone. Calling her friend. Calling the clinic. The whole day keeps passing before me, like I'm on my deathbed."

"I'm telling you, it's just nerves. You had a bad scare there for a while," Joe said. He put a piece of chewing gum in his mouth and smacked noisily.

"Did you notice anything weird at Dena Armstrong's, Joe?"

"Nada. We checked it out. There was nothing."

"What about Marlo's, when we were looking for Sellers?" Martin stroked his chin, scratching at the stubble.

"Just people drinking and dancing and having a good time." Joe turned up the radio. They listened to a call, but it wasn't for them.

Martin shook his head to get rid of the feeling, but it wouldn't go away. After a while he said, "I have this gut feeling. I keep going over it, from the beginning. Ginny's moving in with that creep. The time she and Sellers lived with Mary. The phone calls in the middle of the night. The breakup. Then when we went down to pick up her stuff. Later when I went with her to Dena's office and saw Sellers pull up afterwards in that big, white Cadillac that used to belong to his father. After all the hell he gave her about the money she took, and he was driving that Cadillac. We thought he'd sold it for the money after his father died."

"What?" Joe shouted. "There was a white Cadillac parked across from the entrance to Mrs. Armstrong's subdivision tonight. Didn't you see it?"

Martin banged his fist on the dashboard. "I can't believe I missed it."

Joe slammed his foot on the brakes and did a sliding U-turn. "Hit the lights and the siren."

Martin held on as Joe got control of their cruiser and sped back toward the west end of the island.

"He must have been there all along. I don't know where, but he must have been there." Martin felt like he'd just been shot in the stomach with a large caliber bullet. "I hope we're not too late." He grabbed his cell and punched in Dena's number.

Chapter Fifty-Eight

DENA

When Dena heard the kitchen door burst open, she dragged a chair to the door and put it under the doorknob like she'd seen in a movie. Sellers hit the other side and twisted the doorknob. She turned her back to the door, digging in with her heels, her eyes sweeping the room for a weapon. There was nothing.

There was no time to call the police or Bob or Martin. She could run into the bathroom and lock the door, but he could get in. He could break in. If the deadbolt on the kitchen door didn't hold him, the other doors wouldn't either. Her only chance was escape. Her eyes lit on the window. She'd have to climb out. But what about the kids? Would he harm them if he couldn't get to her? She didn't think so. He wanted her. And climbing out the window would lead him away from them.

She could hear his rapid breathing on the other side of the door as he pushed up against it. For a brief moment she had a fleeting thought that she should yell to him through the door, try to talk to him, tell him of their relationship. "Listen to me," she called out. "Mr. Sellers ... Alan ... you don't know what you're doing." She felt him throw his weight against the door again. It held for the moment.

Dena darted to the window, yanked the blinds up, and unlatched it. She grabbed the aluminum window rim with both hands and tugged on it. It wouldn't budge. She heard his body hit the bedroom door again. The wood around the lock cracked. Oh God, oh God, why wouldn't the window open?

After tugging on the window rim again, Dena finally checked the lock. The dowel. Her hands shook as she reached for the little piece of wood that blocked the track. She pulled it out, grasped the rim with both hands, and pulled with all her might. The window opened. The door cracked, louder this time.

She beat at the screen with the flat of both hands. As it fell outward, Dena put one bare foot up on her night table, grabbed hold of the windowsill, and hoisted her body into the opening just as Sellers broke through the door.

"I'm your sister," she screamed as she twisted around and dropped to the ground. Before she could let go of the sill, he lashed out with his knife and punctured the back of her left hand right in front of her wrist, ripping through her skin toward her fingers as she released her hold on the ledge and pulled her hand away. The pain was at first sharp and then dull.

She slipped on the wet ground and fell against the brick veneer, then pulled herself up, her feet catching for a moment in the length of her nightgown. She ran sideways like a crab toward the darkest part of the yard. She looked back over her shoulder and, in the dim light of her bedside lamp, she could see Sellers' silhouette as he climbed through the window.

Pressing her sliced hand against her chest with her other one, she tried to stop the sticky blood flowing freely between her fingers. She searched for a means of escape. Sellers was between her and the gate, near her bedroom window. She had to get out of the light, out of Sellers' sight, run farther into the darkness of the yard, then try to escape.

Chapter Fifty-Nine

MARTIN

ena's number rang and rang as Joe urged the police car faster and faster down the center lane of the wet pavement. Martin laid the phone down on the seat, still ringing, and sent a radio message for backup. It was almost time for shift change. Backup, if any, would probably be slow in coming. Thank God he and Joe hadn't received any calls to another location, or they wouldn't have had a straight shot down the seawall.

"Geez, I hope we're right," Joe said after Martin got off the radio. "If we're wrong, we're going to look like a couple of fools."

"I'm right. I'm right. I wish I wasn't. I knew something was wrong." He slammed his fist on the dashboard again and wished he were behind the wheel so he could make their unit go faster. "I can't believe I let that Caddy slip by me. I looked right at it and didn't see it."

"Take it easy, Man. It's not your fault. You weren't thinking about anything but Ginny."

"Hell, Joe, don't you see? If I'd seen it, I mean if I'd really seen it earlier, we could have stopped him right then. It might be too late now. That poor lady…those kids …"

"She's got a gun though, remember?"

"But she was going to bed. She was going to sleep. And she's totally unaware that he's after her."

"Yeah, you told me."

"Damn. Can't you make this thing go any faster?" Martin glared at Joe. He could see Joe's fingers were white knuckled, but it didn't matter. The only thing that mattered was they get there in time. They passed Gaido's restaurant with its giant crab out front, and Martin realized they were still thirty blocks away. "Damn." he said again.

"Calm down, Martin. If I kill us, we'll never get there."

"I can't. I'm afraid of what he'll do to her. You don't know him. He's crazy."

Chapter Sixty

DENA

*D*ena ran for the garden shed. Behind her, there was a splat that she assumed was Sellers hitting the ground when he jumped from the window. Then another splat—he must have fallen—and then the slapping of footsteps in the wet grass. Her cell phone rang—or was that just a ringing in her ears?

He hit the ground again. She hoped the fall had knocked the breath out of him.

She reached the shed and felt her way around it. Yanking open the door, she stepped inside and pulled it closed as quietly as she could. With her uninjured hand, she reached into the darkness. She kept her left hand up against her chest, hoping in the back of her mind that it would slow the bleeding. She stepped forward and stubbed her toe on something hard. Pain shot up her leg, but she could only tough it out. Crouching down, she touched the thing. It was the base of the lawnmower. She put a bare foot on it, got her balance, and then stepped up. She eased her way around, until she touched the back wall.

The rain pattered on the shed roof. She leaned against the rear wall, catching her breath, faced the door, and braced herself. With her legs spread apart, one bare foot against the base of the lawnmower, she began scratching around, searching for something, anything she could use to defend herself should Sellers find her.

She felt a wooden handle, a thick wooden handle. She tried to lift it, but it was too heavy. Her fingers groped around some more. She found another, smaller, wooden handle. She pulled up on it. It weighed a lot less. Squatting, Dena ran her hand down the length of the handle until she reached the blade, the shovel. It would have to do. She stood again and picked it up. With her throbbing left hand, she clasped the handle the best she could and tried to ignore the pain. Her hand was weak, but it could support the other one. She maneuvered the shovel around until she had the blade up, the backside out, and the handle down. Gripping it with both hands, she stood ready to strike if the door opened.

She tried to hold her breath, so she could hear better. Nothing but rain. Thunder. Lightning. What if he went back inside? He must know she had kids. He'd come in from the garage.

Oh God, please don't let him hurt her babies. Poor little Melissa wouldn't stand a chance. She'd be crying for her, and Dena wouldn't be there to help. Five years old was still a baby. Would he hurt a baby? Paul was only a year older. What would he do to him?

Her rapid breath was loud in her ears. She shivered, but with fear, not cold. Why didn't he come? Did he know the shed was there? He'd had time to find out by now. What was he doing? What was he planning? Dena stood tensed to strike the second she heard him at the door.

'He's crazy,' they'd said. 'Dr. Jekyll and Mr. Hyde.' How crazy was crazy? Crazy enough to come into her house to kill her. Oh, Lord, please don't let him do it.

"Zack, Zack," she whispered. "Please come home now, Zack." She touched the pulse beating in her throat. Her mouth was as dry as desert sand. Her knees quivered. Tears streamed down her face.

Should she leave the safety of the shed and go back to the house to see about the children? She had to protect her children. Would he leave them alone if he got her? Anger built inside her at the thought of his hurting her kids. She couldn't let him hurt her kids.

The door flew open. Intense, bright light blinded Dena. "No," she cried, striking out with the shovel in the direction of the light. She felt and heard the shovel make contact.

Sellers' flashlight flew to the ground. He howled and raged like a wild animal.

Dena worked the shovel up for another strike. At the same time, she hollered, "I'm your sister. You're my brother."

"I'll kill you," he screamed, his voice sounding high-pitched like the cry of a banshee. He lashed out with his knife, slicing the back of her right forearm.

Dena gasped at the pressure of the tear in her arm and moments later, the searing pain, but she forced herself to concentrate on positioning the shovel for another blow. It was her only chance. "Please, Alan, don't you feel it?" She stumbled over tools on her way to the opposite corner of the shed. The fallen flashlight cast enough light that she could see the tools' long shadows. If he would only stop long enough to hear her out. She didn't want to hit him. Why wouldn't he listen? "Your mother was my mother."

"My mother's dead. You're trying to fool me." But he hesitated, the knife in hand, ready to lunge at her.

"No," she yelled. "Rebecca Lowell was my mother's maiden name. Your mother's name was Rebecca Lowell Sellers."

With all her might, she smashed his head with the shovel, but she didn't have much strength left. It wouldn't have much effect.

He stumbled backward out of the doorway and into the yard. Dena lifted the shovel again. Blood flew from her open wounds. She could barely make him out as she scrambled from the shed toward him.

He cursed and screamed obscenities and jumped up off the ground. He turned his head away from her, his attention on something else in the yard. She started to swing the shovel until she realized what he saw. It was Zack. Thank God. It was Zack.

Chapter Sixty-One

ALAN SELLERS

ellers' head swam with confusion. The lawyer. His sister? Their mother? It couldn't be. His mother was dead. His father had told him, ever since he was little. First, she had abandoned him; then she had died. But why would Dena Armstrong tell him that? She had yelled something about feeling it. Had that been what he'd felt the first time he saw her in court?

Was that why he'd had such a hard time letting go of that picture in her den? That woman in it had seemed so familiar. He'd had a picture of his mother once. He'd found it and kept it hidden from his father. One day when he got home from school, his father was sitting on Alan's bed and held the picture in his hands and tore it into little bits right in Alan's face and then whipped him until he couldn't sleep, he hurt so much. He tried to remember, was it the same face? She'd said the name, too. How had she known his mother's name, if it wasn't true?

What was the husband doing there, standing in the yard in the dark and the rain? He was supposed to be thousands of miles away.

Fog surrounded his brain as he looked from the husband to her. She stood there in her long, wet, white nightgown. Dark spots of blood splattered across her face and arms. Her hair was dripping wet. He heard her call out.

"Zack. Zack, help me."

Sellers looked back at the husband.

"Why haven't you killed her yet?" the husband called in a loud, flat voice. "Kill her now." Sellers raised his knife, then the husband pulled his hand from his jacket pocket. A nine-millimeter caught the light from the lightning and the moon and glinted in the husband's eyes. With clarity, Sellers realized he'd been set up. The man had never intended to pay him the rest of his money. As soon as he finished off Lawyer Armstrong, the husband would shoot him.

As if in slow motion, Sellers glanced back at the woman and saw surprise and terror reflected in her face. She had to have heard what her husband said. Instead of lunging toward her, Sellers went for the husband. It didn't matter to him whether or not she was his sister. No one welshed on a deal with Alan Sellers.

Sellers saw the whites of the husband's eyes as he leapt on him, knocking him to the soggy grass, and plunging his knife into the man, raking it through his body before pulling it out and slashing it across the man's neck. He turned back to the lawyer, sister or not, he didn't care. He took a step toward her, reaching out with the knife.

The lawyer slammed the shovel down sideways on Sellers' arm, slicing a chunk of it. He dropped the knife and went down on one knee. The shovel came at him again, at his head. He used his other arm to shield himself. With his uninjured arm, he grappled around for the knife. Just as he glanced to the side, the shovel swung at him sideways. For just a moment, he tasted fear on his tongue as the shovel hit him again.

Chapter Sixty-Two

MARTIN

*M*artin and Joe pulled up to the Armstrong house just seconds after another unit arrived. The light of the moon and the headlights from both police units illuminated a white Lexus SUV in the driveway. An officer stood at the front door, banging on it and punching the doorbell. Another ran toward the backyard, his right hand gripping his handgun in his holster. Martin followed the second officer. If Dena was asleep, they could alert her from her bedroom window, in the back.

He reached the gate and moved the other officer aside. "I know this lock," he said unlatching it in record time. A raspy voice was saying, "No. No," over and over. His weapon in one hand and flashlight in the other, Martin ran toward the speaker.

Dena Armstrong held a shovel over her head. She swung it down, striking what looked like two bodies in the wet grass. A mask of blood covered her face.

Martin holstered his handgun and dropped the flashlight onto the ground beside her. When she struggled with the shovel, trying to raise it again, he stopped her. "Let go. It's all right." He took the shovel and threw it to the side and pulled her to him. Blood covered much of her body. It oozed from her hand and arm, but not her face or head. He breathed a deep sigh of relief.

"Call nine-one-one," he hollered over his shoulder and held tight to her hand and arm to stem the flow of blood.

She resisted him, trying to pull away, her eyes held a wild, wide-eyed look.

"It's Martin. You're okay." He wanted to wrap his arms around her, but there was so much blood, he didn't dare let go of her limbs.

The whites of her eyes were huge in the moonlight.

"Lieutenant?" A uniformed officer's flashlight illuminated the ground at their feet. Joe came around and checked for a pulse on one of the men. He looked at Martin and shook his head. He picked up Martin's flashlight and said, "No hurry on this one."

The other officer stood. "This one's dead, too. Worse than dead." He looked like he wanted to puke.

Martin said, "That's Alan Sellers. If I had to guess, I'd say the other one is Zachary Armstrong, this woman's husband. Looks like he returned home just in time to save his wife, only it didn't work out that way."

A third officer came up. "Lieutenant, I got inside. The kids slept through all this."

Dena whimpered and became a dead weight against Martin. He held her up. It was awkward holding on to her like that, but he didn't know how much blood she'd lost and didn't want to risk her losing anymore. A siren in the distance grew closer.

Martin looked down into Dena's face. Her eyes studied him. She had grown quiet and let him hold her arms. When the ambulance showed up, he stayed with her while the emergency medical technicians bandaged her wounds. He spoke reassuringly to her that she would be all right, that her children would be fine.

"Call my friend," she whispered. "Call Ellen." Her eyes searched his. The wild look he'd seen earlier had gone. "Her number … her phone number is on the kitchen bulletin board."

Her hand had a deep slice, but the one on her arm was shallower, though longer. The EMTs strapped her on a gurney. Martin walked beside it until they slid her into the back of the ambulance. The two technicians climbed out and walked around to the front where they spoke with Joe.

Dena held an arm out toward Martin. "My children?"

"Don't worry," Martin said. He leaned halfway in and halfway out of the back of the vehicle. "I'll take care of them. I'll get your friends' information and call them."

"No—that's not what I meant. I have to ask you something." Her eyes got that wild look for a moment. The blood having been wiped from her face made her look more normal, except for that glint in her eye. "Come closer. I want only you to hear."

Martin scrambled the rest of the way into the ambulance and knelt next to where she lay. There were still smears of blood at her hairline and across her face. For just a moment his mind flashed on how close he'd come to losing her, yet he knew she wasn't even his to lose. His eyes met hers. Her lower lip trembled as she started to speak.

"What is it? It's okay now. You can tell me. Only I can hear."

"Promise me one thing," she said, studying his face.

"Anything."

"Promise me that no one will tell my kids their father tried to kill me."

Epilogue

SIX MONTHS LATER DENA

"It's a boy," the doctor exclaimed so loudly Dena could hear him through the birthing room door. She and Martin had been standing outside for the last hour of Ginny's labor. Mary coached, so she got to stay inside. They all had been at the hospital since eight that morning after Ginny had called to say her water had broken.

"Congratulations, Lieutenant," Dena said.

"Congratulations, yourself, Counselor," Martin said.

"I'm glad it's a boy," Dena said. "A new year. A new baby. In a way, it's like giving him another chance. Alan never had much of a chance."

She recalled the story she had pieced together since the night Alan Sellers and Zack had died. Between discussions with her cousin, Luke, the papers she'd found of her mother's, and further use of the private investigator, Dena had a pretty good idea about what had happened those many years before, and what had made Alan Sellers, Jr., into the mad dog he had become.

By looking into their bank accounts, she also figured out what had transpired most recently between her husband and the man who had turned out to be her brother.

"With a father like Senior, Alan Sellers, Junior was doomed from the very start," Martin said.

"Makes me wonder what his father's father was like, and his father before him, and his father before him——"

"You've made your point." Martin smiled down at her and touched her shoulder.

His touch was gentle. Dena didn't shy away from it. "We're going to break that cycle of violence. We'll all love this little boy so much he'll never have a chance to turn bad."

"I'm going to have to spoil him a little bit," Martin said.

"Of course you are, Uncle Martin."

"And you're not, Aunt Dena?" There was a twinkle in Martin's eye.

"Sure I am. Right now, let's spoil his mother. Let's go to the florist's to buy her the biggest bouquet of flowers she's ever seen and one of those 'It's a Boy' door hangers."

"I'm game," Martin said. "And while we're at it, may I treat you to a late lunch?"

Her eyes met his. It was as if he could see through her, but in a good way. "All right. You've been patient a long time. I think I'm ready for that lunch."

"I'm glad." Martin helped her on with her jacket and shrugged into his own. He paused at the nurse's station on their way out and left a message for his sisters. Then he held the door for Dena as they left the hospital.

"Take my car?"

"Fine by me." Martin said.

As they approached her new, larger Ford sedan, she held out the keys to him. When he reached for them, he took her hand. Dena's heart thumped. The past few months had been so filled with mourning and therapy and spending quality time with her children and moving into her new offices that she had put Martin off each time he had tried to see her. Only twice had she come into contact with him. Once had been at Ginny's apartment when Dena had been helping decorate the baby's room. The other was when Martin had been waiting for her outside the courtroom when she had been in trial. He had insisted they at least have coffee together.

He had phoned her numerous times after Zack's and Alan Sellers' funerals. Dena had paid for both. But she had left strict instructions with both Meredith and Juliet that she didn't want to talk to anyone except Ginny or, maybe, Mary. Several months had gone by before she began accepting his calls. She was ready now for their relationship to move to the next level. Well, really, for their relationship to get started.

Martin held her hand until they reached the car. He opened the passenger door and helped her in. He leaned down and kissed the scar that ran across the top of her hand. Dena shivered and smiled at him.

Closing the door, he walked around to the other side and let himself in. After he started the car, he turned to her and said, "I'd like to do more than just take you to lunch if you think you're ready. You know how I feel about you."

"Yes, I'm fully aware of that." She caressed the place on her scar where he had kissed her. "I guess I'm just scared, that's all."

Martin ran a finger down her cheek. "I can understand that, but I guarantee you I would never hurt you. Never. I care deeply about you, Dena. I'm just asking that you give me a chance, that's all. I want us to take care of each other."

"We're a package deal, you know." She put her hand over his and squeezed.

"I know that. I want to be a father to your children, if you and they will let me, and we'll all watch out for our new baby nephew. Could you do that?"

For some reason, Dena felt shy when Martin began talking like that, when she realized how much he cared for her. He was so different from Zack. With Zack, she was never sure where she stood, never sure he really loved her. Martin made his feelings known—made her completely aware that finally someone loved her for herself. He seemed too good to be true. She leaned across the bucket seats and kissed him on the cheek. "I think I can do that. At least, I sure want to give it a try."

Thank you for reading!

If you enjoyed reading *Unaware*, I would appreciate it if you would help others to enjoy this book, too.

Lend it. Recommend it. Please help others find this book by recommending it to friends, readers' groups, and discussion boards.

Review it. Please tell other readers why you liked this book by reviewing it at Amazon or Goodreads. If you do write a review, please send me an email at susan@susanpbaker.com so I can thank you with a personal email.

Mailing List. To subscribe to my mailing list, visit: www.susanpbaker.com

Susan P. Baker

ABOUT THE AUTHOR

Susan P. Baker is the author of six novels and two nonfiction books, all of which are related to the law because of her career in the justice system. As a judge, for twelve years she dealt with murder, kidnapping, incest, stalking, child support, child custody, and divorce. Prior thereto, she practiced law for nine years, spending much of her time in the courtroom. While in law school, she worked as a probation officer. Her worst experiences at that time, besides driving 50 miles each way on I-45 from Galveston to Houston for classes several times a week, were making home visits to some scary neighborhoods.

Susan's father was a lawyer and a judge. She remembers him parking the family outside the old county jail while he went in and made bail bonds. She'd stare out the window at the broken glass lining the tops of the walls to prevent escapes and wonder what the jail was like inside. Later, she became quite familiar with the interior of the jail but luckily could leave whenever she wanted.

Susan is a member of Women Fiction Writers Association, Authors Guild, Sisters in Crime, Writers League of Texas, and Galveston Novel and Short Story Writers.

She has two children, eight grandchildren, and lives in Texas. She loves dark chocolate, especially with raspberries, and traveling around the world. An anglophile, her favorite country is England where she likes to visit relatives (her mother was a British war bride) Roman ruins, anything Shakespeare, and just about everything else she comes across.

Find out more about Susan and her books at
www.susanpbaker.com. Like her at
www.facebook.com/legalwriter.

Follow her @susanpbaker.

Also by Susan P. Baker

Novels:

Death of a Prince

Ledbetter Street

My First Murder

Suggestion of Death

The Sweet Scent of Murder

Nonfiction:

Heart of Divorce

Murdered Judges: Of the Twentieth Century